THE SNOW

THE EXODUS PLAGUE
BOOK 1

It came with the snow. Overnight the world changed. Bodies lie unburied. Gangs of bestial semi-humans roam the streets hunting for prey. But for one man the end was a new beginning.

Snowbound, in an isolated cottage, Jonathan Richards wakes from illness to discover that the world he knew has gone. He sets out on a perilous journey across Britain, searching for safety – but finding only death, destruction and danger.

When the final pandemic arrives, will you be ready?

The Snow takes you into a post-apocalyptic world where survival is the only goal. But survival at what cost?

HUW COLLINGBOURNE

dark neon

ISBN: 978-1-913132-10-1
Published by: **dark neon**

http://www.darkneon.com/

DOWNLOAD FREE STORIES

To download **free stories** now and to be the first to hear about new books, join Huw's mailing list at:

http://www.darkneon.com/newsletter

or scan this QR code:

Also by Huw Collingbourne

The Exodus Plague

Book 1: The Snow
Book 2: Imprisoned
Book 3: Escape

The 1980s Murder Mysteries

Book 1: Killers In Mascara
Book 2: The Glam Assassin
Book 3: Death Wears Sequins

Table Of Contents

PART I – CRISIS

Part I – Crisis

1

There was blood in the snow. It was the first sign of life I'd seen for over a week.

I'd been snowed in for about ten days by that time. I don't remember much about the first couple of days. I was too sick to get out of bed. I had no idea where I was or what was happening. I lay staring into the darkness for hour after hour. The darkness was filled with shapes: luminous creatures whose heads were all eyes and whose bodies were like eels squirming across the ceiling and slithering down the walls. Fever raged in me. I couldn't tell what was real and what was delirium. When I woke on the third day, the bedsheets were soaking with sweat. That was the day the power went off for the last time.

I think there'd been a power cut the day before too. I'm not sure because I wasn't thinking straight at the time. And even if I had been, I wouldn't have paid much attention to it. In the depths of the countryside, you get used to power cuts. They happen all the time. The power flicks off for a few seconds, or sometimes for a few hours. Then it comes back on again. So when the power went off for the final time, it took me a while to notice. Night fell and the room was pitch black so I forced myself to get up and look for candles. That was when the cold really started to get to me. Power lines must be down, I told myself. After all the snow we'd been having, that was only to be expected.

The snow had started falling in early January. Small flurries at first. A light dusting over the hillsides. It was picturesque, people said. Like a Christmas card. In the second week of January it began to fall in earnest. There was something weird about it. On the first night anyway. The snowflakes seemed to shimmer in the darkness. It was at about that time that I started to feel a bit under the weather. I'd never seen such heavy snow before. Relentless. Day after day it kept on falling. Soon the fields and the roads were buried under deep mounds. Little wonder if some powerlines had come down, then. That was only to be expected. The power would be back on again soon, I thought. But, of course, it wasn't.

I stayed in bed. I piled blankets on top of me but I still couldn't get warm. The sheets were cold and clammy. When, after a few days, the fever started to abate, I couldn't bear to lie in damp sheets. The cold in my unheated bedroom was bitter and penetrating. The windows were covered in hoar frost. Ice had formed on the surface of the glass of water I kept on my bedside table. I had to do something or I would freeze to death.

I went downstairs, into the kitchen. There's an old cast-iron, wood-burning stove there. I made up a fire and I settled down on the settee. I wrapped myself in a duvet and I heaped up some blankets and an old overcoat on top. I sat there, in front of that fire for a few more days, adding logs to keep it going every once in a while. And then, one morning, the fever finally broke. And, although I was frail and tired, I felt almost human again. The headaches had gone, the retching coughs and the hallucinations had gone, I no longer felt the leaden weight of tiredness that had drained my energy to the point where I had barely been able even to think.

I was consumed with hunger. I hadn't eaten anything for days. I looked in the fridge to see what food there was. There was a bit of hard cheese, a few withered-looking vegetables and some sour milk. I had better luck when I searched the cupboards. There were plenty of tins: beans, soup, sardines, fruit. I reckoned I'd manage to keep going until the snow melted and then I would go into the village to buy some more food. You have to remember that I had no idea how bad things were. I still thought this was just a bit of cold weather we were having, that the snow had brought down some power lines and everything would get back to normal pretty soon.

Still the snow kept falling.

With no electricity, I was totally cut off. There was no TV, no Internet. The battery in my phone was dead and there was no way of recharging it. Which meant that I had no news of the outside world. I was isolated. Now that I was feeling better, I didn't mind that too much. At least it kept the stress at bay.

The fact of the matter is that I'd been going through a bad time. Before the snow, I mean. The usual stuff. Too much work, too little money. I worried about the work and I worried about money. Most of all, I worried about the way my life was going. I'd started to have panic attacks. My friend Marie warned me that if I didn't slow things down I was heading for a breakdown. Whatever happened to Marie, I wonder? The last time I saw her was on Christmas Eve down in the Farmer's Rest, which is a pub in the village. I don't suppose I'll ever see her again now.

Over the next couple of days, after the fever broke, there were times, while I was sitting by the fire reading a book or drinking a glass or two of wine, when it seemed to me that being cut off by the snow wasn't such a bad thing after all. Even the power cut had its good side. With no phone and no Internet, I couldn't take on any new students or upload any new lessons. My time was my own; I could spend it doing whatever I wanted.

I'd better explain about my students. I'm a guitar teacher. Well, I was, anyway. I'm not sure what I am now. Back then, I spent my time teaching students to play whatever type of guitar music took their fancy. Usually they came to my home. Occasionally (for an additional fee) I went to theirs. When I first started, I had been expecting all my students to be teenagers wanting to learn to play hard rock. In fact, most of my students were over thirty. A couple of them were pensioners who wanted to play like Buddy Holly and Hank Marvin. One enthusiastic woman in her forties had taken a fancy to playing classical guitar "just like Segovia". I taught her as best I could but I explained that playing like Segovia was an ambition that neither she nor I could ever expect to achieve. If I'd been honest, I would have added that she would have had a better chance if she'd started learning about thirty-five years earlier. But when your students are your livelihood, sometimes it doesn't pay to be too honest.

Just in case you think that teaching guitar is a fast route to easy money, let me put you right. The guitar lessons didn't earn me anything like enough money to live on. So I also taught online. I recorded a couple of video courses, I taught one-to-one lessons via Skype. I also published a few books.

It's not what I wanted to do. What I wanted to do was play Heavy Metal in a band. I'd tried it once or twice but it had never worked out. I won't give you all the sordid details. It was the old story of bad management, clashing egos and not enough work to go around. Not that it would have made any difference in the long run. Once the snow came, all that ended. Ambitions, careers, the things we'd always taken for granted – abruptly they all became things of the past.

2

The great snowfall started on January 13th. It was January 23rd when I saw the bloodstains. I'd gone outside to get some wood from the lean-to shed that abutted the back wall of my house. I'd chopped up a good stack of wood in the summer, which was just as well because it seemed to me that I was going to need to burn a lot of it just to keep the kitchen warm.

When I saw the blood, my first thought was that an animal had been injured. Then I saw the footprints. The falling snow was already starting to cover up the footprints, smoothing out the edges and filling them in, but even so it was obvious they had been made by a person rather than an animal. The footprints had come from the direction of the woods that lie at the far edge of the field to the west of my house. The footprints arrived at my house, wandered around a bit and then backtracked into the woods again. There was no way that I was going to follow them. Whoever had been there had gone, I told myself. But I was wrong.

The day after that, the dog came. It was about half past nine in the morning. I'd just eaten a breakfast of tinned pilchards and digestive biscuits and I was having a shave by the table. My rechargeable shaver had lost its charge but luckily I had some disposable razors. I'd heated up some water in a saucepan on top of the stove and I'd smeared a bar of soap over my face. Then I'd propped a mirror up against a mug on the table. The most difficult thing was seeing what I was doing. You don't realise what a slave you are to electric lights until you have to do without them.

I was towelling off my face when I heard a scratching at the front door. It gave me a fright. I hadn't seen or heard a single living soul in ages. Apart from the footprints and bloodstains in the snow, there had been no indication of any living thing beyond the walls of my house. And now, out of the blue, something was scratching at the door!

For a few moments, I imagined that there must be a person out there – maybe the person who'd left the bloodstains and made the footprints. But when the barking started, I realised that it was a dog. Either that or somebody who did a very convincing impression of a dog. Even so, before I opened the door I took a surreptitious glance out of the window. To check that it was a friendly dog rather than a huge, slavering, rabid one. I've always been cautious. It was a medium-sized black and white dog and from the way it was wagging its tail it looked friendly enough. It was the sort of dog you see on many of the farms in these parts. I think theoretically they might be collies but I doubt if they come with a pedigree. I assumed the poor animal had lost its way in the snow. I went to the door and opened it. The dog ran straight into my house, barked twice, then ran straight back out again.

I called after it but it was already plunging through the snow away from me. I was about to shut the door but then the dog came leaping through the snow towards me again.

"Make up your mind," I said, and opened the door for him to come inside.

Once again, the dog went through the same procedure. It came into the house, woofed a couple of times, then ran out again. This time it ran off a few yards and stopped. Then it ran back towards me. It woofed and ran off, stopped, ran back again – and, well, that went on for a little while before I finally cottoned on. The dog was trying to get me to follow it.

I had nothing to do that day except sit by the fire and stare out of the window at the snow. So I thought, what the heck, I may as well go and take a look to see if I can figure out what all the fuss is about. I grabbed my overcoat, wrapped a scarf around my neck, put on gloves, wellies and a tweed cap and set off after the dog.

I must have followed that dog for over a mile. The journey wasn't as difficult as I'd feared. Although the snow lay in deep drifts around my house, once we got onto the narrow country roads, the going was easier. The snow had mainly drifted at one side of the road. On the other side, it lay at a depth of just a foot or two. No snow was falling by that time and, with the sun shining, I began to hope that maybe a thaw was about to begin. If I'd known then what I know now, I wouldn't have been so keen to see the snow thawing.

But I was ignorant or innocent or just plain stupid and I thought a thaw was the answer to all my problems.

Everywhere I looked, the landscape was strangely featureless. As far as the eye could see, everything was white. Most of the distinctive landmarks had been smoothed out so that after a few minutes of trudging through the snow I had difficulty working out precisely where I was.

I didn't pass any other houses. Beyond the dry-stone walls and banks at either side of the narrow roads, snow-covered fields and moorland stretched into the far distance. It must have been about half an hour, maybe a bit longer, before I saw the farmhouse on the brow of the hill up ahead of us. It looked like so many of the farms around here. A wooden gate at the side of the road opened onto a narrow track leading to the old stone house. Various ramshackle buildings were scattered around the house but whether they were intended to contain cows, pigs or tractors I couldn't say; the life of a working farm is a mystery to me. There were a few frosty-looking sheep in the fields. They were huddled together against a line of hedges where the snow lay thinnest.

Smoke was coming from the chimney so I assumed that someone must be at home. I thought there was a chance I might be offered a cup of tea and maybe a slice of cake. I pictured a smiling, rosy-cheeked farmer's wife full of joy and gratitude when I returned her dog. But there was no farmer's wife. And no tea and cake.

The front door was ajar. Which explains how the dog had got out in the first place. I knocked anyway. The dog meanwhile ran into the house, barked a couple of times, then ran out again. I knew the signs by now. This was his way of telling me that he wanted me to follow him. But I didn't want to barge into the house uninvited so I knocked again. And I waited. The dog was yapping at me, scurrying into the house then out again, giving me a look that suggested he thought I might be mentally deficient if I couldn't understand the message he was trying to get through to me.

Clearly nobody was going to come to the door so I followed the dog inside. Other than the light from a few glowing embers in the grate, the house was in total darkness. Heavy curtains were drawn across the windows. I could barely see anything. Instinctively I looked for a light switch on the wall, found one, and flicked it down. Nothing happened. Obviously my house wasn't the only one that had been affected by the power cut. There was no reason for me to stay, I reckoned, so I might as well go back home. I'd done my duty, as far as I could see. I'd accompanied the dog back to what I presumed was its home. As nobody was there, it seemed to me that there was nothing else for me to do. I turned to leave. The dog ran in front of me so rapidly and so unexpectedly that I nearly tripped over it. It stood there, barking at me. I moved to one side with the intention of walking past the animal. But as soon as I moved, it moved too. It was determined to block my exit.

I knelt down and stroked its head. I hadn't had a dog since childhood, but I had the feeling that stroking a dog's head is generally regarded as a good strategy when you want to calm it down. I stroked its head, I fondled its ears. The damned dog barked right into my face! And then is darted across the room, sat on the floor and barked again.

It seemed to me that there was something to which the dog was trying to attract my attention. In the gloom, I couldn't make out what it was. I went to the heavy curtains and pulled them back. Light flooded through the frost-covered windows. That's when I noticed just how bitterly cold it was in the house. My breath made plumes of vapour in the air.

Then I saw the body.

3

It was an old man, slumped in an armchair in front of the open fire grate. The fire had dwindled away, leaving nothing in the grate but a few smouldering sticks surrounded by mounds of black ash. The man's face was pallid, his eyes closed, the wrinkled skin drawn tight over his skull. I assumed he must have died after the snow came; with no effective source of warmth he had succumbed to hypothermia. My first thought was to phone the emergency services. Call an ambulance to deal with him. There was a cordless house phone sitting on a sideboard. I picked it up but there was no sound. How helpless we are without electricity! With power, we can video-chat to someone on the other side of the world. Without power, we can't even make contact with someone half a mile away.

I was debating what to do – whether I should try to walk on to the village in the hope that they still had power there or that someone might have a fully-charged mobile phone – when I heard a low, rasping sound of breathing.

The man opened his eyes, turned to look at me, said, "What the bloody hell!" and jumped out of the chair faster than any corpse had a right to. I was forced to conclude that my initial diagnosis had been in error. The man wasn't dead after all.

"What the hell you doing in my house?" he snapped.

He was holding a knife in his hand. A big, sharp knife. The sort of knife a butcher uses to cut the bone out of a leg of lamb. The knife was pointing in my direction. I smiled. I tried to look friendly, which, when someone is pointing a knife at you, is a hard thing to do.

I babbled a bit and mentioned the dog. The dog, for his part, did his best to corroborate my story by licking my hand and staring up at the knife-wielding man with big, brown soulful eyes. Between the two of us, we finally managed to convince the man that my intentions were benign.

"You'll be wanting a cup of tea, I suppose?" he said at last.

"That's very kind of you."

"So it may be but you can't have any because I haven't got any. And even if I had, how the hell would I boil any water?"

"How long has the power been off?" I said.

"What business is that of yours?"

"None. I was just wondering..."

"I tell you one thing, I shall refuse to pay. The electric bill. Not a penny will they get out of me. I shall demand a rebate."

"Good idea," I said, "In the meantime, if there's anything I can do..."

The man sat back in the chair with a sigh – "The thing is, I'm so damn' tired all the time. Light-headed, you might say. I had a touch of flu."

"So did I," I said, "Must be going around."

"It's the sheep I blame," he said.

"The sheep?"

"Dirty animals. Any disease that's going around, the sheep will be sure to have it."

"Is that a fact?"

"Are you doubting my word, boy?" His eyebrows quivered accusingly.

"No, no. It's just, well, I don't know much about sheep."

"Not much to know. They are stupid, dirty, nasty animals. Full of parasites. And you can't trust the buggers. A sheep will stab you in the back as soon as look at you." He waved the knife menacingly.

"I had no idea."

"How old are you?" he snapped suddenly. The knife was pointing straight at me.

"Twenty-seven, I answered. Twenty-eight in February."

"Young," he said and gave me a suspicious look from under his bushy, grey eyebrows.

I laughed. "That's the first time anyone's said that to me in a while."

"Aye," he said, "Young. But not so young."

I wasn't sure what he was getting at, so I let it pass without commenting.

"You heard the wireless, at all?"

I shook my head. "Like I said, the power went off."

He smiled. "Modern technology! Absolutely bloody useless just when you need it. I always keep a good stock of batteries. Aye, batteries. You can't beat batteries. I heard all kinds of stuff on the wireless. I don't mean the BBC. They tell you nothing. The shortwave is what you want. I heard stuff from all over. America. Canada. Somaliland… You listen to the shortwave, boy?"

"Well, not often," – I smiled inanely because I didn't have a clue what he was talking about. As far as I knew, I'd never listened to a shortwave radio in my life. But he was getting so worked up on the subject that I didn't think it would be diplomatic to tell him that. You couldn't be sure how he'd react. He might turn violent. It crossed my mind that he might, in fact, be a bit strange in the head. Simple. Or drunk. At any rate, with that knife in his hand, I saw no reason to risk provoking him.

"It's young people you got to watch out for," he said, "They are the worst."

"Yes," I said. By now, I was desperate to get away. Get back home. "Well, I brought your dog back, so if it's all right with you…"

But he wasn't listening. He had slumped back into the chair and was sitting there as still and cadaverous as when I had first entered. I thought – Oh, God, no! He's had a heart attack! He really is dead now.

But then I heard the wheezing. He had dozed off. Which didn't seem entirely natural. I mean, one moment he was ranting and raving about sheep and shortwave radio. And the next moment, he was fast asleep. The dog started whining and licking the old man's hand. It occurred to me that if he was left there, that old man, all alone in that bitterly cold house with no warmth and no food, then he would certainly die. The dog knew that too.

Actually, it was even worse than that. At least, so it appeared. Not only didn't he have any food, he didn't have any water either. I turned the tap on and nothing came out. The water had frozen solid in the pipe. Or maybe the pipes had burst? That was one problem I hadn't had in my house – yet. I guessed I was just lucky. Maybe the water pipes that led to my house were further underground so they hadn't frozen. Or maybe my pipes were better lagged. I'd heard people talk about the importance of lagging your pipes even though I had no idea how to do it.

I patted the dog on the head. It was following me wherever I went. I told it that I'd be back soon and that this time I'd bring some food and water. How stupid is that! Explaining myself to a dog. But the dog made little huffing noises in reply which made me think that maybe it got the general idea of what I was saying.

I had a look around the house to see if there was anything I could use to heat the place – a paraffin heater maybe. Or some more wood for the fire. I couldn't see a heater but I soon found plenty of wood, stacked in a shelter outside. The only trouble was that there was nothing to light the fire with: no newspapers or kindling. I couldn't even find any matches. The embers in the grate were no longer glowing and even if they had been I wouldn't have known how to work them up into a decent blaze. I decided the best course of action would be to trek back to my cottage. I had a few firelighters, so I could bring those, and also some food and water. Potty as the old man might be, I couldn't just leave him there to freeze or starve.

The dog followed me all the way back home. Once there, I found an old rucksack and filled it with tins of soup and beans and fruit. I added a couple of firelighters and a box of matches. Then I had the problem of finding a container for the water. The only thing I could find was an empty screw-cap wine bottle. I didn't think that would hold enough water to keep the man going for very long. Not if the freeze continued for more than a day or two. Then it occurred to me that taking water to him was a stupid idea. The one thing he wasn't short of was water. It was everywhere. Piled up around his house in the form of snow. Once I'd lit his fire, I could melt some snow in a saucepan. So I set back off in the direction of the man's house. Snow was falling again. Little more than an hour had passed since I'd left the old man: it had taken me twenty-five minutes or so to walk from his house to mine, ten minutes to fill up my rucksack, and another twenty-five minutes to walk back.

The man was no longer there.

The blankets he'd had around him when last I'd seen him, asleep in the armchair, were heaped up on the floor. I walked through the house, shouting. I went upstairs. There were two rooms up there: one was full of junk, the other contained a rumpled double bed that smelled of rotting fish. There was no sign of the old man. I looked in the kitchen downstairs and in the small bathroom. Then I went to the back door to see if he might be outside, in one of the barns or outbuildings. He was nowhere to be seen. But I did see footprints. They led away from the house, up the side of a low hill. The snow was falling heavily by now, great goose-feather flakes, the kind of snow that quickly settles into deep drifts. If I didn't hurry, I might not be able to make it back to my own house. The snow would be too deep. So I didn't try to follow the old man. If he was well enough to go climbing up a hill in this weather, I reasoned, he was well enough to make his own way back without any help from me.

The dog seemed less convinced. It kept running up the hill, then back to me, letting out a whine or a bark every once in a while by way of emphasis. I got the strong impression that it wanted me to go looking for its master. Sorry, I told it, but that would be well above and beyond the call of duty, old chum.

I went back into the sitting room and put a few of the tins of food, plus the firelighters and some matches, onto the mantelpiece above the grate. When the man came back – *if* he came back – he would at least have something to eat and some way of getting warm. Then I left.

The damn' dog followed me. I shooed it away. "Back!" I said, "Go on! Go back home!"

It was having none of it. Wherever I went the dog was determined to follow. I continued trudging through the snow in the direction of my house and the dog kept darting around me, leaping through the snow, from one side of me to the other. I hoped it would eventually tire of the game and trot off back where it had come from. But, no way. Once it had decided to stick with me, it was not to be deterred.

If it hadn't been for the dog, I might not have found the boy in the woodshed.

4

The dog was scratching at the door of my woodshed and barking. I yelled "Shut up, you stupid mutt!" but that was either a command that he didn't know or else one that he chose to ignore.

I went inside and took off my gloves, coat and scarf. The fire was still smouldering in the stove but the wood had mostly burned down to ashes. That meant I'd have to go out again to get some logs. I wrapped my scarf around my neck but didn't bother with the coat and gloves because I didn't intend to be outside for very long.

When I got outside, the blasted dog was still there, alternately scratching at the woodshed door and barking at me. I was going to the woodshed anyway so if there was anything in there both the dog and I would soon see what it was. I suspected it would be rats. Or maybe a cat. What I didn't suspect was that it would be a seventeen year-old boy covered in blood. But that is exactly what it was. Slumped on the floor in front of the stack of wood was Geoff Parkham. Geoff is one of my guitar students. As a rule, he was a sensible lad – studious, polite, intelligent and level-headed. To say that I was shocked to see him sitting in my woodshed with blood soaking through his denim jacket would be an understatement.

You are probably thinking to yourself that I must have immediately realised this was a medical emergency, asked Geoff what had happened and then dealt with the problem swiftly and efficiently. Sadly, you would be wrong. The truth of the matter is that I couldn't make any sense of what I was seeing and I couldn't think of anything sensible to say. What I did say was, in fact, pretty damn' stupid in the circumstances: "Hello, Geoff. What are you doing here?"

It was a few seconds before he answered. He was looking at me in a very strange way. As though he was frightened of me. As though he didn't trust me.

"Hello, Mr Richards," he said, "I was taking shelter. From the snow."

Suddenly the ludicrousness of this conversation stuck me.

"Your arm," I said, "You're hurt. What the bloody hell…"

He smiled feebly but it was obvious he was in considerable pain.

"Got shot, didn't I."

"What d'you mean, you got shot? Who shot you?"

"A farmer, I guess."

"Who?"

"Not sure. I mean… it was snowing and… you know. I couldn't see…"

"But why did he…? Oh, never mind that. You're losing blood. We need to get you to hospital."

He laughed, but without humour. "How you going to do that then, Mr Richards?"

"Jonathan," I said, "Call me…"

"Whatever I call you, I don't see how you're gonna get me to no hospital. Not the state things is in."

He had a point, of course. The roads were blocked with snow and the snow was continuing to fall. There was no power and the battery of my mobile phone was flat. An idea occurred to me – "You haven't got a mobile phone on you, have you, Geoff?"

"Yeah."

"Charged?"

"Don't know. I think so. But that's not gonna do you any good. Who d'you think you're gonna call?"

I thought I was going to call the hospital, of course. They had a helicopter that they used in emergencies. It's not that unusual in rural areas. But first things first. I had to get the boy out of the woodshed and into the house. Keep him warm. Get him somewhere comfortable to lie down. I wished I'd paid more attention to the First Aid lessons we'd had at school. I couldn't think what you were supposed to do when someone was injured. I had a feeling a tourniquet was involved. Or was that only if an artery had been severed? I knew you were supposed to give them sweet tea. Or was it brandy? Oh well, those were minor details. The most important thing was to get him out of the shed and into the house.

I reached down and tried to grab Geoff around the chest with the intention of pulling him to a standing position but he immediately cried out in pain. I'd accidentally brushed against his wounded arm, I think. So I knelt next to him and he put his good right arm around my shoulders. Somehow or other, we managed to arrange it so that I was holding on to him and he was holding onto me without causing him too much pain and in that way I slowly hoisted him to his feet. He was trembling. I didn't know if that was from the cold or the shock. Maybe from both?

"Hello Bobby," he said, "What are you doing here?"

Bobby, it seemed, was the dog's name and he and Geoff knew one another. The dog rubbed its head against Geoff's jeans while Geoff tried to pat the dog's head – not entirely successfully – with the injured arm which was hanging limply at his side. At least he still has the ability to move his fingers, I told myself. That's got to be good.

Let me be honest: I've never been any good around blood. I cringe at the sight of it. The stink of blood on Geoff almost made me gag. I got him into the house and told him to lie on the settee. He refused. He said the blood would make a mess. I told him not to be so damn' stupid, a bit of blood on that old settee was neither here nor there. But he was adamant.

"How did this happen, Geoff? I mean, how the hell did you manage to get yourself shot?"

There were only two explanations I could think of. Either someone had been out hunting – shooting deer or foxes or pheasants – and they'd been careless, fired into some trees maybe or shot off into the distance and they'd hit Geoff by mistake. Or else Geoff had been doing something he shouldn't have been doing, somewhere where he shouldn't have been doing it, and a farmer had fired off a shot to deter him. But neither scenario seemed all that likely. What fool would be out hunting in this weather? And as for Geoff doing something bad, something criminal – well, that was impossible to imagine. He was always so well behaved, so damned polite. I wasn't even sure if he used swear words, let alone anything worse.

"It's just the way things is now, ain't they, Mr… I mean, Jonathan?"

"What do you mean?"

"Well, nobody trusts anybody now, do they? Especially not someone like me."

"Like you?"

"Someone my age, I mean."

I can't remember what I replied. Jonathan wasn't making much sense to me. I assumed it was the shock. Making him say irrational things. The important thing was to get some medical help. I asked him for his phone and he handed it over but told me I was wasting my time.

The phone was still charged. I had no idea what the hospital's phone number was so I dialled 999 to get through to an Emergency hotline. With no success. The phone just said "No service".

"I told you," Geoff said, "You're wasting your time."

My house was at the bottom of a shallow valley and the phone reception there was intermittent at the best of times. What with the bad weather and the power cuts, I assumed the mobile network must be in an even worse state than usual.

"I'll try again in a few minutes," I said, "I can't leave you like that. I have to get you to a doctor."

He shook his head, "There isn't anyone."

"Of course there is. I just have to…"

"You really don't know, then?"

"Don't know what?"

"What I said. There isn't anyone. Not any more. There's nobody. No doctors. No hospital. Nobody."

He's in shock, I told myself. He's talking nonsense. Just like the old man. The man the dog had taken me to. There's nothing to worry about, I told myself. And I felt my blood run cold. Because I wasn't sure that the things I was telling myself were true.

"I reckon you'll have to do it," Geoff said.

"Do what?"

"Get the bullet out. Strap up my arm."

"I don't know anything about…"

"Unless you're too squeamish, that is." – he was smiling as he said it. In the circumstances, Geoff seemed to be coping a lot better than I was.

"Well," I said, "I'd rather get someone who knows what they are doing, but..."

"But there ain't nobody. There's just you."

He was right. But I was scared. Because I had no idea what I should do.

"Let's ease you out of that denim jacket," I said.

The blood had seeped right through the material and had congealed. I was afraid I might open up the wound and make matters worse if I wasn't careful. I tried pulling the jacket collar back over his shoulder, aiming to draw out his arm as slowly and carefully as I could through the sleeve. But whenever I tugged at the denim sleeve, Geoff winced and gave a gasp of pain.

"I reckon you better cut it off," he said, "The jacket, I mean."

"I was hoping that's what you meant."

"Cut the sleeve off anyway."

"Are you sure?" I said, "This is a new jacket, isn't it?"

He laughed so loudly it was like a donkey braying. In fact, he laughed so much that tears started rolling down his cheeks. The laughter was infectious because soon I was laughing just as much as he was. When we'd finally calmed down a bit, I said, "I have no idea why we are laughing."

"You!" he said, laughing still, "I've been shot, you're probably going to have to cut my arm off with a kitchen knife, and as if that wasn't bad enough, it's also the end of the soddin' world. And all you are worried about is spoiling my denim jacket!"

I was laughing again now. "Yes," I said between guffaws, "I suppose that is a bit funny."

But when the laughter eventually subsided, I knew that it wasn't funny at all.

"There is no way I am cutting off your arm," I said solemnly, "With or without a kitchen knife."

I got a large pair of scissors from the kitchen and I cut all the way through the arm of the jacket from the cuff to the shoulder. Then I had to take off his watch. He was very proud of that watch. It had Bluetooth, Wi-Fi, GPS and calendar. It even told the time. Then I cut through the arm of his shirt underneath. I had to use a wet kitchen towel to dab at the dried blood from time to time so that I could peel away the material without hurting him too much.

His upper left arm, just beneath the shoulder, was a mess. To my untutored eye it looked like a piece of tenderised steak. I couldn't see a massive hole though, so it wasn't quite as bad as I'd feared. It wasn't good either. All I could do was dab at it gently with some cotton wool dipped into TCP and then put a bandage over it. TCP and a bandage was about as far as my home First Aid supplies stretched to. I wasn't sure that my treatment was likely to make any improvement. I only hoped it hadn't made matters worse. Once he'd been patched up, I found an old pullover for him to wear. It had the benefit of being sufficiently baggy to slip over his injured arm without causing too much pain, sufficiently thick to keep him warm and sufficiently old for a few bloodstains here and there not to be a problem.

"Why didn't you go home after you were shot?" I said.

"I ran away."

"Ran away from what?"

"I ran away from home. That's how come I was out in the fields in the first place."

I couldn't make any sense of what he was saying. I knew Geoff's family slightly. His father was a good-natured, hard-working dairy farmer. His mother ran a small grocer's shop in the village. He had a young sister, Greta, who was about twelve or thirteen, I think, and always seemed very serious and studious. As far as I knew they were an entirely happy family.

"Running away sounds a bit desperate. What happened? Did you have an argument with your mum and dad?"

"My sister. Me and her had an argument."

"You ran away from home because you had an argument with your sister?"

"Yeah, well, it was a bit more than an argument. She went for me. Attacked me."

I couldn't help smiling. Greta was so small, so fragile.

"My dad took her part, of course. My mum was still feeling pretty sick so she never really stood up for me. So I had to clear out. There was nothing else I could do."

"Geoff," I said, "You have to go back home."

"I can't."

"You have to. I mean, what will your parents say when they find you've been here and I haven't even let them know?"

"Oh, for God's sake!" – the sudden anger in his voice shocked me – "You keep going on as if everything is like it used to be. As if nothing's changed. The world has ended, man!"

I kept my cool. I told myself again that this mood swing was a symptom of the shock. I sat there and I let him rave at me for a while. I thought it would do him good to get it out of his system. When he'd finished telling me what a stupid fool I was in words of one syllable, I said, very calmly, "OK, Geoff, so you think the world has ended…"

"Listen to me, man! I don't *think*…!"

"OK, OK," I said, "So tell me about it."

And he did.

5

"It started with the snow. That was over a week ago. Ten days maybe. The heavy snow, I mean. I thought it was great. I looked out of my bedroom window that morning and everything was white. It reminded me of when I was a kid. There was always snow in winter in them days. My little sister, Greta, she wanted to go out and build a snowman, so we had breakfast and then we… well anyway, that was before she... before she got sick."

"Greta got sick?"

"I told you."

"You said your mum was sick. You never said…"

"I told you she got violent. I told you she attacked me. It's all the same."

I didn't see the connection but Geoff had already snapped at me once and I didn't want to set him off again, so I said nothing.

"Yeah, well anyway, never mind about Greta. You know where my dad's farm is, don't you? Up on Windicott Hill, so we get a good view for miles around. Everywhere was covered in snow. It was as if Windicott Woods and the village and the fields and farms for miles around had all vanished. Apart from the old church steeple and one or two of the big old barns in up in Biddeman's farm, off in the distance, there wasn't much you could see. Only the snow."

"I know," I said, "It was the same here. Worse because my house is in the bottom of the valley so I couldn't even see the church steeple, never mind Biddeman's barns."

Even though it had been snowing on and off ever since Christmas, the heavy snowfall came as a shock. In late December and early January, the snow had mostly been the sort of snow that doesn't settle: fine, powdery, wet snow that sifts down like icing sugar and melts away beneath the watery sun. That changed on January 13th. That was when we had the first of the blizzards. We'd had plenty of advance warning. The Met Office had been tracking a 'cold front' moving in through Sweden, Denmark, Germany and France. The newspapers were calling it the Siberian Snowstorm. It arrived in the South-east of England first. Then it moved west. With so much advance warning, you'd think we'd have been well prepared. But, of course, we weren't.

"I always loved the snow," Geoff said, "Not any more though."

"It's been a damn' nuisance," I said, "But hardly the end of the world."

"Maybe not. Not yet. But things are only going to get worse, ain't they?"

"I didn't think you were such a pessimist. OK, so the weather is bloody awful, the power's off and the phones are out of action. That's only temporary. Everything will be back to normal pretty soon."

"You reckon?"

"I do."

"The way things are going, I reckon there'll be nothing much left. Nothing that works, anyway."

"What makes you think that?"

"The riots and stuff."

"Riots?"

"You're not going to tell me you never heard about the riots, are you?"

"That's exactly what I am going to tell you. I honestly have no idea what you're talking about."

"How come you don't know?"

"I don't watch much telly. I prefer to read. And play guitar."

"The Internet though. You must have seen it on the Internet."

I shook my head – "I had a touch of flu. I was completely out of it for a few days. Well, more like a week, I think."

"You got better though."

I nodded, "I got better."

"Some people do." It struck me as an odd thing to say. A lot of what Geoff was saying struck me as odd. He told me about the looting then. It had started in London. Random gangs of youths smashing shop windows and taking things for no reason at all. Mass looting is not a commonplace occurrence in London but it happens from time to time. In London, almost anything could trigger a riot.

Hot weather, flooding, a confrontation with the police, someone having a private argument that suddenly escalates into a fight that eventually turns into mob rule.

"This wasn't the usual sort of riot," Geoff said, "There were rumours going about that it was something that got started on the web. You know, like flash mobs an' that. The news on telly was full of stuff about looting and smashing up shops in big cities – not just London. Birmingham too, Cardiff, Plymouth, all over the place. Round here, we thought we were safe. Out in the sticks. What goes on in the cities don't have anything to do with us. But then the riots started spreading. Breaking out all over the place. Not only in Britain. There were riots in France and Germany. I seen it all on the telly."

I remembered seeing some reports about trouble in France and Germany, just before I got sick. Civil unrest is what they were calling it. People burning cars, fighting on the Champs Élysées. A couple of mass shootings in Berlin. I hadn't paid too much attention at the time.

Those were the sorts of things that happened all too often abroad. If you'd asked anyone around here they'd all have told you that 'abroad' is a dangerous place. The only ever news that got reported from France and Germany was bad news: clashes between political rivals, unrest in the banlieues, terrorism, crooks, nutcases…

"Some mobs went into the Vatican, smashing stuff, nicking stuff. The police couldn't stop them, or so they said. If you want my opinion, I think half the police was probably in there nicking stuff themselves."

I laughed. I assumed Geoff was making a joke.

"Then it got worse."

"Worse?" I said, "How much worse can it get?"

"A lot worse. You sure you don't know anything about this?"

"I must have missed it all. When I was in bed with flu. By the time I got over that, there was no power."

"It's been going around," said Geoff, "Russian Flu. One of the bad sort, so they say. It laid my mother pretty low. My dad got over it. I think. I never got it at all. But my sister, she got it bad. My dad locked her in her bedroom. You could hear her in there. Screaming. Smashing things."

"Not exactly the usual symptoms of flu," I said.
"It takes people different ways."
"But Greta wouldn't harm a fly!"
"She changed."

6

I tried Geoff's phone a few times more. For a while the "No service" message went away, which gave me hope. But when I tried phoning 999 again, there was no answer. I tried phoning some other numbers – a friend, a couple of local businesses, even the Inland Revenue in London on the basis that the tax man is a creature that never sleeps. Nobody answered. Then the phone reverted to "No service" again. I still refused to be as cynical as Geoff. He had tried to convince me that the world as I knew it had pretty much pulled down the shutters and gone into administration. That prospect seemed so absurd that I didn't bother worrying about it. The only thing I was concerned about was Geoff's injured arm. Somehow I had to get him to a doctor.

"I think we'll have to see if we can get you into the village," I said.

"Why?"

"To see the doctor."

"There's no doctors in the village."

"Of course there are. There are two doctors."

"There's a doctor's surgery," Geoff corrected, "But the doctors don't live there. They live miles away."

It hadn't occurred to me that even the doctors would be cut off from the village.

"Looks like we're screwed, don't it," Geoff said.

I slumped back into an armchair. "Yes, it certainly does."

The blood was starting to seep through the arm of the pullover that I'd given Geoff. I was worried about him but tried not to show it. He wasn't losing huge amounts of blood but I had no idea how badly injured he might be where it didn't show. I had horrible visions of him suddenly keeling over and dying on my kitchen floor. But I couldn't think of anything else I could do.

Geoff seemed to be more worried about the dog than about himself. "Poor old Bobby. He wants some food. Don't suppose you got any dog food?"

"Not something I keep in stock," I said, "As I haven't got a dog and have never acquired a taste for dog food myself."

"Better make him some scrambled eggs then. Or a tin of tuna might do."

I didn't have eggs or tuna. I soon discovered, however, that a few pilchards in a saucer made an acceptable alternative."

"How come old Bobby is here?" Geoff asked, as he patted the dog.

I told him about my strange encounter with the old man in the farm house.

"Old Douggie Lampton wouldn't let Bobby out of sight. He loves his dog almost as much as he loves his sheep."

I told him that as far as I could figure out, he didn't seemed to love his sheep very much at all. He'd said that sheep were diseased animals that couldn't be trusted.

"Don't sound like old Douggie Lampton, that don't. I reckon he must have got a touch of it too."

"A touch of what?"

I knew what Geoff was going to say before I'd even asked the question. And say it he did – "The Russian Flu."

If Geoff was to be believed, this mysterious Russian Flu had the strangest set of symptoms. It could do everything from making little girls throw temper tantrums to causing a sheep farmer to take against his own sheep. The symptoms I'd suffered weren't anything like so exotic. I'd had alternating bouts of sweating and freezing-fits with added hallucinations. In fact, I'd had a set of symptoms that you wouldn't want to have one at a time, and you definitely don't want to have all together: sneezing, coughing, headaches, vomiting, diarrhoea – well, you get the picture. While everyone else was watching the country collapse under the devastation of the snow-storm of the century, I was wrapped up in my own private fever dreams, oblivious to it all.

"There must be someone in the village who has some medical knowledge," I said, "A nurse maybe?"

"There is Dr Prentiss, I suppose," Geoff said after a moment's thought.

"Who's Dr Prentiss?"

"He used to the be the doctor here but he retired years ago. He's ancient. Must be about a hundred, if not more."

"And he lives in the village?"

"Yeah."

"Right then. I'll take you to Dr Prentiss." An ancient and geriatric doctor was, after all, better than no doctor. "Where does he live?"

"Oh, he won't be at home."

"No?"

"But I bet I know where he will be…"

7

So that's how we came to be trudging through the snow just as twilight was falling. We'd been walking for almost an hour when we saw the dead sheep. It was Bobby the dog who noticed it first. He must have caught its scent and went scampering off in great excitement, leaping and diving through the snow and barking at us until we followed. The sheep's throat had been cut and it had bled out into the snow.

Then we saw another. And another. And another. Scattered at irregular intervals, the blood-drenched bodies of the sheep were already being covered by the falling snow. Then we saw a human body. It was the old man I'd talked to in the farmhouse. Douggie Lampton. His throat was cut too and he lay in a mush of red-tinted snow. He still held the knife in his hand, its blade red with blood.

I had never seen a dead body before. I mean, yes, I'd seen them on films and on TV. I saw my Uncle Ray's body too, when I was about seven or eight; he was made up to look as lifelike as a waxworks figure that someone had put, as a joke, inside a satin-lined coffin. But seeing dead bodies in films and on TV, or seeing the carefully arranged body of my Uncle Ray, that's different, totally different, from seeing a human being, a man I'd been talking to just a couple of hours earlier, lying cold and dead in a snow-covered field. I've got used to seeing dead bodies since then. We all have. But that was my first and I didn't take it well.

My legs almost gave way. I'm not normally squeamish but this was something I couldn't control. For a second, everything became brightly-lit as though someone had turned on high-powered floodlighting, the kind of lights they use in stadiums and football pitches after dark. I felt light-headed, dizzy. For some reason, I felt like laughing. It was as if I was looking down on the scene from a distance. I was detached, uninvolved – and then *bam!* I slammed back down to earth with a jolt.

There, lying a few feet away from me, was the dead body of Douggie Lampton. He was lying in a mess of his own blood. His throat gaped, as cleanly sliced as a joint of meat. This was real. This had happened. It was too big a thing for me to take in. I kept saying to myself, "This is not real. This can't be real." But, by God, it was!

The dog lay in the snow, licking his dead master's hand and whining. I said we should do something. Geoff said there's nothing we can do. I said, he might not be dead, which was obviously absurd. Geoff said we had to keep walking. I said the least we could do was notify the authorities. Geoff said there were no authorities. Not any longer.

And so we left the man, lying there, alone, his body fading away beneath the falling snow. At the time, this seemed like a terrible thing. Later on, I came to realise that Douggie Lampton had taken the easy way out. Other people would not be so lucky.

It had been Geoff's idea to come that way, past Lampton's farm. The village lay two miles or so beyond it. But in the bitter cold, trudging through the deep snow, we were making desperately slow progress. Geoff was still in pain. I could see it on his face. He made light of it, said he was fine. I suggested we go back to Lampton's farm. See if he had a Land Rover we could borrow. I said "borrow" but I meant "steal". It was no great crime. A Land Rover would be no use to Douggie Lampton any more. Geoff said a Land Rover would never be able to make it through that depth of snow. He was right, of course.

"How about a tractor, then?"

"He was a sheep farmer," Geoff said, "He had a 15 horse-power tractor."

"Is that good or bad?"

"In this snow, it would be useless. It's just a tiny thing. It probably wouldn't take the two of us very far on a sunny day in the middle of summer let alone in this weather."

"If only we had transport…"

"I think he had a digger."

"A digger?"

"A kind of excavator. You know, one of them things with caterpillar tracks and an hydraulic neck at the front with a scoop on the end."

"That would be perfect," I said, "We could dig our way through the snow, couldn't we?"

Geoff didn't look convinced. "It's for mud mostly, not snow. Anyway, it'd be bloody slow."

Even so, as we were only about a quarter of a mile away from the farm, we decided – well, to be honest, *I* decided – that it would be worth going back for a look. When we got there I could see what Geoff meant about the tractor. It was barely bigger than a ride-on lawn mower. The digger on the other hand, was plenty big enough. Only problem was, it didn't work. The hydraulics were leaking and when I tried to start it, the digger just shuddered and died.

But while we didn't find any means of transport, we did find something of interest: the old man's shortwave receiver. We also found that he'd been lying through his teeth when he'd said he didn't have any food or water. He had a whole room full of food, water, beer and much more bedsides, all neatly stacked and labelled. We didn't notice the room at first. It was entered via small door in the wall just under the staircase. It looked like the door to a store-room. But inside there was another door. That door led to a cellar. The cellar had been turned into a kind of survival bunker. It was almost as though he'd been expecting something bad to happen and had laid in supplies to make sure he could survive it. In which case, why had he killed himself?

The shortwave radio was really something. Not the kind of piddly little transistor radio I'd expected. It was a serious bit of kit. A big black box studded with dials, buttons and knobs. I tried lifting it and I reckon it must have weighed six or seven pounds. Maybe more. It's what I think is called a transceiver – something that can transmit as well as receive. It was plugged into some sort of power device – I'm not sure if you'd call it a battery or a generator. It was a big square box with knobs and dials all over the place. I'm guessing it was some sort of electricity-storage unit. Anyway, when I turned on the radio and tried moving a dial, I heard a noise like eggs frying and the occasional word or two in some language I couldn't even identify. Then I tried pressing some of the buttons. That was a bit more successful. I guess they must have been tuned into specific channels. There was one that claimed to be broadcasting from Canada but all I got was music – John Denver, I think – and a message saying what time the next live broadcast was. That didn't mean much to me because I had no idea what the time was in Canada. Then I got a religious station, I think from America, that had someone ranting on about the End Of Days and why we must atone for our sins. At first I thought there were no British stations but after a while I eventually heard a crackly jingle – three synthesized tones: *Zink, Zink, Zonk*, followed by a man's voice – "Radio True Britain, your only source of true news. Coming soon on…" and then giving a wavelength that I didn't bother to remember.

I shone my torch around the room. If we'd wanted to, we could have stayed there for weeks. It was stocked up with everything you'd need. I remember thinking that the only thing it lacked was a generator. In fact, I was wrong about that too. The generator was in one of the barns. It was diesel powered so I guess it couldn't have been brought indoors because of the fumes.

"We could take some of this stuff," Geoff said, "The tins of food could be useful anyway."

"Too bulky," I said, "The radio would have been handy. Just a pity he didn't have a smaller model!"

I didn't seriously consider the possibility of taking the radio with us. It would have been different if we'd had a vehicle of some kind. But as we hadn't found any usable means of transportation, there was nothing for it but to continue on foot. As long as we had to walk there would be no way we could cope with the extra weight of tinned food and radios.

So we went outside again, heading in the direction of the village. The thing I remember about that walk is how beautiful everything was. How white and clean and pure the landscape looked, how crisp and sparkling everything was as the snow kept falling in big, feathery flakes. In the deepening twilight the landscape looked almost blue. We walked along twisty, narrow country lanes flanked on each side by smooth snowdrifts covering the banks and hedges. It was a long, difficult journey. In places the snow lay so deep that it filtered down into our Wellington boots; and the snow also tugged hard at our boots when lifted our feet out of it. There wasn't much to see on those little roads. No people, no cars. No houses, even. Just undulating white fields on either side, occasionally dotted with unhappy-looking sheep or cows. As we walked, we talked. About this and that. Not about the snow. Not about Geoff's injury. Just ordinary, everyday things, as if we were on an ordinary, everyday stroll.

"You got any family?" Geoff asked.

I told him my mother shared a house in Guildford with an interior decorator half her age. My father had left years ago and my mother neither knew nor cared where he was now.

"No brothers or sisters?" Geoff said.

"No."

"Girlfriend?"

I shook my head.

"Boyfriend."

"No. There was somebody once. But it didn't end happily."

"Runs in the family, 'eh?"

"What?"

"Like your mum, I mean. You said your dad left her?"

"Oh, that ended very happily as far as she was concerned. Remember the interior decorator I mentioned, half her age?"

"Oh, yeah. There is that, I suppose."

"Let's just say he satisfied her cravings."

"Sex?"

"Soft furnishings. And sex too, I suppose, though that's not something she's ever discussed with me."

"So why did you decide to move down here? It's a long way from Guildford."

I smiled, "That was the main reason. Also, there were things I wanted to get away from. I had a bit of a bad time."

"How'd you mean?"

"A breakdown."

"Wow!"

"Yes, wow, indeed. I needed to get away and make a fresh start. A friend of mine happened to have inherited a little cottage around here and offered it to me at a low rent. I jumped at the chance. That was two years ago. The life here suits me fine."

"Suited," Geoff corrected, "I know you don't believe me, but that life's all gone. It's never coming back again."

Eventually we came to a rise in the ground and when we reached the top of it we could see dimly see the village in the gathering darkness. It was maybe half a mile distant, down at the bottom of a shallow valley. It looked like the sort of English country village you might see on a Christmas card but never expect to see in real life. The buildings there are all quite old. A few houses have thatches. It's what you'd call picturesque even on a normal day. But now with the roofs all covered in snow and smoke gently rising from a few of the chimneys, it looked perfect.

"Well, at least the world hasn't ended just yet," I said, "There are fires lit so some people must be at home."

"Don't go into the village," Geoff warned.

"What? That's why we've come here, isn't it? At least, we can see if the doctor is at home. He should be able to do a better job of your arm than I've done."

"Too dangerous."

"The village?" I said, "Dangerous? I hardly think so."

Geoff gave me a hard, bitter look – "Yeah, well, nobody's shot you, have they?"

It was Geoff's opinion that it would be safer to make for the Church, which was situated at the top of a long lane to the west of the village.

"I didn't know you were religious," I said.

"I'm not. It's where the Church Hall is. You can bet the Colonel will have gone there. And if the Colonel is, Doc Prentiss will be there too."

"Who's the Colonel?"

"You don't know the Colonel? You don't know much about anything, do you! He's the only one who ever gets anything done around here. He organises stuff. Flower shows, fêtes, street parties. If anything needs organising, he's the one to do it."

"What's that got to do with the Church Hall?"

"That's the centre of things. F'rinstamce, when we had that flooding a few years back… You probably wasn't here then though, was you?"

I shook my head.

"Yeah, well, the village, being at the bottom of a valley, like, it gets flooded every now and then. And a few years back we had a big one. Most of Fore Street was under three feet of water. All the shops was flooded. Well, the Colonel took charge, didn't he. Got everyone into the Church Hall. Organised search parties to see if anyone was trapped in their houses. Then, when the military arrived, he told them what to do like as though he was in command or something. Take my word, if anyone is in charge, it'll be the Colonel."

"And if the Colonel isn't in charge?" I asked.

Geoff smirked. "Then we're really screwed."

8

It was fully dark by the time we started climbing the hill towards the Church Hall. I'd brought a small torch and we needed it because there was no moon showing and the snow was falling heavily again. The Hall was just a one-storey oblong building with a corrugated metal roof. There was a dim light showing through its windows. A short path led from the road to the Hall and the snow there had been churned up by numerous feet so I guessed there must be quite a few people inside.

When I walked onto the path, Geoff held back. "You go first," he said, "That would be better. Then, if everything's OK, you can come back for me."

"If everything's OK?"

"If they don't mind. Me, I mean."

"Why should they?"

"I'm seventeen."

"And…?"

"Young."

"So?"

"Just check, that's all."

It dawned on me then. Most of the rioters and looters were young. That's what Geoff had said. And that's what the old farmer, Douggie Lampton, had said too: "It's young people you got to watch out for," he'd told me. With so many young people on the rampage, I guessed that Geoff might be worried that people in the village would be prejudiced against anyone under thirty.

"You think they won't want you in there because you're young?"

"I just think it's worth checking is all."

"But wait a minute," I said, "What about me? I'm twenty-seven."

"That's what I mean. You're old."

"Hmmm. OK, I'll let that pass. For the time being."

Geoff was determined to stay outside, hiding behind a bush. Until I gave him the all clear. The arrangement was that I was to go into the Hall, find out who was there and if they seemed friendly. Then I was to break the news gradually that I had a young companion who was at that very moment freezing to death behind a bush in a snowstorm and if they didn't mind, would it be all right if I invited him inside for a cup of tea and a game of darts. Or something to that effect.

So I left Bobby the dog with Geoff and I walked up to the Hall intending to push open the double doors and stroll inside. It was not to be that easy. The doors were locked. I knocked on them. After a few moments I heard a deep, gruff voice on the other side call out "Who's there?"

"Jonathan Richards," I said.

There was a pause. Then – "Jonathan Who?"

"Richards," I replied, and added – somewhat irrelevantly – "I'm a guitar teacher."

"Never heard of you," said the voice, "Sorry, we're full here. You'll have to find somewhere else."

I confess this was not the fulsome welcome I'd been anticipating. I was debating whether we should trudge all the way back to my house or call in at one of the village pubs when a woman's voice called out from within the Hall.

"Is that Jonathan Richards from Heather Cottage?"

"It is indeed!" I replied, foolishly happy that somebody actually knew who I was.

"This is Millie Jenkins. The postie. I deliver your post. In a red van."

"Millie!" I said, "How are you?"

"Oh, can't complain," she said.

Then there was some sort of mumbled conversation behind the doors. I couldn't hear what was being said but I got the impression that the gruff-voiced man was asking Millie the postie if she was sure I was who I claimed to be and whether, even if I were, they should consider letting me into the Hall.

Finally they came to a decision. I heard bolts being pulled back on the inside of the door. Then the door opened a crack and a single eye peered out at me. It was one of Millie's eyes. "Yes, it's him," she said.

I smiled to show that I was pleased to receive confirmation that I was who I said I was. The gruff-voiced man mumbled something. Millie said, "Yeah, I think so. He seems all right."

"Oh, I am," I said, "Just a bit cold, that's all. Because of the snow out here."

"Yeah, well then," Millie said, "I s'ppose you better come in then, hadn't you?"

The door opened and in I went. There must have been a thirty or forty people in there. Most were sitting on chairs. A few were sitting on the floor. There were no children, I noticed. No teenagers either. In fact, I was probably the youngest person in the room. Two things struck me. One: the stink of paraffin; there was an old paraffin heater in the middle of the Hall; and two: the air of sickness; most people where sniffling and wheezing, coughing and sneezing.

"Ah, so you are our famous guitar virtuoso!" boomed a fruity voice from across the Hall. This voice was as sound as a bell – with no hint on a wheeze or a sniffle. I couldn't see who it was at first, because the lighting was so dim. In fact, the only lights they had were one small camping gas lamp that was suspended from a ceiling joist and about a dozen candles stuck onto saucers resting on tables or on the floor.

"Pleased to meet you, old man," the same fruity voice boomed as a tall, white-haired man advanced towards me with his hand extended. I am not, as a rule, one of Nature's born hand-shakers but it was clear that when this particular individual extended a hand to be shaken, there was no alternative but to bloody well shake it.

"We got sandwiches," Millie the postie interrupted, pointing towards some plates on a table. And she sneezed, pretty much in the direction of the sandwiches. I was hungry, but not that hungry.

"And we got beer," said a plump, ruddy-faced gent whose gruff voice gave him away as the bloke who had initially refused to let me in. He was all smiles now, as though his previous aim of sending me to my certain death in a blizzard had been just a minor lapse in politeness. I didn't bother replying to him, though I did take note of the stack of crates in which the beer, presumably, was stored.

Apart from the Mille the postie, I didn't know anyone there. I mean, I recognised a few faces vaguely. I think one woman worked in the Post Office. And there was a man I'd seen cutting hedges last autumn. But I've never really thrown myself into the life of the village so most of them were complete strangers to me.

"How're you bearing up, old man?" said the chap with the plummy voice.

"I've been better," I said.

"Ha! Yes! Haven't we all! Haven't we all! However, I'm sure this is all a passing phase as it were. The Government will no doubt have contingency plans for this sort of eventuality. But it all takes time, it all takes time. Feel free to avail yourself of the hospitality. Tea, coffee, alcoholic beverages…"

By now the interest in my arrival had worn off among the other people in the Hall and they went back to doing what I supposed they must have been doing before I had turned up. Some of them started talking to one another, punctuated by bouts of coughing, a few sat around reading books by the flickering light of candles. The plummy voiced man was clearly in charge of everything so I decided that I would have to ask him if it was OK to bring Geoff inside too.

"Would I be right in supposing that you are the Colonel?" I asked.

He gave a short grunt. "That's what they call me. The rank, however, is not mine. I run a small antique business. But for some reason, people call me Colonel. I really can't think why."

"What should I call you, then?"

"Whatever you like. Reginald is my name, Reginald McPherson, but nobody would have a clue who you were talking about if you called me that."

"Shall I call you Colonel, then?"

"Might as well. Everyone else does."

"Well, you see, Colonel, the thing is, there's someone else. With me, I mean."

"Someone else?" He looked around the Hall theatrically to indicate that he was unable to see any companion of mine.

"He's outside," I said.

"In this weather? Seems rather eccentric. Who is he? Anyone I know?"

"Geoff Parkham," I said.

"Ah, yes. I know him. Nice lad. Better get him inside, then."

I told him about the gunshot wound. The Colonel seemed genuinely concerned. He immediately took charge of the situation, barked out an order to someone sitting on the floor to get a camp bed sorted out. Snapped his fingers at an elderly white-haired, tweed-coated gentleman who had been sitting at a table, reading – "Walter! You're needed!" – then strode to the door, opened it and bellowed into the darkness, "Geoffrey Parkham, you stupid damn' fool. Get yourself in here before I come out there and drag you in!"

That was when a shape leapt out of the darkness towards us. The Colonel jumped back, bumping into me and nearly knocking me over. It was Bobby the dog. Fortunately, Bobby and The Colonel knew one another and clearly liked one another's company. My heart sank as I realised I was going to have to explain how Bobby had adopted me and what had happened to his master.

9

Walter Prentiss may have been old but he carried himself with the authority of youth. He took Geoff over to the far end of the hall, sat him in a chair next to a table and called for someone to bring the gas lamp over to assist in his examination. He took off Geoff's watch and handed it to the Colonel. He carefully removed the pull-over Geoff was wearing and cut off the bandages I'd put on. He chuckled to himself when he saw those. I gathered my bandaging did not entirely suggest a high level of medical competence. He asked me to shine my torch on Geoff's arm. The arm looked, to me, worse than ever. It was not only swollen but it was also now crusted with congealed blood. Doctor Prentiss tutted to himself.

"Is it bad?" Geoff asked.

"It depends on the angle from which you look at it," said the doctor, "From your perspective it is no doubt worse than it is from my perspective. From my perspective it is merely an interesting problem. From your perspective I should imagine it is moderately painful."

Geoff went for the stiff upper-lip approach. "Oh, it's not too bad, really."

"How about now?" The doctor pressed his thumbs into Geoff's arm and Geoff yowled like a dog. He yowled so convincingly that, for a while, Bobby joined in.

"Sorry about that. I was just testing the accuracy of my diagnosis."

"What is it?" Geoff said, his upper lip showing definite signs of weakness this time, "Did he get an artery?"

"I think," said the doctor, "that we may safely discount that possibility."

"Why's that?"

"Mainly because you are still alive. Had you suffered a severed artery you would certainly have expired long ago."

"Ah…"

"Fortunately, I have all the equipment I need to operate upon you. The facilities here are somewhat primitive, but all the same, I think I should be able to do a moderately satisfactory job."

The doctor then set about giving instructions to various people who had been standing around watching and ten minutes later a table had been laid out in readiness for the operation. There was a bowl of tepid water, some methylated spirits and cotton wool balls, some towels and plasters. And some kind of forceps. While all this was being assembled, Doctor Prentiss had said nothing about what he was preparing to do and Geoff's face, I noticed, had become quite pale.

Eventually, the doctor took a flannel and dipped it into the water. "The first thing we have to do is clean up the wound," he said, "And then I shall ask someone to go and get the meat cleaver and bread knife from the kitchen so that…"

Geoff fainted clean away.

"Oh, dear," the doctor said, "That was just my little joke. It's surprising how often my patients don't see the funny side of things."

It turned out that Geoff's injury wasn't quite so bad as it looked. Once the arm has been cleaned up, you could see that it was dotted with a whole bunch of little holes. They looked red and swollen. Geoff had regained consciousness just in time to be able to watch the proceedings with a detached interest. He had been peppered with shot – little lead pellets. Doctor Prentiss spent a happy half hour or so removing a dozen or so of them. There were a few more that had penetrated more deeply and would probably work their way out in their own sweet time.

The doctor used a pair of tweezers to squeeze out the pellets that were close to the surface of the skin. A few of them popped out quite easily. Each time one did, Geoff gritted his teeth and made a little moaning sound. I got the impression that having gunshot tweaked out of your body was not the most pleasant experience you can have. Some of the pellets took quite a bit of probing and squeezing. One in particular took about five minutes before it finally popped out.

"I haven't any painkillers or antibiotics," the doctor warned, "so don't bother asking for any. Naturally, if you have the chance to go to a better equipped facility than this, I should do so. But, at any rate, I'll patch you up as best I can."

Doctor Prentiss clearly enjoyed his work. He gave a broad smile of triumph with each pellet that he extracted and dropped into a small metal dish. Everyone in the Hall had gathered around to watch. Someone actually clapped after a particularly painful pellet was removed and fell into the bowl with a tinkle.

"I wonder why anyone would shoot you?" Doctor Prentiss said, "I hardly think you could be mistaken for a pheasant!"

Geoff shrugged.

"Who was it?"

Geoff shrugged again. "A farmer, I suppose."

"You can't have failed to recognise him at that distance," said the doctor.

Geoff didn't shrug that time. Doctor Prentiss was a wily old bird and he knew more than he was letting onto.

"It was snowing," Geoff said.

"Let me see, from the depth of the wounds and the fairly narrow range of scatter, I'd say he must have shot you from a distance of about fifteen yards. Possibly twenty. If you didn't recognise him at that distance, it must have been snowing very heavily indeed."

"I didn't say I didn't recognise him. What I'm saying is, with the snow an' all, maybe he didn't recognise me."

"And that's why he shot you? Because he didn't recognise you? Ah well, as motives go that's a new one to me. So who was it, this farmer who shoots people he doesn't recognise?"

The assembled crowd waited for an answer. Geoff looked around at them and then mumbled something.

"I beg your pardon?" said the doctor.

Geoff mumbled again. More loudly this time – "Douggie Lampton. It was Douggie Lampton who shot me."

"Indeed?" said Doctor Prentiss, "I shall have to be careful, then, if I happen to be wandering near Lampton's Farm. To make sure he recognises me from afar. I don't want to get peppered with birdshot."

"You don't have to worry about Douggie Lampton," Geoff said, "He's dead."

There was a silence.

Someone in the crowd said, "Douggie Lampton dead? I don't believe it. I saw him a couple of days ago and he was right as rain."

Then I told them how we'd found his body in the snow, with his throat cut.

10

Nobody batted an eyelid when I told them about finding Douggie Lampton. They seemed more shocked when I told them about finding his sheep with their throats cut. "He loved those sheep more than he ever loved any people," someone said. Someone else said, "At least, he went quickly." "Yes," another voice added, "And at a time of his own choosing."

I heard someone say, "How do we know it wasn't them who killed him?"

By "them" he meant me and Geoff.

Someone else said, "If it was them who killed him, why'd they be telling us about it?"

"To cover their tracks," said the first voice.

"You've said some stupid things in your time, Fred Weaver," said another voice, "But that just about takes the biscuit." I took that to mean that we had been judged and found innocent.

Then they started telling funny stories about the dead man. "Do you remember the time one of his sheep fell into his septic tank and, oh, but the stink it made when he fished it out again!" "And then there was the time when he was cutting Margie Melthorpe's hedge and he mowed down all of Albert Melthorpe's prize marrows by accident…" And so on and on. It sounded as though they were sharing reminiscences of someone who had died happily in his sleep rather than an old man who'd slit his own throat, alone on a hill in a snowstorm.

But if they weren't shocked by what I had to tell them, the same can't be said for me when I heard what they had to say. By all accounts, Geoff's description of the country falling into anarchy under the combined pressures of riots, looting, sickness and the never-ending freeze, was not an exaggeration.

The Colonel, however, was sanguine about it all – "Oh, the chaps in Whitehall will have everything under control soon, mark my words. There are contingency plans for all sorts of disaster, you can be quite sure of that. The Army will get everything sorted out."

"What makes you think the Army haven't been infected?" mumbled the doctor.

"What? Oh, no, there are vaccines and whatnot, all kinds of measures in place. Have no doubt about that."

Doctor Prentiss grunted. "We can only hope that the Army has been recruiting old age pensioners then. Still, the Generals will be all right, I suppose. Geriatrics to a man."

"I fail to see the point you are making," said the Colonel, rather grumpily.

"The point I am making is one that should be obvious to any dispassionate observer. Namely that the malaise disproportionally affects the young. All the rioters are, as far as one can tell, in their teens or early twenties."

"The 'malaise'!" snapped the Colonel, "What the Hell d'you mean by that, exactly? You medical chaps over-dramatise everything. A bit of winter flu and you'd have us believe the Black Death had come upon us!"

Someone at the far end of the Hall sneezed violently.

"There!" said the Colonel, triumphantly, "Flu. Coughs, sneezes, headaches."

"Yes, yes, you are probably right, Colonel," said the doctor, "Just a touch of winter flu. A symptom of which is that young people lose all inhibition. Engage in excesses of Dionysian proportions. Go on rampages of orgiastic violence. Quite, quite. Winter flu, as you say."

It was obvious that the Colonel and Doctor Prentiss were enjoying themselves. They were clearly two old friends who liked nothing better than a good argument.

"Drink is probably a more likely cause," said the Colonel, "And drugs. Isn't that what they were saying on the wireless before the power went out?"

"Were they?" said the doctor, "If so, that would be a most extraordinary conclusion. The country is experiencing a devastating outbreak of an as yet unidentified disease, flu-like in its initial stages, and somebody on the wireless thinks that booze is behind it."

"Excess of alcohol is often the precursor to violence," said the Colonel.

"Why, then, is the violence confined to young people? Do not older people also drink alcohol?"

"Oh, really, Walter! You are being deliberately obtuse. Remember the Mods and The Rockers fighting in Brighton? Skinheads. Punks. Young people, the lot of 'em. Football hooligans, for God's sake. What about the Poll Tax Riots? The London riots of 2011. Battles on the streets. Buildings burning. That's what young people are like. Always have been, always will be. It's not a new phenomenon."

"Perhaps, perhaps…" said the doctor.

"But you don't think so?" I asked.

"Oh, I can only speculate. I note the facts, I form a hypothesis. But the facts are few and, I suspect, much of what we have been told is inaccurate. I am an old man and my knowledge of these sorts of things is probably quite out of date."

"'These sorts of things'," the Colonel said, "And what sorts of things might those be?"

The doctor gave a chuckle. "My friend, the Colonel," he explained, "likes to think of himself as a down-to-earth, rational sort of fellow. By which he means that if he can't see something with his own two eyes, then in all probability it doesn't exist. In his view, I am more of a fantasist. I believe that the entire progress of human history has been largely dictated by things that we cannot see."

The Colonel made a noise that sounded a bit like a car tyre deflating.

"The Black Death, for example…"

"There! What did I tell you? I knew he'd bring the Black Death into it before long!"

"Or, for another example," continued the doctor, "the tularemia outbreak at the Battle Of Stalingrad. Then again there is AIDS. SARS. Ebola. COVID-19. The Spanish Flu pandemic of 1918 which killed over fifty million people and, incidentally, disproportionately affected the young. In all those cases, there is nothing to be seen. Not with the naked eye, at any rate. And yet the effects of those 'nothings' could hardly have been more profound. Or more catastrophic."

"You don't seem to have the flu," I commented.

"Immunity," said the Doctor, "In my professional career I must have come into contact with countless varieties of flu bugs. Built up immunity over the years, no doubt."

"And you?" I said, looking at the Colonel who also gave the impression of robust good health.

"Same thing," he said, "In my career I've been in all kinds of desperate situations."

"In the antique business?" I said.

The Colonel raised a disapproving eyebrow. "'Scuse me, old chap. I see someone is trying to contact me," and off he wandered to the far end of the Hall, leaving my question unanswered.

By that time, Doctor Prentiss had finished removing pellets from Geoff's arm. There remained two or three pellets that had penetrated too deeply for him to get at. He said they might work their way out of their own accord in a few weeks. Or they might stay there for ever and Geoff would just have to learn to live with them. The show, as far as everyone else in the Hall was concerned, was over and they had drifted back to their tables and camp beds to natter or play cards or read books.

That just left the three of us: Geoff, me and Doctor Prentiss. The doctor was dabbing some kind of disinfectant on Geoff's wounds and patching him up with clean bandages.

That evening passed slowly. The fact of the matter is that there was nothing much to do in the Church Hall. They had some paperback books there but none that I felt inclined to read. I didn't feel like playing draughts or Happy Families either.

Someone had a transistor radio. The only station they could get was Radio 4. That was promising at least. It meant that the good old BBC was still operational. Up to a point anyway. They were broadcasting repeats of old programmes: Just A Minute, I'm Sorry I Haven't A Clue, Gardener's Question Time. Every so often an announcer's voice would say: "You are listening to Radio 4. Due to the current emergency situation, we are unable to broadcast our scheduled programs. Normal service will resume as soon as possible."

So mostly I sat around talking. Even though the Hall was pretty packed, most of the people in the village had decided to stay at home. The people who'd gathered in the Hall either lived alone and had come for the company or else they had some other reason for leaving their house. Frozen pipes. No food or water. Or, quite simply, they were frightened.

I soon discovered that I wasn't the only one who'd been ill. More than half the people in the Hall had suffered from the flu, though whether of the Russian variety or some more commonplace sort nobody seemed entirely clear. Not even Doctor Prentiss. Some of the people had experienced little more than a cough and a runny nose. Others had been confined to bed. Some said they'd recovered but clearly a good many of them were still pretty sick. I asked if anyone had died. Three, they said. There had been three deaths in the village, not counting Douggie Lampton. The doctor told us that the ones who'd died had been frail. They'd had "pre-existing conditions," he said. The Colonel pointed out that this was entirely consistent with a flu epidemic.

At least, I felt I'd done something useful by coming to the Hall and getting some proper medical attention for Geoff. Now that my duty was done, I had every intention of getting back home as quickly as possible. Looking through the window, however, it was obvious that I wouldn't be able to make it back that night. Not only was it pitch black, with not so much as the hint of moonlight, but the snowfall was heavier than ever. I had to reconcile myself to spending the night in the Hall.

"Once the thaw sets in," said the Colonel, "everything will get back to normal in no time at all."

"On the contrary," said the doctor, "The snow is our only protection. It's like a defensive wall around the village. As soon as that wall is gone..." – he shrugged but said no more.

11

About two o'clock in the morning there was a tremendous crashing sound. The Hall was entirely in darkness. Most people were asleep but everyone woke immediately. People flicked on torches. There was broken glass all over the floor.

The Colonel took charge at once. He went to the window and shone his torch through it. Someone outside shouted at him. I couldn't make out what he said but it didn't sound complimentary. Then a couple more voices yelled at him. The Colonel, however, was not so easily intimidated. "Come up here and say that again to my face!" he yelled. Then I saw him duck away from the window and a rock about the size of a grapefruit whizzed past his head.

That was the final straw as far as the Colonel was concerned. He drew the cord of his pyjama trousers a notch tighter, requisitioned the nearest torch and strode out through the front door of the Hall. We could hear some more shouting. I looked through the window to see what was going on. There were three young men down on the road. They were screaming and cursing for no reason that I could make any sense of. One of them kept laughing. Then one of them threw another rock at the Colonel. There was a plentiful supply of rocks around there due to the old dry-stone wall that separated the Hall from the road. This one hit its target. The rock caught the Colonel on the side of the head and he staggered back. Just then there was an enormously loud bang. I looked across to the next window on my right. An old man in a tweed jacket had opened that window and fired a gun at the youths. It was the sort of gun I've seen people hunting deer with. A rifle of some sort. A serious gun. Not the sort you'd use to shoot pheasants. Whether or not he had been aiming at the youths I don't know. Since they were all still standing, all I could be certain of was that he hadn't scored a direct hit.

But it scared them. They called out a few choice obscenities and vanished into the night. The last thing I heard was a voice calling in the darkness, promising that they would be back and that next time they'd be armed with more than rocks.

The Colonel had a nasty looking gash on his cheek but the doctor said that, luckily, no bones had been broken.

The following day, the thaw came.

12

The first thing I noticed was the water dripping from the icicles above the windows. I went outside. The sun was shining in a cloudless sky. The Colonel felt this was a good sign, that soon everything would be tickety-boo, ship-shape and Bristol fashion, the power would come back on, the BBC would resume its scheduled programs and we would all be able to carry on as if nothing had happened.

Doctor Prentiss was not so sanguine.

As for me, I thought the change in the weather could only be for the better. After breakfast (cornflakes with reconstituted dried milk, which was revolting), Geoff, Bobby and I set off on the road back to my house. Heather Cottage had been my home for the last two years. I'd grown very fond of it. So when I saw the state it was in, I was shocked. The broken window was the first thing I noticed. The second thing I noticed was the trail of footprints leading to and from the front door. People had been there. Difficult to guess how many. They'd gone in through the window and, as far as I could see, they'd left by the door.

Once inside, I could see that they'd done a pretty thorough job of wrecking the place. I wasn't too worried that they might have stolen things because I haven't got much worth stealing. A tatty old computer. Some books. A cheap TV set. The only things of any value… Oh God, no! I rushed upstairs. My guitars. They'd wrecked my guitars. An Ibanez RG, a Harald Peterson classical guitar. A Gretsch 6120 'Chet Atkins'. Sacrilege. The Grestch was a work of art. I could imagine somebody wanting to steal it. I couldn't imagine why would anyone would want to destroy it. But that is exactly what they had done. Its gorgeous orange flame-maple body had been smashed with great violence and now lay scattered across the floor.

"I'm sorry," Geoff said.

"About the Gretsch?" I said.

"About your house."

Ah, but it wasn't my house, was it. I was just the tenant. I think I mentioned earlier that an old college friend had rented it to me. Fully furnished with good antiques. I looked around the place. Windows had been smashed. Legs had been broken off chairs, the drawers had been taken from a chest of drawers and smashed into fragments, great gouges had been carved into the wood of a 19th Century sideboard. How was I going to break the news of all this destruction to Justin? That was the friend who had rented the house to me: Justin Davenant.

Then another thought occurred to me. Maybe Justin wasn't alive any more. I don't know why I thought that. I still hadn't formed a clear impression of the true extent of the catastrophe that had hit the country. I think it was the sheer wantonness of the destruction, the desecration of the antique furniture, the ruin of my beloved guitars that made me conceive of the idea that Geoff might, after all, be right. That Douggie Lampton's madness might have been closer to sanity than I'd thought. That Doctor Prentiss's cynicism might have been all too justified. That the world was no longer as it had been.

"What do we do now?" Geoff said.

"I don't know."

But I pretty soon came to a decision. There was nothing keeping me or Geoff here any longer. Neither of us had a proper home to go to. As for me, I wanted to find out what had happened to my country. I would go to the village. And if I couldn't find the truth there, I would go to the town. And if I couldn't find the truth there, I would keep on going until I did find it.

The sun was still shining as we set off towards the village. The snow didn't melt all at once but at the sides of the road there were some places that weren't shaded by hedges and banks where the snow was starting to turn to slush. I thought of the doctor's warning. The snow is our only protection, he'd said, like a defensive wall around the village. Doctor Prentiss had formed the opinion that it was only a matter of time before the mass violence that had sprung up in the towns would spread into the surrounding countryside. The thaw was not yet well enough advanced to diminish our 'protective wall' to any significant extent so I didn't think this was a problem we would be forced to confront quite yet.

It was a long slog through the snow, back the way we had come – past Lampton's Farm, past the road leading to the Church Hall. But this time, instead of turning up the hill towards the Hall we kept on going down into the valley, towards the village. From a distance, everything looked peaceful. The roofs of the stone-built houses and shops that straggled along Fore Street sparkled, white and brilliant, beneath the clear blue sky. At the far end of the street, smoke rose from the chimney of The Farmer's Rest – the old, thatched pub that was the social centre of the village.

Fore Street, which runs through the centre of the village, was eerily empty. The Lettuce Leaf grocery was shut. So to was Barnford's Bakery. There were no people on the streets but the snow had been well trampled on the pavement, mainly in the direction of The Farmer's Rest. That seemed as good a direction to take as any so that's where we went.

The Farmer's Rest is one of those comfortable, old-fashioned pubs that have all but vanished from the towns of Britain but can still be found out in the depths of the countryside. It has just one bar with wooden settles against the walls and a couple of rough oak tables and chairs standing on the slate-flag floor. There is a glass fronted case on the wall in which a stuffed fish is mounted – in memory of some angling achievement that occurred so long ago that nobody knows who caught the fish or why it was thought worthy of preservation. There is a big open fireplace in which a pile of burning logs provides heat enough for all that big room even in the coldest depths of winter.

When I opened the big oak door and stepped inside, the heat hit me at once. I unbuttoned my coat, took off my gloves and unwrapped my scarf. Two old gents were sitting on stools by the bar. The landlord, Alan Pendelin, was standing behind the bar, as he always was, drying glasses with a towel.

"Afternoon gents," he said, just as he always did, "And what'll it be today, then?"

"Two pints of bitter," I replied though I wasn't at all sure that Geoff was of legal age to be served with alcohol.

"The pumps isn't working," Alan Pendelin said, "But we have barrels of Stormy Bay or Otterly."

"Stormy Bay," I said.

The two barrels were resting on a trestle behind the bar and while Alan Pendelin poured two glasses straight from the tap, one of the old gents at the bar nodded to me, smiled and said, "Cold enough for you, lad?"

"Warmer in here anyway," I said. It was meaningless chatter. The kind of thing you say to strangers in a pub.

The other old gent, who had been eating from a packet of crisps, leant down and offered a crisp to Bobby, who had strolled in with us. "That dog you got there could be the twin to Douggie Lampton's dog," he said.

I smiled. I hoped the old man would be content to think there were two dogs that looked alike. I didn't want to get involved in a discussion of Douggie Lampton and how we came to have his dog.

When Alan Pendelin pushed the two foaming glasses over the bar towards us, I handed him a ten pound note and he went to the till to get my change. At least, the normal business of everyday commerce hadn't yet been disrupted in the village.

"You're Eddie Parkham's boy, ain't you?" said one of the old gents to Geoff, "I heard young Greta got taken bad with this flu that's doing the rounds."

"'Tis a bad to-do," said the other old gent as he took a handkerchief from his pocket and coughed into it wetly. "It's the phlegm that gets you."

"I haven't been into the village for a while," I said, "On account of the snow."

"You that newcomer ain't you?" said one old gent, "The one what lives up in Heather Cottage."

"That's me."

"You'd have been snowbound up there, I suppose?" Alan Pendelin said.

"Pretty bad," I said, "But that's not the worst."

"Oh no?"

"This morning someone broke into my house."

"Burglar?" said one old man.

"Not sure. Didn't steal much as far as I could see. Just wrecked stuff."

"That's the way of the world," muttered one of the men impassively.

"You was there when they broke in?" said the other man.

"I was up at the Hall. Last night, I mean."

"The Church Hall, was it?" said Alan Pendelin.

One of the old men laughed. "Emergency Operations Centre, that's what they call it. Lot of bloody rubbish, that is. Just a chance for the Colonel to swank around and tell people what to do."

"He isn't even a proper Colonel," said the other old man.

"'Tis Colonel they call him though. Too good for the likes of us he is, if you ask me. Put another pint in there, Alan."

Alan Pendelin took the empty glass and filled it from the cask.

"Why was you up at the Hall, then?" asked one old gent.

"I hurt my arm," Geoff said, "Jonathan here took me to see Doctor Prentiss."

"I thought he retired years ago," said Alan Pendelin.

"He'll be up at the Hall, I expect," said one old gent, "Him and the Colonel swanking it over everyone."

"That dog do surely look like Douggie Lampton's dog," said the other old gent.

It was a nice pub, the beer was good and the heat of the fire was welcome but I didn't feel this conversation was leading anywhere. So I took a more direct approach: "How many people in the village have had the flu?"

"Look at the pub," said Alan Pendelin, "Normal times we'd be packed."

"People is too damn' scared to leave their houses," said one old gent.

"Why's that?" I said.

"Oh, you know," he said vaguely, "One thing and another."

"So what'll you be doin' now, then?" asked Alan Pendelin.

"Oh," I said, "I was thinking of taking a look around town."

He shook his head gravely – "From what I been hearin', 'tis best to keep clear of town."

13

We followed the road out of the village. It took us past the village green which is a square of grass with a duck pond in the middle. In summer they have a farmers' market there on the weekends. It's full of noise and laughter then. Today it was as silent as the rest of the village. As silent as the grave.

There were no ducks on the pond. The water had frozen and a layer of snow had settled over the ice. Snow so completely covered everything that I nearly missed the old woman's body. She was lying on her side at the edge of the pond. The body was covered by just a thin crust of snow so I guessed she hadn't been there long.

"Aggie Wilton," Geoff said, "She used to run the sweet shop years ago. Sold sherbet and old-fashioned mint humbugs."

We carried on walking and soon we passed two more mounds in the snow. They must have been there longer. The bodies were more deeply covered. I didn't look closely. I'd had my fill of death. All I wanted was to get away from this place. I wanted to get away from a place where bodies could be left outside and nobody came looking for them, because nobody cared. We passed half a dozen more bodies before we were outside the village.

"They said there'd only been three deaths," Geoff said, "When we was in the Church Hall. Three people had died. That's what they said."

"They can't have known the full extent," I said, "Maybe there'd only been three deaths when they'd gone to the Church Hall."

"Or maybe they was lying," Geoff said.

"Either way, the sooner we get into town the better."

"And how are we going to do that? It's over twenty miles. We'll never walk that distance in this snow."

"We'll need a Land Rover."

So we stole one. It was in a farm about half a mile further along the road. I suggested trying to hot-wire it, even though I had no idea how that was done. Geoff saved me the trouble. He noticed that the keys were in the ignition. I didn't feel bad about stealing the Land Rover. The farmer and his wife wouldn't be needing it any more. We found their bodies in the kitchen. Someone had beaten them to a pulp with a crowbar. The crowbar was still there, lying next to the bodies on the floor.

The world had gone mad. What I didn't know was that we were heading deeper into the insanity.

Part II – Anarchy

1

It was a dark, litter-strewn lane on the northern fringes of the town. The left-hand side of the lane was bounded by a crumbling red-brick wall. On the right-hand side there was a wire-mesh fence beyond which was a big yard of some sort. A couple of derelict trucks stood in the yard, surrounded by heaps of wood and metal pipes. It looked like the yard of a builder's merchant.

The moon, which was nearly full, was all the light there was. I dared not switch on my torch for fear of being seen. Up ahead, about two hundred yards away, was a bridge – it looked like a railway bridge – that spanned the lane I was walking down. The bridge was barely visible, its outline faintly silvered by moonlight.

The lane, the bridge, the yard and the town beyond were all silent. Well, not completely silent because, from time to time, I heard sounds – shouting, breaking glass, once a noise that sounded like guns being fired – but they were in the far distance; away on the other side of town.

I was in an industrial area. From its air of dereliction, I surmised that its industry no longer functioned and any people who might once have been there had departed. There was nobody: no night-workers, no long-haul drivers, no watchmen. Only the rats remained. The unexpected desertion of their domain had given them a new boldness. A big black rat strolled across the lane in front of me, stopped for a moment to look at me while it preened its whiskers, decided I was of no interest and casually moved on.

The wire-mesh fence began to rattle. My heart skipped a few beats. There it was again. The mesh rattled, fell silent, rattled, fell silent. There was a rhythm to it. It wasn't shaken by the wind – there was none – and no wind could create a noise with such a regular beat. A person created a noise like that. Someone grasping the wire-mesh then releasing it, grasping it then releasing it.

I flattened myself against the wall. Should I run? Go back the way I had come? Or should I stay there, hidden in the darkness? Hoping that whoever was approaching wouldn't notice me?

I strained to see who, or what, was coming towards me, causing the fence to rattle, fall silent, rattle, fall silent. For a moment or two I could see nothing. But then, as it came closer, the moon shone upon it and I could make out the shuffling, shambling silhouette of a man, clutching the wire with both hands to support his weight; then releasing his grip with one hand, grasping the wire again about a foot or so distant from his previous hand-hold, taking a step, then going through the same routine with his other hand. And in that way, he was making slow and difficult progress, reeling himself in along the meshwork fence, handhold-by-handhold, step after shuffling step, moving slowly and painfully towards me.

That he was in pain was self-evident. With each shuffling step, he made a slight noise, a groan as though through gritted teeth. When, at last, he was just a few yards away, I could hear his laboured breathing, like air bubbling through liquid. Then he stopped. He clung to the fence, his body sagging, the strength in his arms barely able to support his weight. He stood there, wheezing laboriously. Then he turned towards me. He looked directly at me. Even in that pale light, I could see that there was something wrong with his eyes. They looked too big, swollen and straining against inflamed eyelids. His eyes were full of pain and terror.

"Help me," the man said.

I didn't know what to do. The man was ill. He wasn't violent. He wasn't dangerous. He was just in terrible pain. My instinct was to go to him. But what then? What in the world could I possibly do to help him? I could give him nothing because I had nothing to give. I could take him nowhere because I had nowhere to take him.

"Help me," he said again. There was such sadness in his voice that I couldn't resist the urge to go towards him. The least I could do was to hold him, relieve him of the struggle of supporting his own weight if only for a few moments. Hold him. Comfort him.

But as I took a step towards him, the man slumped down, his fingers losing their grip on the wire fence. As he fell to the ground, he vomited. I jumped back. He was vomiting blood. It flew from his mouth explosively. Finally, he lay on the ground, at peace, alone in tatters and rags while blood continued to gush from his mouth and nostrils. A few yards away a rat sat watching, preening itself, waiting…

For a while, I stood there, shaking. It was an uncontrollable reaction. I couldn't stop my body from trembling. Maybe there are those people who can stay calm when faced with sudden death. And maybe, eventually, I will be one of them. Because the way things are now, death is something you get used to – something you experience every day. Even now, after everything I've seen and experienced, I am still not hardened against death. When that man bled out in front of me, it made me feel physically ill. For what seemed like an awfully long time I did nothing but stand and stare. A man I'd never met, had asked for my help and then died and I couldn't think what to do next.

The only thought I had was that I had failed him. I was his only hope and I had done nothing. I wondered who the man was. It was so dark and he was in such a terrible state that it was almost impossible to guess his age. He could have been anywhere between twenty and fifty. Did he have a wife? A girlfriend? A boyfriend? Children? What had his job been? What had he liked doing? What music had he listened to? What books had he read? Had he been planning a holiday, saving to buy a house? Was he rich? Or on the breadline? Were there people alive who missed him? Or was he alone?

This was what life had become now. This man's death was the way we would all die. Alone. Unmourned. A crumpled heap of diseased flesh for rats to feed upon.

I turned away. Angry at myself for wasting time. One man's death was of no consequence. Not to me. Not any longer. I had my own life to think about. If I intended to survive, I had to put myself first. My main concern now was to find somewhere safe.

Geoff and I had split up to reconnoitre this part of town half an hour earlier. Geoff had taken the dog with him. I was glad he had. I wasn't sure that Bobby would have been helpful in my encounter with the dying man.

I looked at my watch. Ten minutes to midnight. I had promised to meet Geoff at 12 o'clock precisely. That was why I'd been in the alleyway. I was making my way towards the industrial estate beyond the railway bridge. I went that way now, trying to forget what I'd just seen. Trying to ignore the sick feeling in my stomach. Trying to pretend that my legs didn't feel like jelly. The truth of the matter is that I was scared that, at any moment, I might meet another sick or dying person, in the dense darkness under the bridge, or just around the corner. That some other monstrous sight would come shuffling towards me, begging for help that I couldn't provide...

But it didn't happen. I passed under the bridge and around the bend in the alleyway. I emerged onto a small road that ran between two-storey buildings, warehouses and office blocks. The signs on the buildings were reminders of the world that used to be: Jenkins Steel, Killforce Pest Control, Davies Precision Machining, First Call Builder's Merchants, XL Tee-shirt Printing, TrustRite Security Systems...

Who needed them any more?

Geoff was standing outside a building that displayed the sign 'Cadwallader's Outdoor Supplies'. He was hidden in a dark niche between that building and a garage next to it. I couldn't miss him though, due to the fact that Bobby ran out to greet me. The dog, I noticed was silent. He came to me, wagging his tail for all he was worth. But there was no yapping or barking. In fact, ever since we'd arrived in town, Bobby had been as silent as a hunting cat. I wondered if he sensed something? Something that made him realise that silence was our friend. Silence and darkness.

"This place has got the stuff we need," Geoff said. He gestured behind him to a large window. The window was open. Geoff had prised it open using a huge metal jemmy that he was still holding. He'd found the jemmy in the garage next door and decided that opening the window that way was less likely to attract attention than smashing the glass. I guessed that there must have been burglar alarm systems which, not so long ago, would have pierced the silence with loud siren-wails if someone had jemmied open a window. Not any longer.

I crawled through the window. Geoff lifted Bobby up and I pulled him inside, then Geoff followed. Geoff had already pilfered a couple of torches and, once inside, we turned them on to see what we could find. It was like an Aladdin's Cave of treasures: tents, knives, cagoules, walking boots, walking sticks, just about everything anyone could ever want before going on a pleasant ramble through the countryside. I wasn't sure if they had everything we'd need to survive the end of civilisation. But it was better than nothing.

We each took a big rucksack – one of those things that fits onto a metal frame that you strap onto your back. Then we got ourselves a good pair of boots each, a few pairs of socks, sheepskin gloves, a couple of fairly ferocious-looking knives, a compass and various other useful-looking items.

We were about to take some cagoules but then I spotted a rack of parkas. The cagoules might have been more waterproof but the parkas were better padded and more suitable for cold weather.

It was then that I noticed the radios. I almost walked past them. I'd had enough of listening to endless repeats on Radio 4 back in the Church Hall. I'd given up believing that normal service would "resume as soon as possible". Radio and TV had died with the old world.

But then I remembered what the old farmer, Douggie Lampton, had said. He'd told me he had followed the news on the shortwave bands. I wasn't sure who broadcast on shortwave any more. I had a feeling that it was a kind of an amateur thing – 'ham radio'. I tried to recall what I'd heard when Geoff and I had tried messing about with the radio receiver we'd found in Douggie Lampton's basement. Crackling noises that faded in and out mostly. But there had also been a station broadcasting from Britain – "Radio True Britain, your only source of true news".

It seemed a long shot but worth a try. I grabbed one of the smaller radios, quite a snazzy little thing, not much bigger than a paperback book and covered in knobs and dials whose functions I could only guess at. I checked the battery sizes it needed and grabbed a handful of batteries too. I didn't know it at the time, but grabbing that radio was one of the best decisions I'd ever made.

"What next?" Geoff asked when we'd looted just about all we could reasonably carry, "Do we stay here or move on?"

I looked around the place. "It looks as though we are the first people to have come into this place since the snowstorm," I said, "So we may as well stay here for the night. Don't you think?"

Geoff nodded. "Suits me. Not the most comfortable place to stay but at least we'll be alone. I reckon we can be sure that there's nobody else in here with us."

But he was wrong.

2

It was just after half-past two in the morning when I heard the noises. I knew it was just after half-past two because the multi-function digital watch with the illuminated dial (which I had stolen earlier) told me that it was just after half-past two. In fact, it told me it was 02:32:54. It was a good watch.

In the sleeping bag next to mine, Geoff was snoring. Quite loudly. I shook him. That stopped the snoring and I whispered "Shhhhhh… we are not alone any more."

Lying in the space between my sleeping bag and Geoff's sleeping bag (the sleeping bags too were part of our recent loot), Bobby sat with his eyes wide open, his ears pricked up and his head angled first to one side and then to the other, listening, as I was, to the sounds coming from the floor directly overhead.

Footsteps.

Barely audible, but definitely footsteps.

The footsteps were moving slowly, padding their way across the floor above us. I tried to work out their direction. They seemed to be heading towards the far-end of the shop, away to my right. The question was, should we ignore them? Should we get out of the shop and make a dash for it? Or should we seize the initiative and confront whoever was responsible for the footsteps.

Geoff decided for me. He wriggled out of his sleeping bag and, using his torch (which I wasn't sure was a good idea but, then again, without it we wouldn't have been able to see a damn' thing), he tiptoed across to a display of walking sticks. These were big, solid oak sticks, the sort that some people like to stride along with over dales and fells. He picked a stout, knotty one about five feet in length with a good, big knob at the top. I don't think he had fell-walking in mind.

Once I'd extricated myself from my sleeping bag, I followed Geoff's example. Geoff had picked the best stick for his own use.

The stick I picked wasn't quite as fearsome but I reckoned that if I gave it my best baseball-style swing and someone's head happened to be on the wrong end of it, the person whose head I whacked wouldn't be picking themselves up of the floor again in a hurry.

Thus armed, Geoff and I tiptoed over to the door. Above the door there was a non-functioning electric sign which should, according to a whole set of redundant laws and bylaws, have been illumined with the words "Fire Exit". I pushed the door open and we crept through into a stairwell. Bobby crept through with us. You might think that taking the dog was a silly idea but, really, we had no choice. As long as he was with us, Bobby was content to remain silent. If we'd left him alone in the downstairs showroom, I had a feeling that he would have set up a racket of howling and barking which would have given the game away!

Before climbing the stars, I turned the intensity of my Cree torch down to its lowest setting. We needed to see where we were going but I didn't want to announce our arrival with a searchlight. Then the three of us (Geoff and Bobby, with me in the lead), started climbing the staircase towards the next floor. When we arrived in the stairwell on that floor, I flattened myself against the wall, grasped my wooden walking stick soundly in my right hand, and glanced surreptitiously through one of the glass panels in the door that opened onto the main showroom area.

There was a light in there. A thin, pale light that barely illuminated much at all. Still, a light is a light. Combined with the footsteps we'd heard, it meant that someone was in there. For all I knew, someone was flattened against the wall on the other side of the door, with a wooden walking stick in his hand, waiting for me to open the door so that he could get a good swing at my head. I wasn't going to make myself such easy meat. I gestured to Geoff to stay back and hold onto Bobby. Then I positioned myself a couple of feet away from the door and to one side of it. My plan was simple. I would push open the door with the end of my walking stick. If anyone was waiting for me on the other side, he would no doubt swing into action with whatever weapon he had to hand. We'd then know exactly where he was and what his intentions were. At which point we would either go inside and confront him or run like Hell in the opposite direction. If, for example, he started shooting at us with a semi-automatic, the run-like-Hell option was definitely the one we'd go for.

I carefully placed the end of my walking stick on the centre of the door. I mimed to Geoff: "One, Two, Three…"

On "Three" I thrust the stick at the door with all my might. And I very nearly dislocated my shoulder. The door didn't budge. I'd forgotten that the bloody doors opened out from the show-rooms into the stairwell. No amount of force would make them open inwards!

I cursed aloud. The time for silence was gone. I'd made so much noise with my damn' fool attempt to push the door open, that whoever was in there must have heard us by now. All we could do was stand our ground and prepare either to fight or run for it.

We didn't have to wait long. Just moments later, the door swung open and what appeared to be a gorilla-like creature with long, dangling ears shambled towards us.

3

"What on earth are you doing out there? Come in, my dear fellows, do come in."

The figure swiftly raised the portable LED lamp in its right hand so that we could all take a good, long look at one another. It was just as well he did this swiftly. Another second longer and Geoff would very likely have bludgeoned him with the stick he was carrying.

What, in darkness, had appeared gorilla-like was, by light, revealed to be a plump, middle-aged man wearing an RAF-style sheepskin flying jacket over a long, woollen dressing gown. The dangling ears were no more than the ear-flaps of the trapper's hat on his head.

"Aha, I see you have selected a couple of good, stout shillelaghs," – he was looking at Geoff's walking stick which was still poised over the man's head, giving Geoff the option of landing him a good thump if things should happen to take a turn for the worse.

"I call them shillelaghs," the man explained, "But that's just my little joke, you know. A small witticism can brighten the darkest of days with a gleam of merriment, don't you think?"

Slowly, Geoff put down the stick. We were starting to get the impression that the man was not an immediate danger to us. This impression was confirmed by Bobby who was wagging his tail and licking the man's hand. In my experience, dogs are generally good judges of character and I was prepared to take Bobby's opinion – for the time being anyway.

I thought it was about time I said something. But I wasn't sure what to say. Finding someone in a locked and (we had assumed) deserted store was surprising enough. Finding a rather posh-sounding middle-aged gent wearing a dressing gown, flying-jacket and trapper's hat, was just about the last thing I'd expected. Eventually, I said, "What are you doing here?"

Predictably, he replied, "I might well ask you the same thing!"

"We've just arrived in town," I said.

"Up from the country, 'eh?"

"You could say that."

"I'm afraid you won't find much to do of an evening. Things have gone downhill recently, as you may have noticed. Would you care for some tea?"

"That would be lovely," I said.

Geoff was staring at the two of us as though we were both insane. I could see his point. We'd just been about to cudgel the old geezer over the head with a heavy stick and now here we were engaging in polite conversation as though we were taking tea with the local vicar.

"Coffee, alas, I am unable to provide. And as for alcoholic beverages, sadly…"

Geoff interrupted – "Never mind all that. Who are you and how the bloody hell did you get in here?"

"Oh, but I was here all the time."

"You can't have been. We checked. The doors and windows were all locked. I had to jemmy open one of the windows to get in."

"Ah, was that the noise I heard? I do hope you didn't damage it."

This was not an answer to Geoff's question, so I added, "So how the bloody hell did you get in here?"

"As I said, I was here all along." He produced a key from a pocket of his nightgown. "Mechanical locks, you see. I can come and go as I wish."

"Where did you get a key?" I asked.

"Where did I get it?" – he looked confused for a moment and then enlightenment broke upon him – "Ah, deary me. I can appreciate your perplexity. I haven't introduced myself. How remiss of me." – he extended a hand to be shaken – "Cardew Excelsior Cadwallader at your service." He said this as though the name would be instantly recognisable. As though he might be a film star. Or the President of the United States. The name meant nothing to me.

"Cadwallader," he repeated, "Of Cadwallader's Outdoor Supplies."

"Ahhhh…."

"You own this shop?" said Geoff.

"And many others like it," said Cardew Excelsior Cadwallader, "I take it you are not regular customers?

"Well…"

"Oh, no need to feel embarrassed. There are many fine, upstanding people who, through no fault of their own, are not regular customers of Cadwallader's Outdoor Supplies. I assume that may be due to ignorance rather than malicious intent. I shall not hold it against you. I have Darjeeling, Lapsang Souchong or PG Tips. Which would you prefer?"

4

It was as though we'd stumbled into the Mad Hatter's Tea Party. We sat around a wooden table, with benches at either side – the kind of table and benches you might expect to see in the garden of a moderately well-to-do country house. Tea was served in floral-patterned bone china cups. A selection of chocolate biscuits and shortbreads had been arranged on matching bone china plates. A Bonio dog biscuit had been provided for Bobby and he was munching away at it under the table.

Mr Cadwallader had been holed up in his old shop ever since the first great snowfall. "That I happened to be here was entirely fortuitous. I had decided to stay late to do a little stocktaking and make some final changes to a new display of gentleman's thermal underwear. I must have become absorbed in the task and it was in the early hours of the morning that I decided to lock up and set off for home. When I stepped outside, I realised at once that a change of plan was in order. Unbeknownst to me, snow must have been falling for some hours and it lay at such a depth that it would have been quite impossible for me to drive through it. So I slept in my office. That is not an unusual occurrence. I keep a camp bed tucked away in there, along with a few essentials to keep body and soul together – Bath Olivers, shrimp paste, Gentleman's Relish, chocolate digestive biscuits, that sort of thing. I assumed that the snow ploughs would be out and about and that, by the following day, the temporary inconvenience of the snow would have been dealt with. Such, alas, was not the case."

On the first day after the snow, the situation in town had been much as it had been in the countryside. Roads were blocked, people couldn't get to work, kids took the day off from school to build snowmen and throw snowballs.

"But then, of course, the situation deteriorated. Thankfully, by the time the looting and violence began, I was still safely locked away in here," Mr Cadwallader gave a snorting laugh, "I watched it all on the TV set in my office. They had all the usual commentators spouting their hare-brained theories. Scientists, sociologists, the Archbishop of Canterbury. But, in truth, nobody knew what was behind it all. As for myself, I put it down to the disintegration of public morals. It's the schools I blame. Did you know they no longer teach logarithm tables? French irregular verbs are, I am given to understand, quite unknown to a large percentage of the younger generation. The inescapable consequence is what we now see. Mob violence. Shops looted, buildings set on fire. Oh my word! You seem to have had an accident!"

"I beg your pardon?" I had no idea what he talking about.

"Your shirt. It appears to have blood stains upon it."

"Oh, that! Nothing to worry about," I said, "It's not my blood."

"Not your blood? Then whose blood is it?"

I told him about the man I'd met earlier, the one who had bled out in the alleyway by the chain-link fence.

Mr Cadwallader looked aghast. "Oh, Good Heavens, how frightful. You must have a change of clothing at once."

"It's nothing," I said, "Really."

"I beg to differ. Blood is never nothing. Especially not when it is somebody else's blood. You never know what's in it."

He found me some more clothes: jeans, a tee-shirt and denim shirt, even a chunky-knit Arran pullover which, in other circumstances, would have been well beyond my means to buy. He insisted that I remove my old clothes carefully, avoiding touching the blood stains. Then he used some tongs pick up the blood-stained clothes and he sealed them inside a plastic bag. To me this seemed to be an unnecessary rigmarole. But I went along with it. Well, after all, the new clothes were much better than what they replaced.

I looked around the floor of shop in which we were sitting. I couldn't see much, due to the dimness of the illumination from the single light – a sort of hand-held torch that had a panel of LEDs in its side; it currently stood in the centre of the table around which we were sitting. From what I could see, though, the shop looked to be in good shape. If the electricity ever came back on it would be ready to start trading again as though nothing had ever happened.

"Nobody has been out here," Mr Cadwallader explained, "Well, I mean, I've seen a few youths staggering around. But one does, doesn't one. Even at the best of times. Over-indulgence in the communion wine, as one might say. But no looting, no destruction. We are out on the fringes, you see. Industrial estate. Not the sort of place young people go for a rambunctious night out. At any rate, the mobs seem to be keeping to the town centres. So, all in all, I've done rather well of it out here. In fact, I could go on living here for quite some time, if necessary. Cadwallader's Outdoor Supplies has everything required for survival *in extremis*. In the circumstances, business should be booming, don't you think?" – he chuckled humourlessly. He glanced at the parkas, wooden sticks and torches that Geoff and I had plundered earlier – "I see you have made a selection from some of our items. Very good choices, if I might say so. No, no, please don't feel the need to pay. I wouldn't hear of it. The fact of the matter is that the outdoor supplies business may be going into a decline."

There was a sadness in his voice that I had not noticed before.

"Three generations of Cadwalladers built this business. My grandfather, Jeremiah Ezekiel Cadwallader opened the first shop in Uttoxeter in 1952. He had come back from fighting in Burma with a wife and, within four years, three children to support, among whom was my father. Being an enterprising fellow, he realised that the tent pegs, knives and jerry cans which he had taken for granted in Burma were rather thin on the ground in post-war Britain. He resolved to make up for that deficit. And thus, the citizens of Uttoxeter were soon to be supplied for a life in the Great Outdoors by 'Cadwallader's Countryside Walking Emporium'. It was my father, Cyril Amadeus Cadwallader, who expanded the business by opening no less than ten more shops and changing the name, wisely, to the altogether snappier 'Cadwallader's Outdoor Supplies'. We now have twenty-seven stores across the length and breadth of the country. Three generations it took. Three generations and a hell of a lot of hard work."

"That's pretty amazing," Geoff said.

"It is," agreed Mr Cadwallader, "as you say, pretty amazing. And all, quite, quite worthless."

"Well, I don't know about that," I said.

He smiled, "Don't you? Come, come, I think you do. All those stores, all those people working in all those stores. All gone, I think. Never to come back."

"We don't know…" I began.

He interrupted me, "Three of my stores were destroyed. That much I do know. Before the power went, when the telephones and the Internet were still operational, I was in touch with the managers of my stores in Aberdeen, Sunderland and Plymouth. Two stores had been burned to the ground. The third had been looted and wrecked, just for the hell of it. The deputy manager in my Doncaster store informed me that the manager, Mr Starke, had been beaten to death on the streets. He was a nice fellow. Had a wife and two daughters."

"I'm sorry," I said.

"Oh, you needn't be. This is all quite commonplace now. This is what the world has become. At least, my store here, remains intact. Though I rather doubt that the spring sale will go ahead as planned. Oh, please, do have some more tea."

"What are you planning to do?" I said.

"Me? Oh, there really is nothing left for me to do, is there? I shall never leave here. My life is…"

He stopped mid-sentence. His face froze as though he were a mechanical toy whose battery had run out. But in the next moment, he was smiling again and continuing as if nothing had happened. "We had a house, you see. Out on the west of the town. We only moved in last year. Quite a grand affair, I suppose. Ten bedrooms. Six acres of gardens. Indoor heated swimming pool. The business was doing well, you see. We moved into the house last July. We had a dog…" – he reached down and stroked Bobby again, "A Cocker Spaniel, called Rickie."

"When the snow melts you'll be able to…"

He shook his head. "We kept in touch with one of these." – He took a small hand-held transmitter out of his pocket. What I would have called a walkie-talkie but which he called a dual-band transceiver. "He called me, but… the house was… the dog…" – he stopped again, "I don't know what happened exactly. There were screams. I could hear the dog howling. I was in a wild panic. I kept shouting, 'What's happening? What's happening? What are they doing to you? For God's sake, what are they doing to you?' And then there was silence. And then there was another voice. A voice I didn't know. A young man, I'd say. Laughing. Gloating. And he told me what they'd done. And I…"

Mr Cadwallader put his head into his hands and cried. He cried in a way I'd never heard a man crying before. It was like a wail of agony. It took him a while to recover. I put my arm around his shoulders and muttered the sort of stupid platitudes I'd heard people saying in films. I knew what I was saying was stupid. But I didn't have anything else to say.

After a couple of minutes, the wailing became sobbing and then the sobbing became a halting, irregular breathing. And then, quite suddenly, he looked up, smiled and said, "Goodness me, I am being a bad host. That tea is quite, quite cold. I shall put on the kettle at once." I could see in his face that his heart was broken. There was nothing left to live for. To all intents and purposes, he was dead already.

5

We must have finally gone to bed again at about half-past four. Maybe five o'clock. I remember thinking, well, at least we are safe. There were three of us now, plus the dog, lying reasonably comfortably inside sleeping bags on metal-framed camp beds set out on the upper floor of the shop. There were sounds in the far distance. Cars screeching. People shouting. Occasional noises that sounded like explosions. But close at hand, everything was, as far as we could tell, peaceful.

I knew we couldn't stay there. Not for ever. I had no intention of living the rest of my life inside a deserted shop in a decaying industrial estate. But, for the time being, this was the best sanctuary on offer. We would stay there, I thought, for a few days. That would give us enough time to work out a coherent plan. We had to have some objective. I didn't believe, *couldn't* believe, that the entire country had fallen into a state of anarchy. Our problems, I told myself, were local. Somebody somewhere must have plans underway to restore power, phone lines, infrastructure. This must be what it is like at times of war, I thought. London after the Blitz. Baghdad in the wake of Shock and Awe. Hiroshima after the bomb. For a while everything falls to pieces. Nothing works as it should. Nobody knows who is in control or how life can ever return to any semblance of normality. But gradually, bit by bit, step by step, people begin to recover from the disaster, the authorities begin to regain control and, eventually, life goes on. Life may never be quite 'normal' ever again – but at least, it goes on.

My mind was racing so much that I didn't think I would be able to sleep even though I was totally exhausted. But I did fall asleep eventually. I was awakened by Geoff shaking me. I asked him what the time was. "Shhhh," he said, "Listen."

I listened. I could hear the dog snoring. I could hear Mr Cadwallader snoring. Apart from that, I couldn't hear very much.

"What am I supposed to be…?"

"Listen!" Geoff whispered again.

I lay as still as I could. In addition to the stereophonic snoring, I could also hear my own heart beating. It was beating fast. Because even though I couldn't hear anything out of the ordinary, I knew that Geoff wouldn't have woken me unless he was convinced that something was wrong.

Finally, I heard it. Laughter. Then someone said something. Then more laughter. There were two people. At *least* two people. They were downstairs. Inside the building. The voices were faint but getting louder.

"How did they get in?" I whispered, "Did you hear anything?"

"Yes. Like glass breaking. That's what woke me. You didn't hear it?"

"Not a thing."

"What d'you reckon? Someone smashed a window. The front door?"

"Wouldn't that be made of tempered glass or something?" I said.

"Not sure. I saw people smashing shop windows in London. On the telly. It didn't look that hard to do."

I leant across to Mt Cadwallader and tapped him gently a few times. That had no effect whatsoever so I tapped him not-so-gently until he snorted into wakefulness. I explained the situation. Then we all listened for a few moments to try to work out the whereabouts of the intruders.

"Hammocks and groundsheets," Mr Cadwallader said.

"What?"

"Hammocks and groundsheets. That is the department where they are currently situated. We have some very nice cotton and polyester hammocks in a cheerful and summery design. Our hammocks are extremely comfortable and strong with maximum load-bearing capacity of 150 kilograms. They have integrated spreading sticks for added comfort."

The sales patter came as second-nature to him.

"How far away from us is the hammocks and groundsheets department and is there anything we can do to stop them getting up to this level?"

"At a brisk walking pace they could be up here in a minute, a minute and a half maybe. I can lock the door to the stairwell but I doubt if that would prove much of a barrier."

"Lock it anyway."

I don't know why I had suddenly started giving orders. Maybe because nobody else was. And I had the feeling there wasn't much time to start a campaign to elect a leader. The position was vacant, so I took it.

Mr Cadwallader tottered over to the door, took a bunch of keys from the pocket of his nightgown and proceeded to lock the only communicating door between this level and the rest of the shop. On the one hand, I was glad that the door had a mechanical lock rather than an electrically-operated one, which would have been useless. On the other hand, I couldn't help noticing how much noise a keyring full of keys made. The jangling was so loud I couldn't believe that the people downstairs could fail to hear it.

"Is there any other way out?" I said.

"The fire escape," he nodded to the far corner of the room. There was a glass door there, next to a wall of windows. It was early morning. Outside, the town stretched into the distance, grey and dismal in the pale light.

"Is it open?"

"It's a fire escape," he said, "Of course it's open."

The voices were getting closer. They were at the bottom of the stairwell now. I could hear talking, interspersed with laughter. Whoever they were, they seemed to be in an exceptionally humorous mood.

"Quick," said Mr Cadwallader, "Behind the ponchos!"

I had no idea what he meant until I saw him pointing to a rack of long, shapeless nylon garments which, according to the sign, were "Rainproof Ponchos – guaranteed to keep you dry in style!"

I had a distinct feeling that hiding behind the ponchos would fool no one. I didn't know if the people who'd broken into the building were looking for a fight but, if so, I thought we stood a better chance if we faced them openly instead of cowering behind a rack of fashionable rainwear.

If we'd had more time on our hands, we might have debated the matter. As it happened, we had no time at all. Seconds later, there was the sound of feet running up the stairwell towards us. Then there was an almighty crash as the glass of the door exploded in upon us followed by a large metal object landing on the floor. It was a fire extinguisher.

Seconds later, they were in the room with us. There were three of them. Young men. All between the ages of about seventeen and nineteen, at a guess. The first to enter was tall and rangy. He had long, greasy black hair and was wearing a fringed buckskin jacket in the 'Davy Crocket' style. There was something of the wolf about him. His movements were jerky and his hands trembled slightly. His eyes looked abnormally large and bloodshot. He was the one we'd heard laughing. He was laughing now. A high, braying laughter that had a touch of madness about it. He was holding a knife. It was a fairly short knife – much shorter than the one that the farmer, Douggie Lampton, had threatened me with – but it had a very sharp-looking serrated blade. I had the feeling that, in the right hands, that knife could do a lot of damage. I was hoping that these hands weren't the right hands.

"Looky, looky, looky, chumsters," giggled the man with the knife, "Looky what we got here. Three jolly victims and a jolly, jolly doggie."

The jolly, jolly doggie didn't take kindly to the description and was crouching, snarling through his teeth, with the hairs on his back standing upright like the spines on a porcupine.

"I see," said Mr Cadwallader, with a calmness that amazed me, "that you have selected one of our premier line of survival knives. This particular model has a drop-point CPM-S30V steel blade and a Japanese white oak handle."

The mad-looking man giggled again, stepped forwards and, with one swift movement, he slit Mr Cadwallader's throat.

6

"That guy talked too much," said the laughing man. He laughed when he said it.

Mr Cadwallader didn't die quickly. He clutched at his throat. He staggered forward. He bumped into a rack of overcoats. He held onto one of the coats with his free hand. Then he sank slowly to the floor and lay there, with his hands around his neck as blood poured between his fingers. All the while, he was making the most horrific sound I have ever heard: a wheezing, bubbling, gasping sound. I turned away. I couldn't bear to look. The laughing man laughed on. His two friends started laughing too. But I could barely hear the laughter. All I could hear was the terrible sounds of the man on the floor suffocating and drowning but, for what seemed a vast eternity of time, refusing to die.

And then, at last, he was silent. I looked at him. Lying, still and white in a growing pool of crimson.

Geoff moved towards the laughing man. I thought at first he was going to hit him. But he didn't. Geoff looked the laughing man straight in the eyes and said: "Cool knife. Almost as good as the ZT 0454."

"What's that?"

One of the other two men spoke then. He was tall and blond. He had the physique of a rugby player and yet he seemed to cringe in the attitude of a hyena. When he spoke, his voice was whiny and uncertain: "We, we don't need, don't n-need knives, Jake. G-guns is what we n-need. Where's the bleedin' guns?"

The laughing man, Jake, spoke over him: "What's a ZT…?"

"0454," said Geoff, "One of these." And he produced a dangerous looking, short-blade knife from his pocket.

Oh God, I thought, Geoff, don't do anything stupid.

"I tell you," the blond man said, "G-guns is what we need."

"It's an outdoor shop," Geoff said, "They don't sell guns."

"What do you mean, they don't sell guns?" said Jake, "Guns is for outdoors, ain't they?"

"This place is behind the times," Geoff said, "You want guns, what you want is a firearms shop."

"'You want a firearms shop…'" Jake mimicked in a high, whiny voice, "And what the hell do *you* know about guns anyway?"

Geoff unbuttoned the top of his denim shirt and pulled it back to show his bandaged shoulder. "I got shot by one."

Jake found that hysterical and doubled over in a fit of laughter. Then, quite suddenly, he straightening up and, without any trace of humour in his voice, he said, "You can't know much about guns if you got shot."

Geoff laughed too. "Nah, it's the bloke who shot me didn't know much about guns. If he *had* known much about guns, I wouldn't be standing here now, would I?"

"He's g-got a p-point, Jake," said the blond one.

Jake thought this over a bit. "Yeah, OK. Maybe."

"The thing is," Geoff continued, "I got shot by some crappy old pheasant-shooting gun. If I'd got shot by, say, a JD5050E, the outcome would have been very different. If you know what I mean."

"I know what you mean," said Jake, belligerently, "Are you trying to say that I don't know what you mean?"

"No, not at all. I can tell you are the sort of person who can size up a situation right away."

"Abso-bloody-lutely," agreed Jake.

"Well then, what you need is a JD5050E – it's powerful but compact, has PTO engagement and synchronized transmission. You don't want to go for one of the flashy numbers. The JD5050E is what a professional would use."

"That's what I been saying all along," agreed Jake, "That's what I need. So where will I get one, then?"

"A firearms shop is where you'll get one."

"And where will I find a firearms shop, my dearest chumster?"

"The best firearms shop in town is Johnson's down on Canal Street."

Jake started laughing again. "Can you believe this world, man? It's like every dream you ever had all rolled up into one."

I was wondering what dreams Jake had? Did he mean nightmares? Apparently not.

"Everything's for the taking man," he went on, "See something you want. Get it. The stuff in this place is shit compared to stuff in town. Come on a looting spree with us, my chummies, and I'll show you stuff beyond your wildest dreams."

"We've got to be off soon," I said, "We have to get somewhere."

"Sod that!" said Jake, "Nobody's got to do nothing no more. Life's for the living, man. You wouldn't believe the stuff I looted this past couple o' days. Booze, watches, an 82 inch colour TV!"

Much good that will do you without any power, I thought. But I kept the thought to myself. I had the feeling Jake might not appreciate my line in humorous irony.

"W-women," the blond one said, "All there for the t-taking."

"That's all you think about," said Jake – then, to us: "You'll have to forgive my thick friend, chums, his brains are in his Y-Fronts."

"So what about the g-guns?" the blond one said.

"OK, OK, I'm coming to that. My new friends here know all about guns. Where we can get some, which one is best. Don'cha, chummies?"

Geoff said, "Like I said, I know the place to get some."

"Come with us," said Jake, "Show us. Then maybe we won't kill you."

The blond one laughed.

Jake snapped at him – "Shut it, you moron. This ain't no laughing matter."

"Sorry, Jake."

"The thing is, we are behind schedule," I said, "We have to be somewhere."

"Who asked *you*?" Jake wanted to know. Then, turning to Geoff, he said, "Why are you hanging out with this geezer, anyway?"

"He's got all the contacts," Geoff said. I had no idea what he meant. From the look on his face, Jake had no idea what he meant either. Geoff stood there smirking at Jake. Then Jake seemed to catch on to Geoff's meaning and he began smirking back. Then he elbowed the blond guy in the ribs, "Why couldn't you think of that?" he said, "Contacts. That's what you need in this world."

While this baffling conversation had been going on, Bobby the dog had been running around, occasionally growling. Now, quite suddenly, he started barking.

"Someone kill that dog!" the laughing man said.

One of his friends – a small, skinny teenager – stepped forward. He wasn't giggling. In fact, he was frowning. "Not the dog," he said, "You can kill people if you like. But if you kill the dog, I'll kill you."

"Calm it, Dink, no one's gonna kill the dog," Jake said, "Just my joke, you know that."

That was the first time I'd got a good look at the man called Dink. He looked sick. His face had an unhealthy grey tinge to it. What should have been the whites of his eyes were dark crimson. A thick trickle of blood was oozing from one nostril. He wiped it away on the cuff of his jacket.

7

"What was that all about?"

"What?"

We were walking down a narrow lane on the far side of town – me, Geoff and Bobby. Doing everything we could to avoid being seen. Not that there were many signs of any people who might see us.

"You and Jake," I said, "All that chummy-chummy stuff…"

"It worked, didn't it?"

""It may have worked but I still don't know what 'it' was."

"Let's just say I'm good at avoiding fights. I'm kind of small. I look like a push-over. So people try to push me over. It happened when I was at school. It happens if I go out to a pub. Some people go out looking for a fight. When they see me, they stop looking."

"You get picked on is what you are saying?"

"That's what I'm saying."

"And…?"

"And I've learnt how to deal with it. You don't argue. Whatever they say, you agree with. If there's a gang of them, you especially agree with whoever's the gang leader. Make him feel big."

"Flatter him?"

"Exactly."

"And then you tell him where to get some guns? That was kind of dumb, wasn't it?"

"It would have been if that's what I'd done."

"I was there, Geoff. That's exactly what you did. I suppose you thought we'd be well away by then so it didn't matter if he went around killing other people."

"What if I did think that? It's true, isn't it?"

He had a point. In this world, it is a case of survival of the fittest. Kill or be killed. The Marquis of Queensbury rules no longer apply.

"Yeah," I said, "I guess so."

"Except that's not what I did. I ain't got no idea if there's any gun shops in town. But I didn't think that's what he wanted to hear. So I told him what he wanted to hear."

"You told him to go to Canal Street."

"Have you ever been to Canal Street?"

"Nope."

"It's where the farmers go."

"For guns?"

"For tractors. It's got one of the biggest agricultural machinery suppliers in the South West."

"But you told him which gun he needed. I heard you. The name, the model number, all the technical details."

"What, you mean the JD5050E, powerful but compact, with PTO engagement and synchronized transmission?"

"That's the one."

"It's a tractor."

"You're kidding!"

"No, I ain't. It's the tractor my dad wanted to buy but couldn't afford. He spent ages ogling the brochures, reading all the specs out loud. I could recite the whole damn' thing. It's the only piece of equipment I could think of that I could bullshit about convincingly. Hey, what are you laughing at? It fooled Jake, didn't it?"

"Yes, but it could also have got us killed."

Geoff shrugged – "Yes, there is that, I suppose."

8

By the time we were back in the suburbs, a fine drizzling rain was falling. Snow still lay in patches, heaped against the curbs but the weather was milder than it had been and the thaw was well advanced.

Most of the streets were deserted. The neat, semi-detached houses were all in neat, semi-detached rows. The hedges were trimmed, the lawns were mowed. It looked like a pleasant area, if pleasant areas are your sort of thing. It also looked entirely normal. Apart from the fact that there was nobody to be seen. Maybe they were all sitting indoors, keeping out of the rain? Maybe if the sun had been shining they would all be out in their gardens tending to the petunias and arranging their gnomes. But I didn't think so. I got the feeling that they had locked themselves away because they were scared.

Most of the streets were deserted, but not all of them. Sometimes as we approached a junction or the entrance to a side-street, we heard something. It might be the screeching of car brakes, motorbikes being revved, windows being broken, or just the hubbub of a gang of people talking and screaming and shouting. Often there was laughter; the sort of laughter that Jake had made; not normal laughter, not happy laughter. It was laughter on the border of hysteria, on the razor-edge of madness.

When we had arrived in town, the night before, it had been dark. I felt safer at night. Now, walking through the empty streets by daylight, I felt conspicuous. I was sure that eyes were watching me from behind all those lace curtains. I felt vulnerable. What if some lunatic in one of those houses had a gun and decided to take a pop at us?

But then, as I glanced into the houses, I realised that I'd got it the wrong way around. We needn't be nervous of them. Because they were terrified of us. Every once in a while I'd notice someone peeping from behind the curtains. As soon as they realised that I'd seen them, they backed away further into the darkness of their houses. As far as they were concerned, we were the enemy, Geoff and I. We were out on the streets. Anyone who was out on the streets had no fear. And anyone who had no fear was dangerous.

We turned into one street and nearly ran, slap bang into a gang on the razzle. This was not the sort of gang you would want to run into. They would be unlikely to give you a warm welcome. They were haranguing an old man. The man was in his garden, standing his ground, determined not to be intimidated. The gang shouted abuse at him. Called him names. The man told them to clear off.

"Or what?" said one of the gang.

"Never mind what," said the old man, "My wife's not well. She's got a bad heart."

Someone in the gang yelled out that all they needed was a good sharp knife and her heart wasn't going to be no problem no more. People laughed. It was that insane, cackling laugh again. Then someone in the front of the gang pushed the man.

"Clear off!" said the man, "I'm not afraid of you."

"He's not afraid of us, fellas," said the loud-mouthed youth who'd been doing most of the taunting, "Let's see if we can make him afraid then, shall we?"

More laughter.

Someone hit the old man with what looked like a baseball bat. There was a horrible thud. The man staggered. He didn't scream. He didn't yell. He tried to say something but the words didn't come out right. Then someone pushed him to the ground. The gang crowded around. I saw the person raise the baseball bat again. And *wham!* down it came. The crowd laughed. Someone cheered. Up went the bat. And *thump!* Down it went. And again, and again and again! I was glad the crowd had gathered around the old man. I was glad I couldn't see what they were doing to him. The gang who stood around watching, found it funny. Hysterically funny. Achingly, side splittingly funny.

Geoff and I were hiding behind a clump of trees at the end of the street. We moved away quickly. As long as the gang was focussed on watching an old man being clubbed to death, they wouldn't notice us. The last thing I saw was an old woman leaning from an upstairs window. She was wailing with a grief that I hope I never experience. Someone in the gang pointed to her. Then they surged forward towards the front door of the house, obviously intending to do something to the old woman too. I didn't hang around to find out what.

9

That night we erected a tent deep inside some woods. We were out on the moors somewhere. The woodlands must have covered hundreds of acres. Narrow, rutted roads wound between the trees. We found an old bridleway that branched off one of the roads and went deeper into the forest. You wouldn't have been able to go down there in an ordinary car. It was a bit of a struggle even with the Land Rover. Geoff and I shared the driving but Geoff was better at it than I was. He'd been driving his father's Land Rover, illegally given his age, for the last five years or so.

The surface of the bridleway was uneven and slippery with mud. The trees on either side grew in so close that the branches scratched the Land Rover's sides and top. Even so, we must have gone over half a mile down that bridleway before we were forced to stop. That was at a point where it suddenly sloped uphill into a denser area of trees that we couldn't have driven through. It was far enough off the beaten track. We just wanted a place that was remote from prying eyes.

We had plenty of food with us. We had cans of food, tea, instant coffee and cartons of long-life milk that we'd taken from a shop in a remote village earlier in the day. The shop had already been looted but the shelves were still well-stocked and there were cans and bottles of food and drink packed in boxes and scattered around on the floor. Whoever had wrecked the place clearly hadn't been impressed by what was on offer and there was plenty left for us to scavenge.

Scavenging is how we thought of it. We didn't think of it as stealing. We were picking up the waste. Waste not, want not. Scavenging that food had been our good deed of the day. It's funny how quickly you can get used to things. The moral compass of a lifetime can be ripped apart and reassembled in the blink of an eye.

Anyway, there had been nobody in the shop. Whoever had owned it must have moved on. Or else something must have happened to them. No point worrying about that. We needed food. Food was going free. If we'd left it, the rats would have had it. That's how I rationalised it, anyway.

We hadn't thought of scavenging soap or shaving kit, though. Even if we had, it would have been too cold to wash in one of the icy pools we saw in the woods. We were beginning to stink, my hair felt dirty and greasy and I was starting to grow a beard which itched like mad.

We made a fire that evening. In a clearing, beneath a canopy of trees. We'd camped out in a part of the forest populated by fir trees of some sort. It was a cultivated forest: manmade, regimented and dense. At other times I would have hated a place like that. I would have raved against the insanity of destroying our beautiful, rambling, native woodlands in order to plant soulless ranks of spruces. But that night I was glad of them. At that time of year, our native trees would be bare of leaf and they would have offered little in the way of shelter or concealment. Under the deadly darkness of those evergreens, on the other hand, we felt safe. Even the flames and smoke from our little fire, drifting up through those tall trees, would (I hoped) be hidden.

After we'd eaten (tinned fish and soup), we sat around the fire and had a few drinks. It was a cold night, but not freezing. We were wrapped up pretty well. The Arran sweater, parka and sheepskin gloves that I'd acquired from Mr Cadwallader's shop kept me pretty toasty. We'd acquired a bottle of whisky from the same shop in which we'd acquired the food. It was blended whisky. Pretty rough. I made a mental note to look for better booze next time – a good Highland malt would hit the spot. But, rough as it was, the whisky did a reasonable job of lifting my spirits. With so much free for the taking, so much waiting to be 'acquired', I told myself, this wasn't going to be such a bad life after all. It was a world well lost.

My good mood didn't last. How could it? Everything I'd ever known was in ruins. The life I'd hoped to live had been taken away – the rug had been pulled from beneath my feet.

After a while, I got out the radio – the one I'd taken from Cadwallader's store. I was hoping that I might be able to find some channels that were still broadcasting: one of the stations I'd heard on Douggie Lampton's shortwave receiver. I remembered the old farmer telling me that he listened to shortwave broadcasts from around the world: America. Canada. Somaliland. Any news would be good to hear. But I wasn't sure if this radio would be up to the job. Douggie Lampton's receiver had been a big, powerful-looking brute. The radio I was holding was like an old-fashioned battery-powered radio. For all I knew, it might not be powerful enough to receive any broadcasts at all. Assuming that there was still anyone out there broadcasting.

I turned it on and twiddled some knobs but the results were disappointing. Just loud static. I think once or twice there were hints of voices wafting in and out through the noise but I couldn't make head or tail of what they were saying. In the end I gave up.

After a few whiskies, I started to get a bit maudlin. I asked Geoff if he missed his family. What he thought would happen to them. He shrugged. "What's past is past." It seemed a callous thing to say. It was as though Geoff was glad to be free of them. Glad to be away from home and all the life he had lost. Glad the Catastrophe had happened.

Not me. For me, the past was a better place. It was a better life. Though, to be honest with you, that life had ended long before the snow had arrived. It had ended two years earlier, before I moved into Heather Cottage. Back then, everything had seemed possible. Love, happiness, wealth, success. I had still believed that one day I'd make it in the music business. In a rock band. And then everything went wrong. I told Geoff about it but I left out the important bits. Just as I'm leaving them out now. There are some things in life that are too painful, too personal, to put on public view.

The only person I had ever really been able to pour my heart out to was an old college friend, Justin Davenant. He took me out for dinner in a restaurant near his flat in Bayswater. We drank far too much wine with our meal and I'd gushed out all my woes to him. I even told him about my breakdown, which is something I'd never admitted to anyone before, apart from my doctor.

Justin said I needed to get away from everything. Get away from London, put the past behind me. Make a new start. I told him that would be wonderful if it were possible. But it wasn't.

That was when he'd told me about his cottage, Heather Cottage. He'd inherited it from a relative but hardly ever had the time to go and visit it. He offered it to me at a ludicrously cheap rent and I jumped at the chance. So I left London, determined to put all my problems behind me. I had no job to go to so I decided to set up as a guitar teacher. I put adverts in shop windows and in the local newspaper and, to my surprise, I actually managed to get some students. Not many. But I just about managed to make ends meet. Most of my students were, to be polite, on the mature side. Geoff, in fact, had been my only teenage student.

"They are all young," I said.

"What?" Geoff was sitting on a groundsheet near the fire, his back propped against the trunk of a convenient tree.

"All the gangs. The street gangs. Everyone you see in the streets. They are all young. Where are the old people?"

"There are plenty of old people," Geoff said, "They don't come out, that's all. Which is why we don't see them. Mr Cadwallader was old. There was that other old guy that we saw in town. The one they were bashing with a baseball bat."

I replayed that scene in my mind. It was so brutal I didn't want to think about it.

"They killed that old man," I said, "There were people living in those houses all around him. Watching through their net curtains. And nobody, not a single person, went to help him."

"Yeah, well," said Geoff, "We didn't neither."

I didn't reply. He was right. We were as bad as the rest of them.

10

We slept in the Land Rover that night. It was a one of those big, old models with solid metal sides and enough room in the back to kip down and stretch out. I slept soundly. I would have kept on sleeping if it hadn't been for the scratching noises.

They sounded like fingernails scraping down the outside of the metal. It was a penetrating noise. The sort of noise guaranteed to wake you from the soundest sleep. I sat up, looked out through the front window and also through the back window. There was nothing to see. Then the Land Rover started rocking from side to side. As if someone, or something, were pushing it. As the sides of the vehicle had no windows, it was impossible for me to see what was going on out there. Bobby had moved up close to me. I could feel him shivering. Geoff was awake too. He lay completely still, in his sleeping bag, his eyes wide with fear.

Then there came an almighty banging. *Bang! bang! bang!* Someone was thumping heavily and repeatedly against the side of the vehicle.

There was no point trying to lie low, no point holding our breath and hoping that whatever was out there might not notice that we were inside. It obviously knew we were there. And it didn't seem to have any intention of going away.

I slipped out of my sleeping bag and took a knife from my knapsack. I crept up to the window in the back door of the Land Rover and, slowly and carefully, I peeped out. There was nothing to be seen other than the long, dark tunnel formed by the trunks of the fir trees stretching away into the distance.

Then, quite suddenly, there was a pair of eyes.

I jumped back in horror. The eyes were huge, bestial, red rimmed and staring.

I wished we had a gun. If we'd had a gun I would have fired a shot. Which, from inside a Land Rover might not have been a very sensible thing to do. Then again, I knew nothing about guns anyway, so even if I'd had one I wouldn't have known how to use it.

Geoff was sitting up in his sleeping bag now. He was panting harder than the dog. All three of us – Geoff, Bobby and me – were staring through the back window. But the eyes had gone. Whatever it was that had looked in at us, had moved away. Then I heard the front door on the passenger side being opened. I hadn't bothered locking it the night before. I hadn't been expecting visitors. And anyway, if you know anything about old Land Rovers, you'll know that a locked door isn't much more of a barrier than an unlocked one.

I leapt up with the intention of holding the door shut. It was a pointless effort. The door was already open and something dark, unkempt and shaggy had leapt inside and was now kneeling on the passenger seat. It grasped the back of the seat, which is all that separates the front from the back of the Land Rover. It crouched there, staring at us through a fringe of long, greasy black hair.

If I'd been quicker witted and more experienced in the arts of self-defence I would have set about it with my knife. Luckily, I wasn't, so I didn't. If I had done, we would never have met Leila.

"What does a girl have to do to get service in this place?" the crouching form said.

My heart was still beating faster than it had any right to be beating and, for a few moments, I could make no sense of the smooth female voice coming from the shaggy anthropoid shape in front of us.

Geoff was the first to speak. What he said was indecipherable but sounded a bit like "Gah-gurkle-gah…" This was probably due to the fact that, in the excitement, his mouth had become entangled with the hood and drawstring of his sleeping bag.

I took up the conversation. My precise words were, I confess, somewhat lacking in diplomacy but they expressed my feelings accurately and concisely in words of one syllable.

"Good morning, gentlemen and dog," said the creature which I was only now starting to think of as an actual woman, "The name's Leila. And who might you be?"

Ten minutes later, the four of us were sitting outside eating cornflakes and long-life milk from plastic bowls while we boiled a kettle of water for tea over a small fire.

Leila was definitely a woman. The ape-like appearance was due to a combination of her enormous black, shaggy coat, a broad-brimmed black hat and her long black hair which had a tendency to drape itself around her face, leaving little to be seen except for her eyes peering through the undergrowth.

She had terrifying eyes. On their own, the silver irises would have been striking and attractive. But combined with the raw-looking red rims, her eyes looked inhuman and brutish.

"I don't look entirely at my best at the moment," she said, as she poured the hot water into the teapot, "I've been a bit under the weather, you see. Sugar and milk?"

"Just milk for me," I said.

"Milk and two sugars," said Geoff.

"Have you any sugar?" Leila asked.

I shook my head.

"That will have to be milk and two sugars without the sugar, then."

"I can't drink tea with no sugar," Geoff mumbled.

"Then we shall drink it for you."

Geoff drank his tea without sugar and complained after every sip.

"What were you doing to our Land Rover?" I asked.

"What did it sound like?"

"It sounded like you were pushing it and thumping it."

"That's precisely what I was doing."

"And scraping your fingernails down it."

"My fingernails? Really? Oh, that must have been this." She reached inside her fur overcoat and produced a long, vicious-looking dagger. It was twice the size of my knife and I had the feeling that, unlike me, Leila knew how to use it. It was probably just as well I hadn't tried to intimidate her with my pathetic little knife earlier.

"Love the coat," said Geoff, "What fur is it? Bear? Or wolf?"

"Bear? Wolf?" she said in a tone that suggested that was one of the stupidest things she'd ever heard, "Oh no, this is buffalo hide."

"Buffalo?" I said, unsure if she was pulling our legs, "Where would you get buffalo hide?"

"Typically," she said, "off a buffalo. You don't have any toast and marmalade, I suppose?"

We didn't. We did have some crispbreads and a pot of strawberry jam, however, so we scoffed that down for our second course.

Leila seemed a nice enough person, once you got past her unusual appearance and eccentric manners. But there was one thing that continued to bother me. Her eyes. They were bloodshot with painful-looking red eyelids. They reminded me of the eyes of the man who'd bled out in the alleyway. They reminded me of Jake's bloodshot eyes when he'd killed Mr Cadwallader. Leila said she'd been ill. I wanted to ask her about that but it didn't seem the sort of subject you could just drop into conversation. She might have taken it the wrong way and I wasn't sure if she was completely sane. She saved me the trouble.

"You keep staring at my eyes," she said, "Quite impolite. But, in the circumstances, understandable. They are symptomatic of an infection. Quite painful, actually. Look." She took the lower eyelid of her right eye between a thumb and forefinger and squeezed gently. A single drop of blood like a red tear oozed from the eyelid and trickled down her cheek. She wiped it away with the back of a hand.

I wondered what infection might cause your eyes to bleed like that. I'd heard of haemorrhagic fever but wasn't sure what it was. I had a feeling that some tropical diseases like Ebola caused people to bleed from the eyes and, well, just about every other bodily orifice. I also knew that Ebola was not at all a good thing to catch. Sitting there on the ground, I shuffled a couple of feet further away from her, almost without intending to do it. The sight of the blood oozing from her eye filled me with dread.

She smiled. "The reaction is a common one. At least you haven't tried to shoot me yet."

"We haven't got a gun," Geoff said. I could have strangled him.

"But you do have a radio which, in the present circumstances, might be of rather greater use."

The radio was nowhere to be seen. It was tucked away inside the Land Rover.

"I was watching you last night," she explained, "Your attempts to tune into shortwave stations were valiant but doomed to failure."

"You were watching us?"

"Oh yes. I am not in the habit of approaching people whom I do not believe to be harmless. Or, at any rate, more harmless than I am."

"Why do you say our attempts to tune into shortwave stations…?"

"…were doomed to failure? I say it because it's true. You need an aerial."

"The radio has an aerial."

"A very inadequate one, however. You need a very long, extensible aerial if you are to have the remotest possibility of hearing anything more than indecipherable crackling."

"Is that a fact? And how do you know that?"

She smiled, "I know a great deal of very useful things, darling. Now are you going to take my advice and get yourself a proper aerial or are you simply going to sit in a forest and feel sorry for yourselves?"

So we set out to find an aerial.

11

Leila led us to a farmhouse a couple of miles distant. We took our walking sticks with us – the ones that Geoff and I had taken from Mr Cadwallader's store. Leila had a stick too, and it outranked ours. It must have been almost six feet long and I had the feeling that she might occasionally use it for activities other than walking. The farmhouse was an old building with rough-plastered walls and a thatched roof. There was a wooden shed out the back and she walked right into it.

"Nothing to worry about here," she said, "There's no one at home. Well, no one that will bother us."

I didn't ask for details. And I didn't look inside the house. I'd seen enough horror over the past few days. It suited me better to think of this as just a deserted house – end of story.

Leila found a roll of wire – thin, electrical wire covered in plastic. She also found some alligator grips and a pair of pliers. She took the lot and then we strolled back to where the Land Rover was parked. The paths we took led mostly through the forest and we didn't see a single soul en route, which suited me.

Once we got back, she unwound about twenty feet of wire, cut the plastic covering off one end and twisted it into the alligator grip which she then clamped onto the aerial of our radio.

"Now all we have to do is get the rest of the wire strung up into the trees," she said.

I looked at the trees. The bottoms of the trunks were bare. Further up, they were dense with the prickly-looking branches of the spruces.

"How are we going to do that?" I said.

Leila gave me a look of withering contempt. Then she took off her huge buffalo-skin coat and hat, clenched the free end of the wire between her teeth and shinned up the nearest tree with the agility of a gibbon. When she got far enough up the tree, she looped the wire around a branch and shinned back down again.

"There you go," she said, as she put her coat and hat on again, "One long-wire antenna. Now, let's see what's on the radio."

Leila tuned the radio with the practised air of an expert. There were a few foreign language stations at first. Although the reception waxed and waned a bit, it was very much better than it had been without the aerial. Finally she hit on an American channel. It came in loud and clear. It sounded strangely normal. A man's voice spent some time talking about domestic news – there'd been a hurricane somewhere and a mass shooting somewhere else. Then he said something about an emergency meeting that the President was having with an Army general and members of the CDC.

"Well, that's good news, at least," I said, "I mean, America seems to be functioning pretty much normally so it's not as if there's a global catastrophe or anything."

Leila shushed me. She was more interested in what the radio announcer was saying than what I was saying.

"...the President said that the situation in Europe was at crisis point but that the American people could rest assured that all necessary measures would be taken to contain and eradicate the problem."

Then there was discussion with an economist about the impact of the European situation on imports and exports. That was followed by someone offering advice to people who had been unable to contact friends and relatives in Europe.

"What's the CDC?" I said.

She gave me one of those "You really are an idiot, aren't you?" looks of hers. "The Centers For Disease Control and Prevention. It's a federal agency. But that's not the important bit."

She turned the radio off.

"Leave it to the Yanks," Geoff said, "They'll get something sorted out. They'll probably be sending food parcels over or something."

"Yes," I said, "And they'll probably negotiate a trade deal while they are at it. You know what the Americans are like!"

Geoff and I were treating it all as a big joke. I guess we were in a good mood. It was a relief to find that life in America was carrying on as usual. I'd been starting to think that maybe everywhere in the world was in as bad a state as Britain. Leila didn't see the funny side, however.

"You do realise what they are talking about, I suppose?"

"Who?" said Geoff.

"The Americans. You do understand what we just heard. What it all means?"

"That America is doing fine," I said, "And help is on its way."

Leila laughed. It was a bitter laugh, completely devoid of humour. "Something is on its way," she said, "But it isn't help. When the President has high level meetings with the top military brass to discuss all necessary measures to contain and eradicate the problem, it's a safe bet it's not food parcels they are talking about."

"What then?" said Geoff.

"A bomb, maybe. Probably more than one. That's just what we need to make everything OK again. Some great, stinking big atomic bombs dropped on us!"

Geoff laughed. I didn't. I was trying to convince myself that Leila was being over pessimistic but I wasn't succeeding. "The Americans think it's a disease, then?" I said.

"Hmmm?"

"The broadcast said the President was consulting with the CDC, some sort of health agency, which kind of implies that…"

"For God's sake, darling! Of course it's a disease. It was the Russians that did it."

"What?"

"It came in the snow. I'd have thought that was obvious."

"Not to me it isn't."

"Of course, I we can't be one hundred percent certain. I mean, maybe it was the Americans. Or the Armenians…"

"Armenians?"

"What I'm trying to say, darling, is that it could have come from anywhere. But since the snow came from Siberia and the Russians have a bit of a history with this sort of thing, one has to draw the most plausible conclusions."

"What history have the Russians got?" said Geoff.

"Are you two really as ignorant as you appear or are you working on a comedy double act?"

"We're planning an act for the Blackpool summer season," I said.

"Then may I suggest you work on better material. You have no doubt heard of Biopreparat?"

Geoff looked blank. I looked blanker.

"The Fifteenth Directorate?"

We continued to look blank.

"The Kirov anthrax accident? The Aralsk-7 smallpox outbreak? Well, crikey, even you chaps must have heard of Chernobyl!"

"Of course, I've heard of Chernobyl!" I said.

"I saw it on the telly," Geoff added.

"Well, then, that's what I'm, saying. This is the same thing that happened with Chernobyl, except this time it's biological rather than nuclear. Isn't it all transparently obvious, darlings?"

Our continued blankness persuaded Leila that, as far as Geoff and I were concerned, it was far from transparently obvious, so she set about explaining. She began with a potted history of the Soviet biological weapons programme. According to her, they'd tried weaponising everything from the plague to dengue fever along with a number of diseases I'd never even heard of. She gave graphic accounts of experiments with monkeys on a place called Rebirth Island. Most of the experiments were unpleasant. Few of them, fortunately, were entirely successful.

"And over the years there have been quite a few accidents. Diseases getting out of the laboratories and into the population. Nobody quite knows how many such incidents there have been because, of course, the Russians don't go around advertising them. They didn't go to great lengths to fess up to Chernobyl either."

"I don't see what Chernobyl has to do with anything," I said.

"Radioactive fallout spread over Scandinavia, Italy, Greece… it even got as far as Scotland and the mountains of Wales. Well then, what do you think would happen if an accident sent a plume of pathogens – viruses, fungal spores, bacteria, something like that – up into the atmosphere and the weather systems carried them across Europe and down into Britain?"

"Can bacteria and viruses live inside clouds?" Geoff said.

"Can viruses live at all is a more pertinent question?" Leila replied, "Most biologists regard viruses as non-living. Little packages of nucleic acids that can't do anything on their own. They just spend their time drifting around looking for cells to infect. My God, you chaps! What does a girl have to do to get a drink around here?"

"We've still got some whisky," I said.

"Sod that! I mean a proper drink. I have a craving for gin. A good dry Martini would go down a treat. Let's go and get one!"

12

We were sitting in a cocktail bar called Miami Nights. It was situated in a dilapidated area on the far outskirts of a small town about twenty minutes' drive from the forest where we'd been staying. Illumination was provided by candles that we'd placed on a few table tops. We'd nicked the candles on our way, from a small, semi-derelict hardware store. Leila was drinking pink gin. Geoff was sipping a glass of cider. I'd decided to stick to wine: a fairly decent New Zealand Sauvignon Blanc.

I'd given up wondering where everyone had gone. We'd passed a few bodies lying in the streets but they didn't account for the entire population. I guessed some people had locked themselves away in their houses, waiting for the Government to take control, waiting for the Army to re-establish law and order, waiting for the power to come back on again, along with the radio and the TV. Waiting for life to get back to the way it was. That would be a long wait.

Others, I guessed, had moved on. Left the area. Gone looking for relatives? Maybe they assumed that the looting and the violence and the killing were just local problems and if they looked further afield they'd find somewhere safe?

And the young people? We'd already noticed that they tended to group together. Maybe they had migrated into the city centres. For all I knew, they might be living in the luxury suites of five star hotels.

"Shame there's no ice," Leila said, "It seems rather common to drink gin without ice."

The gin was so cold it would have made no difference. It had been a long time since there had been any heating in the Miami Nights Cocktail Bar. The three of us were wearing hats and gloves. Our breath made plumes of steam in the air.

"Who the hell are you, Leila?" I asked.

"You really don't know?" she said, her mouth and eyes wide with astonishment, "I might be quite insulted."

"What?"

"'The Return Of The Native'…"

"What?"

"Thomas Hardy. Mini-series. Eustacia Vye, the exotically beautiful but ultimately tragic heroine. It was a smash hit. On the telly last year."

"You were in that?" Geoff said, "I saw a bit of it. It was OK. Bit old-fashioned. But OK."

"You're an actress?" I said.

She put a hand over her breast and nodded in acknowledgment.

"And you played Eustacia Vye. On the telly?"

"Ah, well, no, not exactly. That was someone else whose name escapes me. I played a milk maid. I had two lines. 'It'll be her up on the heath that you'll be a-lookin' for, young sir,' and 'Oh, 'tis a terrible hot day today.' Still, the lines were said in two different episodes and my agent managed to negotiate twice the fee as a consequence."

"So how come you know so much about shortwave radio and biological warfare and… well, everything?"

"That might be because I was researching a part for a TV series all about a glamorous Russian assassin who is trained in the art of survival."

"Were you? Researching a part for a TV series all about a glamorous Russian assassin who is trained in the art of survival, I mean?"

"No."

"Well, then?"

"It might be because there's much more to me than meets the eye. What's the time, dearheart?"

I looked at my watch. "Nearly half past eleven."

"Better get going then. We don't want to be here at midnight."

"Why not?"

"It's not a good time to be here, that's all."

"You are superstitious!" I said.

"Either that or I have premonitions. Either way, we don't want to be here at midnight."

It was about ten to twelve before we finally left the Miami Nights Cocktail Bar. We took a couple of bottles of gin and a box containing twelve bottles of wine with us. In case of an emergency. Geoff drove the Land Rover. Leila sat in the passenger seat. Bobby and I roughed it in the back.

If you've ever ridden in the back of a long wheelbase Land Rover, you will know that when I say we roughed it, I mean it. There are no seats. There are, however, two long box-like ridges, that run along either side of the vehicle from front to back, about the width of the gym benches they have in schools, only much less comfortable. I sat precariously on one of the benches. Bobby stretched out full-length on the other. Every time the Land Rover bounced over a pothole, we got bounced on the benches. Bobby didn't seem to mind. I wasn't so keen.

At first the streets seemed deserted. Geoff drove down the hill that led from the bar towards a roundabout at the edge of the town. There were no street lights and no moon, so he had his headlights on. That may have been a mistake.

As we approached the bottom of the hill, we saw some shadowy forms moving towards us. A crowd of people. They were staggering slightly as though they were drunk. They reminded me of a crowd of football fans I'd once got caught up with after a big match at Wembley. I'd been visiting friends. I hadn't even realised there had been a match until I found myself mixed up in the crowd. The Wembley crowd I got mixed up in had been chanting and singing, most of them had been drinking pretty heavily; they had gone staggering down the road, often right down the middle of the road paying no attention to oncoming traffic. It was as though they had stopped being individuals. They had stopped being rational, sensible human beings who paid attention to the laws of the land and who had retained at least some basic concern for their own safety. They had become a single, moving, swaying, chanting creature. Like a massive, human colony of army ants on the march, sweeping away everything in their path.

The crowd that was lumbering towards the Land Rover had some of that same ant-colony look about it: an animalistic mass that was heading straight for us. At first it was just a dark, amorphous shape bubbling out of the distant night. As we got closer, our headlights illuminated them, picking out individuals. There must have been thirty or more and they were heading towards us with deliberate intent.

"Turn back!" I yelled, "Geoff, for God's sake…"

Geoff slowed the Land Rover and began to turn the wheel. Leila grabbed the steering wheel – "Don't you dare go back!" she said.

"They won't let us through," I shouted, "If we go that way, we'll have to stop."

"Stop?" said Leila, "I don't think so! Put your foot on the accelerator, dear boy, we are going through!"

"Don't be so bloody…"

But Geoff had already made a decision. Given contradictory advice from me and Leila, he had clearly decided that Leila had a better grasp of the situation. The Land Rover picked up speed and now we were hurtling towards the approaching crowd. I expected to see shock and horror on their faces. But all I saw was blank determination. I expected to see them jump out of the path of the Land Rover. But they carried on moving towards us, implacably.

Then came the horror of the collision. Geoff swerved to avoid the first of them but, having done so, he hit another. I remember the sound of impact. A sickening thump. One moment a young man had been standing there, staring through the windscreen at us. The next moment, he was gone, his body collapsing under the moving vehicle.

But there was worse to come. Because a few yards behind him there was a great mass of people blocking the road. At the speed we were travelling, Geoff wouldn't have been able to stop even if he'd wanted to. He ploughed straight into them. I closed my eyes. Leila whooped and cheered. *Thump, thump, thump!* I felt each collision reverberate through the Land Rover. Afterwards, the vehicle bumped up and down, over the fallen bodies, as though travelling over a badly pitted road surface.

Finally we were past them. Geoff took the left-hand turning from the roundabout, taking the road that led back towards the forest. On the journey there, Leila told us all about the films and TV plays she'd appeared in. She'd been in a detective series on the BBC.

She'd played an alien in Doctor Who? She'd played a Viking maiden in a film I'd never heard of. Geoff and I said nothing.

I was starting to think that Leila might be insane.

That night, it snowed again.

13

When I woke up, Leila had gone.

Geoff and I sat inside the back of the Land Rover eating Corn Flakes with evaporated milk. We poured milk into a saucer for Bobby. He lapped it up without enthusiasm. Then, as there was nothing else to do, I started messing around with the radio. We were inside the Land Rover, so I hadn't connected the long wire antenna. Shortwave reception was abysmal. I switched it off.

Geoff wasn't ready to give up. He turned the radio back on and played around with it for a bit. He tried other wavelengths. In addition to shortwave, the set was supposed to be able to pick up FM, Longwave and Mediumwave. We listened to some old comedy show on the BBC for a while. The BBC was still broadcasting repeats most of the time.

Every ten minutes or so a pre-recorded voice would interrupt to say: "You are listening to Radio 4. Due to the current emergency situation, we are unable to broadcast our scheduled programs. Normal service will resume as soon as possible."

"They're taking their bleedin' time," I said, "To resume normal service."

I was about to turn it off when, quite unexpectedly, there were the pips: the electronic beeps that the BBC had always played in the old days to mark the time on the hour. Then a voice said: "It is twelve o'clock. And now the news."

I couldn't believe it. It sounded just the way Radio 4 used to sound. In the old days.

"The Government has announced plans to make more hospital beds available for emergency treatment during the present emergency. The acting Prime Minister promised that, while the recent problems have been exceptional, the restoration of a fully functioning Health Service is the Government's top priority.

"The President of the United States said today that the planned State Visit will go ahead as scheduled. However, the date of the visit has not yet been confirmed and it is expected that it may now be delayed until later in the year.

"The Met Office has issued an amber weather warning for all of the UK and a red warning for the South West of England. Heavy snow and high winds are expected with the potential to cause damage to property. You are advised to avoid travelling whenever possible.

"And in sports news. Tottenham Hotspur won 3-2 in their match against Everton. This means that Tottenham will be in the Champions League next season, whatever happens when they face Liverpool.

"Next on Radio 4. A classic episode of 'Dad's Army' in which Captain Mainwaring…"

I turned the radio off.

"It all sounds so bloody normal," I said.

"That's good, ain't it?" said Geoff.

"*Too* bloody normal," I said, "I don't believe a word of it. Who's the 'acting' Prime Minister, anyway? Where's the real Prime Minister?"

"Could be sick," said Geoff.

"Or dead. And what's all that bollocks about football matches. Tottenham Hotspur, Everton, the Champion's League. Are we really supposed to believe that the bleedin' football season is carrying on as if nothing had happened?"

"Maybe things are all OK in London."

"Maybe. And maybe the BBC is lying to us. Maybe the Government is lying to us. Or whatever's left of the Government. Whoever the acting Prime Minister may be. I don't believe a word of it. It's all lies."

Later that afternoon, Geoff and I were sitting in the front of the Land Rover with Bobby sleeping in the back, when suddenly something slithered down the windscreen in front of us. It was a dead animal. Grey, furry and bloody. Its blood left a red smear on the glass.

I looked at Geoff. "Looks like Leila's back."

And sure enough, there she was. She had three more dead animals strung together over her shoulder. Geoff and I got out of the Land Rover. Bobby leapt over the seat and followed us.

"While you boys were sleeping, I've been out getting dinner."

"What are they?"

"What do they look like?"

"Dead animals."

"Was that just a guess or did you work it out?"

"Worked it out. The only thing I can't figure out is what sort of dead animals."

"Rabbits, darling, rabbits."

Bobby was supremely interested in the furry corpses. He was leaping up at Leila, sniffing and licking his lips and woofing and wagging his tail. "Don't worry, old boy," she said, "I got one for you too."

So we collected some wood and we made a fire in a clearing beneath the trees while Leila explained how she'd caught them. She'd used some of our antenna wire to make a snare. In the weeks she'd been living in the forest, she'd become expert at catching rabbits. The rabbits had some runs in fields and hedgerows nearby. Leila had made little frameworks of branches and set up wire snares that the rabbits would run into. Once snared, they'd start struggling to get away and would end up strangling themselves.

"I collect them before they are dead, of course. Best to get them when they are still fresh and wriggling. Then one bump over the head with a good stone and they are done for."

The way she described it made me feel a bit sick. I felt even sicker when I saw Leila take her knife and skin the poor creatures. She sliced each of them neatly through the belly, then pulled the skin over the rabbit's head the way you might pull a tight glove off your hand. I kept thinking of the pet rabbit I'd had when I was a kid. Geoff, being a farmer's boy, wasn't in the least bit squeamish. Nor was Bobby. In fact, he stood there entranced and drooling.

Once again, I wondered how Leila knew how to do all these things? I wouldn't have had a clue how to snare and skin a rabbit. She did it as though it was an everyday activity. I suppose it was possible that she might have been researching a role for a film about

Neanderthal hunters or early American settlers – a remake of The Little House On The Prairie, maybe? But that didn't seem likely.

"If only we had a gun we could probably catch something a tad bigger," she said.

"Bigger? Like what?" I was thinking maybe a hare or a pheasant.

"A deer maybe. Or a cow."

"A cow?"

"Or maybe a dog."

Bobby whimpered. I saw a television documentary once about a dog that understood over a thousand English words. I wondered how many Bobby knew.

"Don't worry," Leila said, "I'm only kidding. About the dog, anyway. I wouldn't mind trying to kill a cow though."

We got one of the saucepans we'd stolen earlier and boiled up some snow over the fire. Meanwhile, Leila swiftly chopped up the rabbits into bite-sized chunks and tossed them into the pot. I searched our store of food and found a bit of salt and some tinned carrots that we added to the mix, then we sat back and waited while the smell was making me and Geoff drool almost as much as the dog.

Leila made fun of my squeamishness. The day before, we'd run down some people with the Land Rover and yet I was still getting soppy and sentimental over a few dead rabbits. That's another thing I hadn't really come to terms with yet. Ploughing into a crowd of people and then just driving away. Leila didn't seem affected by it. She said it was a case of us or them – kill or be killed.

"I suppose we could try it with a knife," she said.

She looked at her hunting knife speculatively.

"Try what?"

"Kill a cow. Or a deer."

I laughed. I assumed she was joking. She wasn't. "Oh, it can be done. If you corner the animal so it can't get away. Might be doable with a cow. If you two lads chase one into the corner of a field. Or into a milking shed. Then all I'd have to do would be to dispatch it. Fairly straightforward, I should think. A deer would be more difficult. I read once about someone who hid up a tree then leapt onto a deer's back, reached around its neck and slit its throat. Seems to me there are a few too many things that might go wrong with a deer though. They can be quite lively when they want to be."

"Especially when someone had leapt from a tree onto its back, wielding a knife with the intention of cutting its throat?" I suggested.

"Precisely. I couldn't have put it better myself. Hmm, a soupçon more salt, I think." – she had taken a spoon and was sampling the broth – "Such a shame we haven't any herbs. A bay leaf and a few sprigs of thyme would have made all the difference."

All the talk about cutting throats had brought back memories of the murder of Mr Cadwallader, his throat sliced open by the madman, Jake. Something must have shown in my face because Leila picked up on my thoughts immediately. "Oh, it wouldn't be like that if I did it. He didn't know how to use a knife."

"What are you talking about?"

I had previously told her all about Jake and Mr Cadwallader. She referred to the killing obliquely, assuming it was obvious what she was talking about. "That Jake fellow. Untrained. Nobody who knew what they were doing would have done it that way."

"What way?"

She slashed her knife through the air in front of her. "Not a reliable killing cut. The victim could have lived for some time. Had medical attention been available, he might have made a full recovery. At any rate, from your description, he took quite a while to die. His trachea was no doubt severed, possibly a jugular vein. He probably suffocated. Or drowned in his own blood. Whereas that farmer chap, the one you said you'd found in the snow…"

"Douggie Lampton."

"The name is irrelevant. He knew what he was doing. Well, as a farmer, I suppose that's only to be expected. You said there was a great gush of blood across the snow, stretching away at some distance. That would have happened when a carotid artery was cut. Which is a much more effective means of killing someone. That old farmer did the job professionally, I'd say. Mmmm, that meat smells delicious. Come on, boys, let's tuck in."

Yes, I was becoming increasingly convinced that Leila was insane. But in this mad world, insanity might be the key to survival. I didn't hold it against her.

14

"This is Peter Quinn bringing you all the best hits from the best decade as we go back to the '80s with Spandau Ballet and 'To Cut A Long Story Short'."

Night had fallen. We were sitting around the fire watching the snowflakes drifting gently through the smoke. We were replete. The rabbit stew had been delicious beyond words. Even without a bay leaf and thyme. Wrapped up in a warm coat, scarf and gloves, sprawling on a groundsheet in a fairly dry spot beneath some trees, I felt that this was a life that was not without its merits. Geoff and I were making inroads into our second bottle of Sauvignon Blanc, Leila was mainlining the gin and Bobby was sleeping off the excess of rabbit which had been his share of dinner.

The '80s music show had been our major discovery that night. Not just because it was good to hear some music (even though I personally would have preferred some classic rock – Ritchie Blackmore maybe, or Eric Clapton), but because the show gave us a purpose and a direction.

We'd stumbled upon the channel entirely by accident. Up to that point, we'd been spending our time trying to find broadcasts on shortwave. Our efforts had met with limited success. Even with the benefit of the long wire antenna, we were able to receive very few stations, almost none in English, and when we did manage to tune in to an English-language broadcast, the reception wafted in and out so that it was hard to make sense of what was being said.

Then Geoff started messing about with the radio, twiddling knobs and pressing buttons in a fairly random way. That's when he heard 'The Damned Don't Cry' by Visage. I happen to like that song so I told him to stay on that station. The next song was Adam and The Ants' 'Kings Of The Wild Frontier'. "That's us," I thought. Kings of all we see. Kings with nobody to rule.

And so we spent the next twenty minutes listening to the Peter Quinn All 80s Radio Show. And for a while it gave us the impression of complete normality. This was the way life had been just a few short weeks earlier. Oldies radio stations. What could be more ordinary than that?

But it was when the Peter Quinn radio show came to an end that we realised that we had really struck gold. Because that's when the news headlines were broadcast. And they were nothing like the headlines being broadcast by the BBC.

"This is the news from Radio True Britain. People Of Britain. The Government does not exist. The country is in a state of civil war. We have reason to believe that up to half the population may have died. Keep clear of the cities. The contagion is spreading. I repeat: keep clear of the cities. The contagion is spreading."

15

We'd been hidden away in the forest for more than a week. Maybe ten days. I was losing track of time. I'd even lost track of my birthday which I'd ignored completely, not realising that I was another year older until Geoff told me that it was February. He knew that because the calendar on his smart-watch told him so. That watch was the last piece of modern technology we had that still continued to function. The weather was cold and we'd had a few moderate falls of snow but nothing like as bad as the blizzards we'd had a few weeks earlier.

Geoff and I had been on a few excursions into some villages round and about and we'd replenished out-of-stock of tinned foods. We'd also found a big free-standing diesel tank in a farm and we'd filled a couple of jerry cans so the Land Rover had plenty of spare fuel. We'd been syphoning diesel from trucks up until that point. This, let me tell you, is not as easy as it sounds. First, there's the problem of getting the fuel cap off. If you manage to do that, you then need a long hose pipe to use as the syphon. Starting the syphon by sucking one end of the pipe isn't much fun since you usually end up with a mouthful of petrol and even then, more often than not, the damn' syphon doesn't work. After much trial and error, we eventually discovered that knocking a hole in a car's fuel tank using a hammer and chisel was the simplest way of scrounging fuel. We once even tried getting fuel from a petrol station but the damned pumps had no power and we couldn't figure out any way of pumping up the petrol manually. The diesel tank in the farm, though, that was no problem at all because it used a simple hand-operated tap. The perfect technology for the modern world!

We relied on Leila for fresh meat. A couple of times she managed to get rabbits. But usually she went scouting around farms and houses in remote parts of the countryside looking for whatever livestock happened to be around. Sometimes she got chickens.

Once she got a small sheep but she didn't bring back the whole carcase – just two legs. I didn't ask how she'd killed it. I didn't want to know.

We were always careful to take circuitous routes when we went out in the Land Rover. I didn't want anyone tracking us back to our hideout. Not that we saw many people. Not alive, anyway. At first we saw a few sickly-looking old people in some of the villages. Some of them were trying to carry on with their lives as though nothing had happened: farmers, trying to feed their livestock, milk their cows. In the villages, some shops were still open for business. But the people were mostly sick. They were pale and drawn. Some of them had to brace themselves against walls and fences as they walked. I remember seeing one old woman suddenly stop half-way down a village street, clutch her stomach, bend over and vomit blood. With every day that went by, there were fewer and fewer people to be seen. The contagion (as Radio True Britain called it) was killing them. Killing the old people. We never saw young people. Not in the countryside.

"This is the news from Radio True Britain. People Of Britain. The Emergency Government has declared martial law. All major cities are now subject to a curfew which will begin at twilight and end at dawn. As far as we understand it, there are no official definitions of 'twilight' and 'dawn'. Reports are coming in of significant civilian casualties in London, Manchester, Birmingham and Glasgow. We strongly recommend that you avoid towns and cities if at all possible. If that is not possible, be sure to keep off the streets after dark. In our earlier reports, we stated that the Army was no longer functional. In light of recent events, it appears this may have been incorrect. We don't know how many soldiers are currently deployed in Britain. In fact, we don't even know how many soldiers managed to survive the contagion. We will try to bring you more information if we are able to do so. Be aware that the Army is not on our side. I repeat: the Army is not on our side. And now back to Peter Quinn's All 80s Radio Show…"

We listened to Radio True Britain every day. Since it was on the mediumwave rather than the shortwave, we didn't have to use the long wire antenna. The simple telescoping aerial on the radio set was all we needed. It was comforting to know that we weren't the only sane people left alive.

Towards the end of our time in the forest, we realised that we were becoming increasingly isolated from such remnants of civilisation as still existed. All around us was silence and death. We no longer saw many signs of life in our excursions to the villages. As each day passed, we saw more and more bodies lying in the streets. Old people who had suddenly lost their battle with sickness and whose bodies had been left to lie where they had fallen.

If it hadn't been for Radio True Britain, it would have been all too easy to imagine that the entire population had fatally succumbed to the disease. But every day, the radio announcer reported that the Army was quelling riots and gunning down looters in towns and cities all over Britain.

"The young people survive," Leila said, "The old people die."

On Radio True Britain they called the young people 'The Infected' or 'The Red-eyes'. The old people they called 'The Sick' or 'The Dying'.

"*We're* not dead," I said.

I had recovered from a bout of flu. Was that the same flu that was killing the old people? Or was it just a regular, everyday sort of flu? I had no way of knowing. Maybe I had caught a less virulent strain and had somehow built up an immunity? Or maybe I was just lucky? After all, not everyone who gets Ebola dies of it. Even when the Black Death ravaged Europe, some people survived. Geoff had never shown any symptoms at all. I wasn't sure about Leila. Her bloodshot eyes were a classic sign of the contagion. The Red-eyes: that's what they called the gangs on Radio True Britain. "Hundreds of Red-eyes were subdued by the Army in Solihull today… A hospital in Sunderland had been looted by bands of Red-eyes…" There was something about the easy calmness with which Leila killed and dismembered animals that gave me cause for worry. But on the whole, I thought there was more of "us" than of "them" in her. Her eyes were wild but she was lucid, intelligent and she had never shown any aggression towards me and Geoff. The fact of the matter is that I liked her.

"This is the news from Radio True Britain. People Of Britain. The time has come to begin the resistance. If we are to survive, we must work together. The towns are still dangerous. The Army is doing its best to restore law and order. But the task is difficult. We are receiving unconfirmed reports that some parts of North London are now under military control and are considered to be safe. The Emergency Government is still imposing a curfew, however. This is for the benefit of the population and all citizens are being asked to cooperate for the good of the country. And now back to Peter Quinn's All 80s Radio Show…"

"I thought the Army was our enemy," Geoff said, "That's what they said a couple of days ago. What happened?"

"Either the Army stopped being our enemy," I said, "Or else the Army has taken over Radio True Britain."

"There's one more possibility," Leila said, "Which is that Radio True Britain is just full of shit."

"At any rate," I said, "We can't stay here for ever. We have to move on. We have to go and find out for ourselves what the real situation is."

So the next day, we packed all our food and belongings in the back of the Land Rover and we set off. I suggested heading back the way Geoff and I had come. Back to the village, back to the Church Hall. Back to what was left of my home. But Geoff didn't want to go. "They'll all be dead," he said.

"Let's go to town," said Leila.

"Which town?" I said.

"There's only one town worth going to, sweetie. London town."

I thought she was kidding. But she wasn't.

"You heard what they said on the radio," I protested.

"They said some parts of North London are under military control," Geoff said.

"And considered to be safe," Leila added.

"And you believe them?"

"Hell, no!" said Leila. And she laughed.

"OK, then," I said, "Let's go to London."

PART III – SOLITUDE

Part III – Solitude

1

Getting to London was easier said than done. We decided to keep to the B roads as much as possible, which meant going via the Mendips, avoiding towns like Bristol and Bath. A full thaw had set in by this time and there were only scrappy remnants of snow visible on the tops of distant hills. Everywhere we went there were the familiar scenes of desolation: deserted villages, bodies left to rot in the roads. Once or twice we saw figures walking along the streets or striding across fields. At a distance it was impossible to tell for sure if they were Normals or red-eyes. I think many of them were Normals, survivors of the plague, who were out hunting or scavenging, just as we were.

We saw other signs of life too. There were numerous stray dogs and cats. Bobby woofed whenever he saw them. Sometimes we saw or heard other motor vehicles. Usually they were at a distance but once or twice we saw cars or vans on the road ahead of us. Invariably they either backed away from us or accelerated to overtake us as rapidly as possible. That, at least, proved that there were still people well enough, and sane enough, to drive. But they mistrusted us, as we mistrusted them.

We avoided motorways, driving instead down bridleways, dirt roads and unsurfaced tracks. It was a good thing we were driving a Land Rover rather than a regular car or we would never have made it over that kind of terrain. It was a bumpy ride. Geoff did most of the driving while Leila and I took turns at sitting in the back with Bobby. It was incredibly uncomfortable there, as there were no proper seats and every bump and pothole rattled through your body and bounced you off the metal sides of the vehicle. I ended up with so many bruises it must have looked as though I'd been the loser in a cage fight.

I wasn't sure that the decision to go to London had been the right one. However, as Geoff and Leila pointed out, the countryside was as dead as a graveyard. Most places we passed through looked empty. We soon realised that this appearance was deceptive. A substantial number of people had survived but stayed in their houses with the doors locked. Once or twice we caught sight of curtains twitching or shadowy figures glancing nervously from windows. For the survivors of the Catastrophe anyone who was living out in the open, as we were, was treated with the greatest of suspicion. We knew from our scavenging exploits in houses, shops and pubs that death lay everywhere. The smell of putrefaction was sickening.

I wanted to try making contact with survivors – to follow people we happened to see on the streets or to go in search of other vehicles. In the long term, it seemed to me that Geoff, Leila and I were too small a group to fend for ourselves. We had to find others who could help us form some kind of self-sufficient community. But I was overruled. Geoff and Leila thought we were safer on our own. There was always the danger that we might meet a gang of red-eyes. Like the gang we had run into, all too literally, after visiting the Miami Nights cocktail bar.

In the end, the decision was taken out of our hands. We were trundling along down a winding country lane when we turned a sharp corner and – Geoff slammed on the brakes! A car was coming up the hill towards us. It was coming too fast. It slammed on its brakes too. But not quite fast enough. It rammed into the Land Rover. Luckily for us, the Land Rover had cattle rails on the front. Cattle rails, I should explain, just in case you aren't familiar with them, are a heavy iron framework of bars that go over the radiator and headlamps. I think the idea is that, if confronted by cows which are reluctant to get out of your way, you can exercise some persuasion by easing the Land Rover forward and using the cattle rails to push them out of the way without causing unnecessary damage to either the cows or the Land Rover.

On the whole, it was lucky for us that the Land Rover had cattle rails. It wasn't so lucky for the car that we collided with. It was a black BMW. Quite a snazzy little number, as a matter of fact, though looking a bit the worse for wear after its disagreement with our cattle rails.

Geoff, who was driving at the time, flew into a rage. "What the bloody hell do you think you are playing at!" he screamed at the BMW. I had to tell Geoff to calm down. These were not normal times and we had more to worry about than reckless driving. The truth of the matter is that I saw this as the opportunity I'd been looking for – to try to make contact with another survivor.

I told Geoff to stay in his seat while I went to see if the driver of the BMW had been hurt. I got out of the Land Rover at the same time as the man got out of the BMW. We stood there facing one another and for a moment I was speechless. The man who'd emerged from the BMW was not, similarly afflicted, however. "Jonathan," he said, "How good to see you!"

Leila had got out of the Land Rover and was standing behind me. "You know this man?" she asked.

"Leila," I said, "Let me introduce you to the Colonel…"

2

"You'll have to forgive the mess," the Colonel said, "Staff shortage, you know."

I think he was making a joke but nobody laughed. We were sitting in the lounge of a small hotel. It was one of those hotel lounges that cram in the maximum possible acreage of floral drapes and lace antimacassars. It had an air of dusty neglect. A grandfather clock ticked languorously in a corner.

"I've been winding it," the Colonel explained, "The tick of a clock soothes the troubled soul, I feel."

I checked the time on my wrist watch. My watch said 12:32. I checked the time on Geoff's watch. It said: 12:32:05. I'm not sure what the '05' meant. It was one of those sort of watches. The hands of the grandfather clock were hovering somewhere around twenty-five past three. The Colonel obviously cared more about the sound of the clock than its intended function. Then again, what did time matter? Nobody had appointments.

We sat at a table drinking wine. A decent enough Beaujolais. Geoff had found a packet of salt and vinegar crisps which he was sharing with Bobby. The Colonel was smoking a Havana cigar. I've no idea where he'd found that. It didn't look like the sort of thing a dowdy little hotel like this would keep in stock.

The way the Colonel had been talking, you'd think it was entirely coincidental that he'd happened to be coming up that hill just as we happened to be coming down it. I don't believe in those sorts of coincidences. Here we are, over two weeks and nearly 200 miles away from our last meeting at the Church Hall, we are in the remote backwaters of the Mendip Hills and we just happen to bump into one another? I don't think so.

"So how did you do it?" I asked, "The truth this time. Did you put a bug on us, some kind of tracking device? Where was it? Hidden in my knapsack?"

He gave that peculiarly fruity laugh of his and blew out a stream of heavily pungent smoke. "You overestimate me, my dear chap. I just followed you, that's all."

"No," I said, "Nobody followed us. Not when we left the Church Hall. We were walking. We'd have noticed if we were being trailed. Then we found the Land Rover. There was nobody after us then either. Nothing on the road. Anyway, the snow was so bad you couldn't have followed us in a BMW!"

"Very perceptive. You are quite right. I did not pursue you through the snow in a BMW."

"What then?"

"I waited until the thaw advanced and then I found you in town."

"How did you know that's where we were headed?"

"Simple. I asked."

"Don't give me that! We didn't tell anyone."

"Oh, but indeed you did. You told Alan Pendelin."

"Who's Alan…?"

Geoff interrupted me. "He's right, Jonathan. Alan Pendelin's the landlord of the Farmer's Rest. The pub in the village. I remember you telling him that we was heading for town."

"So you really followed us?" I said, incredulously.

"I would not say 'followed', exactly. I found you. Quite easily done, you know. You weren't at all clandestine in your operations. And when you went to Gissom Wood…"

"Where?"

"The woodland where you stayed for some considerable time, it seems. Ah, you did not know its name? Suffice to say, I noted your location."

"You were watching us all along?"

He laughed again – "Ha! No, no, my dear fellow. I had other business to attend to. You err if you suppose I have sufficient leisure time to observe you, as it were, from a distance. I merely noted where you were. And when you departed, I followed in your tracks. Or, at any rate, such was my intention. But rather soon I lost you, I'm afraid. The tracking of vehicles is not one of my more accomplished skills, I fear. However, I made the assumption that you would most probably be heading North and East rather than backtracking in the direction from which you had come. I further made the assumption that you would keep to the minor roads rather than risk being conspicuous upon the motorways. It appears my assumptions were correct and thus, eventually, we 'bumped into' one another. Have some more wine, my dear fellow."

Lying back in a well-stuffed arm-chair (which was covered in a hideously twee material featuring lots of pink roses), I was beginning to relax at last. I hadn't realised how tense I'd become over the past few weeks. It was a tension that was always there: a slight cramp in my legs and shoulders; a slight ache across the front of my head; the clenching of my jaw for no reason at all. A constant sense of alertness, always looking, always listening, always determined that nothing will take me by surprise.

Now here, sipping wine, listening to the gentle tick-tock of the grandfather clock and the deep, soothing rumble of the Colonel's voice, I began to unwind. But for the lack of electricity, which accounted for the all-pervading gloom, this could have been a scene from the old world, the world as it had been before the Catastrophe. We could have been old friends chatting inconsequentially, after a hearty but tasteless meal served by a hearty and tactless waiter; we would have migrated to the hotel lounge to relax over a bottle of wine and a cigar and contemplate the indigestion to come. Apart from the fact that, in the 'old world', the cigar would not have been permitted, as the sign over the fireplace made clear.

"...relocated to Cambridge. Quite a convenient location in many respects. Just far enough from London but not too far. Then, what with the colleges, the science park, the Cavendish Laboratory..." – the Colonel had been talking for some time and I had lost the thread of what he was saying.

"What's Cambridge go to do with anything?" I asked.

"The Government. As I was explaining, it is where the Government has relocated..."

"To Cambridge! You mean, the Houses Of Parliament..."

"Oh, the situation in London is quite impossible. Downing Street, Parliament, Whitehall... Command and control centres have been established at COBRA, the Cabinet Office Briefing Rooms. And also at Pindar."

"Pindar?"

"One of the principal underground military citadels in London. Had Britain found itself under nuclear attack, the Cabinet might have relocated to Pindar too. Given the actual nature of the emergency, however, it was decided that Cambridge would be altogether more congenial."

"How lovely for them all," said Leila.

The Colonel stared at her for a moment and was about to say something but then thought better of it.

"What happened to the Prime Minister?" I asked.

I was thinking about what we'd heard on Radio True Britain. They had mentioned the 'acting Prime Minister'. I wondered what that meant.

"The Prime Minister is in Cambridge, naturally. Overseeing things."

"He's alive, then?"

"It would be difficult to oversee things if he were not."

I wasn't sure who to believe. The Colonel who, by all accounts, wasn't a Colonel at all. Or the announcer on a radio station I'd never even heard of until a few weeks before and which was broadcasting on a frequency where no radio station should, by rights, be expected to be found.

"What about the Army?" I said.

"What about them?"

"Are they on our side?"

"The British Army?" he said, raising a shocked eyebrow, "What possible *other* side *could* they be on?"

"So, according to you, everything's under control."

"I would not go that far. But progress is being made. Riots are being quelled. Power stations are being restarted. Order is being restored. Wherever possible."

"How do you know all this? Nobody else seems to know anything about what's going on. You seem to know everything. How does an antique dealer manage to keep so well informed?"

"Ah, yes. I can see how that might be surprising. An explanation might be in order. I wonder if any of you have heard of the Civil Defence Corps?"

I looked at Geoff. He shrugged. I looked at Leila. She smiled.

"How about the Royal Observer Corps?"

I looked at Geoff. He shrugged again. I looked at Leila. She smiled again.

"I take it that the young lady is perhaps more informed on the matter than either of you two gentlemen."

"CDC and ROC were two civilian volunteer organisations," said Leila, "The ROC kept a lookout for enemy aircraft and bombs. If any bombs should happen to be dropped, the ROC would report them. The CDC would then take control of the country after the event. That is, after the bomb had been dropped. They would go around telling people what to do, clean up the corpses, organise village fêtes, jam-making competitions and so forth."

"Somewhat of a simplification," said the Colonel, "But near enough to the truth for our purposes. At one time the CDC alone had over 300,000 volunteers spread right across Britain. Both organisations were disbanded some time ago. After the Cold War came to an end it was though they were no longer needed. In hindsight, their disbanding might appear to have been precipitate. After all, the threat to Britain never really went away. It merely changed in nature. Russia, North Korea, Iran, Islamic terrorism… the threat of a cataclysmic attack was always there.

"That is why another, and very different organisation was created. Of which I am a member. Suffice to say we are not exactly a volunteer organisation. We have been specifically recruited. Until now, our existence has never been officially acknowledged. In the case of a national crisis, we have been trained to observe, report and liaise."

"Why you?" I said, "An antique dealer!"

"Suffice to say, I was not always an antique dealer."

Leila laughed. "I bet!"

"Do they know what caused the disease?" I said, "Have they got a cure yet?"

"Disease? Cure?" The Colonel took a languorous puff on his cigar and blew out a perfectly formed smoke ring, "You are starting to sound as cynical as my dear friend, Walter."

He was talking about Walter Prentiss, the retired doctor who'd tweaked the gun pellets out of Geoff's arm.

"It's too early to know if there is a disease. As such," the Colonel continued, "And, if there is, what that disease might be, where it came from or how to treat it. It might, after all, be no more than an unusually virulent strain of winter flu."

"You didn't catch it though, did you?" I said.

"That is true. I did not."

"Nor did Doctor Prentiss."

I recalled that just about everyone in the Church Hall back in the village had been coughing or sneezing or showing some other flu-like symptoms, with the sole exceptions of the Colonel and the Doctor.

"That also is true," he agreed.

"Would I be right in thinking that the Doctor is a member of this secret organisation, the same one as you?"

He smiled. "If he were, that is something which I would not be at liberty to disclose."

"Which means that you must have known – the Government must have known – about the infection before it happened. So you, the doctor, all the important people I'm guessing – the colonels, the generals, the Prime Minister, the Royal Family – they were all vaccinated. While the rest of us, all the expendable people..."

"Let me stop .you there. You are now drawing unsupported inferences."

"Then how else do you explain the fact that everyone else in the village was infected. But you and the doctor weren't. Another coincidence?"

"Ah, but Walter and I were not the only people unaffected by the, ah, flu. A substantial number of people suffered symptoms and made a full recovery." He puffed his cigar again and fixed me with a piercing stare – "You among them."

As far as I could recall, I had never mentioned that I'd been ill. Once again, I was forced to wonder how the Colonel knew so much about so many things. And, in particular, how he knew so much about me.

"There were others, indeed, who suffered no symptoms at all. Were there not, Geoffrey Parkham?"

Geoff shifted uncomfortably in his seat. He was in an age-group that had been most ravaged by the disease. Most teenagers had not only suffered the debilitating flu-like symptoms but had also been most affected by the after-effects which seemed to cause a mental change, a break-down of inhibitions, an increased propensity to violence. Not to mention the tell-tale red eyes. Geoff had suffered from none of that. What a strange place this world had become when it appeared incriminating that a person had not fallen ill!

The Colonel, I noted, made no mention of Leila. He could not have failed to have noticed the prominent redness of her eyes. In the case of Leila, his reticence alarmed me. If indeed he was working for some quasi-military governmental organisation which aimed to take control in a national emergency, what implications would that have for someone like Leila? Someone who clearly demonstrated signs of the infection?

In spite of the fact that he had gone to some lengths to find us, the Colonel did not stay long. He had, he said, 'important business' to attend to. But, of course, he would not tell us what that business was. In spite of the accident, his BMW had not been significantly damaged and he was soon ready to set off again.

As he was leaving I said, "I can't believe you found us just by chance."

"Oh, no. Not by chance. I trust I did not give that impression."

"Not by following us either."

"I found you. That is all that matters."

After he had gone, we decided to stay at the hotel for the night. The Colonel had recommended two bedrooms on the ground floor. I assumed that might be because the bedrooms on the upper floor were already be occupied. And not by anyone who would be inclined to conversation, if you get my meaning. We were by now well used to the ever-present odours of decay and putrefaction. The smell was not especially noticeable in the hotel and it was, to a degree, masked by the bowls of potpourri, overflowing with highly-scented dried flowers and petals. Even so, we decided to take his advice and stick to the ground floor. Leila took a small single-bedded room. Geoff, Bobby and I occupied the twin-bedded adjoining room. Once again, the floral motifs all over the wallpaper and furnishings, added an oppressive air of cosy decay. But the beds were comfortable and weren't infested with bedbugs. I reckoned I would be able to survive a close encounter with the interior design.

3

That evening, I continued to think about the Colonel. The 'coincidence' of our meeting bothered me. I didn't know what technology he had access to or how much of it was still operational. But I felt sure that he hadn't just 'bumped into' us out in the middle of nowhere. Would it be possible to pinpoint a Land Rover using satellite imaging? Or had he found our location by tracking Geoff's smartwatch? I had a feeling that watches like that one had some kind of Global Positioning System functionality built in. Were the GPS satellites still working? And, if so, how long would they continue to function? Especially if the USA fell into anarchy.

Or maybe the secret organisation the Colonel mentioned had observers dotted around the country? One, or more than one, of these observers had seen us and reported our position using two-way radios. Strangely enough, I found that idea comforting. You might think it's odd that I wasn't worried that we were being spied upon. All I can say is that the possibility that an organisation existed that was able to function with that degree of efficiency gave me hope for the future. And, in those days, hope was in short supply.

But a bigger mystery than *how* the Colonel had found us was *why*? Why would he bother? Why were we even worth the trouble?"

4

We approached London by night. We had taken two days to get there, travelling by a circuitous route. We had gone to the north, skirting Didcot and Dorchester, then down through the Chiltern Hills, which at times give the deceptive impression of being in the remote countryside even though they are situated quite close to the north-western boundaries of London. Then we came down past Beaconsfield and the Colne Valley, Brent Cross and Hampstead.

The closer we got to London, the busier the roads became. By now, we were used to the empty roads and deserted streets of the countryside. At first, it came as a surprise to see so many other vehicles. By the time we got to Ruislip and Harrow, there was barely a road that was completely devoid of cars, trucks or motorbikes. Many vehicles were being driven erratically as though the drivers were drunk. Some drivers didn't bother using headlights even in the pitch darkness. We, however, kept our headlights on. The biggest danger to us was not, as it had seemed in the countryside, the risk of being seen by other people. On the contrary: now the greatest risk was that other drivers wouldn't see us and would slam into us at catastrophic speed.

There were a fair number of joyriders around. On the A40 at Hillingdon, we nearly had a crash with a Porsche that must have been going at close to 200 miles per hour on the wrong side of the road. From all the burnt-out wrecks of cars scattered around, it looked as though not all joyriders survived their rides.

Apart from the hazards of navigating roads where traffic lights no longer worked and where drivers no longer obeyed the speed limits, we weren't put in any obvious danger by the people we came across. Our Land Rover was old, the paint was flaking and its top speed hovered around 60 mph when going downhill. It wasn't worth a second glance from a would-be joyrider. In fact, as far as I could see, nobody paid any attention to us at all. Not in the suburbs. But as we drew closer to the centre, the situation changed.

We took the A502 from Golders Green to Hampstead. It was gone ten o'clock at night and the streets were pitch black. One thing that struck me as odd was that the stars were visible. Whenever I'd been in London before, the brightness of the city lights had masked the night sky. Now I could see the Plough constellation with startling clarity. I could even make out the faint band of the Milky Way.

Hampstead itself was eerily busy. Crowds of youths were strolling along the pavements or down the middle of the roads, many of them drinking from bottles of beer, wine or whisky as they went. As far as I could see, they were in good spirits. There was almost an atmosphere of celebration. The Good Times had come and everyone was out to make the most of them. Some of them shouted at us as we passed or banged on the Land Rover's bonnet and sides. I couldn't tell what they were shouting. They were largely slurred and incoherent. But at least they didn't sound threatening.

There were some people sitting at tables set on the pavement outside a wine bar. Portable LED lights had been set upon the tables. On a warm, sultry night of summer, it would have looked quite normal. In the bitter cold of February, it was surreal. Many of the people weren't wearing pullovers or coats. They sat there in T-shirts and blouses. One young man was wearing nothing but a pair of jeans; he was bare-chested and wore no shoes. His companion, a girl of about eighteen, was only wearing a bra and panties. They seemed oblivious of the freezing conditions.

We carried on down Hampstead High Street, past shops whose broken windows littered the pavement with heaps of shattered glass. The glass glittered like ice in our headlights. Going down Fitzjohn's Avenue, we passed some big, expensive-looking houses that wouldn't have left much change from eight million pounds or so a few weeks earlier. Now the front doors were open and teenagers were lounging on the steps, drinking, smoking, fighting, having sex. In some places, furniture had been brought out onto the streets: expensive-looking armchairs and sofas, a silk-covered chaise-longue. I wondered what had happened to the people who had owned those houses.

It looked like the grown-ups had all gone away and the kids were making the most of it. They were having a whale of a time. The best time of their lives. I saw two boys playing a sort of football match. The ball looked heavy and didn't move far when they kicked it. Then I saw that it wasn't a ball. It was a child's head.

We turned left before arriving at Swiss Cottage and went via Chalk Farm and Belsize Park, then along Mansfield Road to Gospel Oak. It was quiet there. Hardly anyone was to be seen. There had never been much to do in Gospel Oak – there were just houses there, a few low-rise office blocks, that kind of thing.

I got the impression that the people we'd seen out on the streets were sticking to areas that had been at the centre of things before the Catastrophe. Maybe that was because the shops and pubs still contained enough things worth looting. Or maybe it was just from force of habit.

We parked the Land Rover in a side street. I wanted to take a look at central London before we ventured any nearer. The ideal place to get a panoramic view was from Parliament Hill which is at the top of Hampstead Heath. Geoff was worried about leaving the Land Rover. He thought that someone might steal it or wreck it. I was of the opinion that when there were so many Porches and BMWs to choose from, I didn't think our clapped-out old Land Rover would be much in demand. So we took our Cree torches and our wooden walking sticks and our knives and we headed up the path from Gospel Oak, past the lido and up to the top of Parliament Hill. We weren't alone on the Heath that night. We heard rustlings and grunts from the bushes. Well, I thought, not much has changed then. Hampstead Heath was always busy on dark nights in the old days – and for the same reason.

From the top of Parliament Hill, we could see London spread out before us. To my disappointment, there was very little to see. In former times, you would have had a view of the city stretching from Canary Wharf to the Shard, from St Paul's Cathedral to the London Eye. It would have been illuminated by thousands upon thousands of lights. Now everything was lost in darkness. There were occasional pinpoints of lights where people were, presumably, using some kind of battery-operated illumination. And there were some fires burning here and there: small fires down on the South Bank,

Primrose Hill, Hyde Park and a few other places. A much bigger fire in the region of Covent Garden that looked as if some buildings had been set ablaze. I wondered if there would be anyone to put those fires out. If the flames spread, maybe London would be ravaged by another Great Fire even more devastating than the one that had destroyed the city in 1666.

"It must have been like this in the War," Leila said.

For a moment, I wasn't sure which war she meant. In its history, London has survived a few of them.

"The Second World War," she said, "The Blitz. When all the lights were out and everything was silent. Until the planes came."

"Well, there are no planes now," Geoff said.

"Thank God," said Leila.

She was still convinced that the Americans had a secret plan to bomb Britain. That they would try to bomb the disease to oblivion and that they would be prepared to sacrifice London, England, maybe all of Europe, to achieve that goal. I thought Leila was nuts. Paranoid. Even so, when I looked at the sky I dreaded the prospect of seeing planes there. If the planes came, I didn't think they would be on a rescue mission.

When we came down off Parliament Hill, I was pleased to see that the Land Rover was just where we had left it. Nobody had tried to steal it. Nobody had smashed its windows or slashed its tyres. We decided to drive on towards Bayswater. I knew someone there. Someone who I hoped could help us.

We got into the Land Rover and I tried to start it up. Nothing happened. I tried again. Still nothing happened. Then I realised what the problem was. Some swine had syphoned the fuel out of our tank!

"People can be so inconsiderate," Leila grumbled.

So we set off with our jerry cans and a length of plastic pipe and started looking for some convenient vans or trucks to syphon fuel from. These days, it's a syphon-or-be-syphoned world.

5

We took a roundabout route to Bayswater, going via Paddington, Kensal Green and Wormwood Scrubs. I wanted to avoid central London as much as possible. I had a bad feeling that going via Oxford Street and the West End would be asking for trouble.

I was looking for a flat close to St Petersburgh Mews, which is up towards the Queensway end of the Bayswater Road. My friend, Justin, lived there. It was Justin, as I think I've already said, who had rented me his country cottage in the back of beyond. I'm not sure how he came to have a country cottage. He was from one of those families that took that sort of thing for granted. I'd known Justin since our college days. Back then he was planning to be a novelist and I was planning to be a rock star. He ended up as a freelance journalist, writing columns and interviews for newspapers and magazines you've probably never even heard of. And I ended up as a guitar teacher. A second-rate guitar teacher, at that.

Notting Hill and Bayswater were in pretty much the same state as Hampstead. Windows were broken, shops had been looted, there were some lights showing in the houses which I supposed must have been battery-lamps or candles. There was some traffic on the roads. There were even some people on bicycles. Random groups of young people were wandering about or sitting on walls, doorsteps and pavements. There were a few older people around too, I noticed. People in their thirties and forties at any rate. Maybe the Colonel had been right. Maybe order was being restored. I didn't see any policemen though.

There's not much more to say about our time in Bayswater. Justin's flat was locked. I hammered on the door but there was no answer. Then a woman's voice spoke from behind me. I turned and shone my torch on the door of the flat opposite. It was open just a crack. I noticed the security chain was still attached. I couldn't see who was behind the door though. The woman's voice said, "He's gone. Went last week."

"Do you know where he went to?"

"The countryside, I think. He has a cottage there, apparently."

Something brushed against my ankles. I looked down and it was a cat. A black cat with a white bib and white paws. "Sorry," said the woman and she opened the door and came into the corridor. That was the first good look I got of her. She was young and undoubtedly attractive with platinum blonde hair that had come out of a bottle. As she stooped to pick up the cat, a little girl ran up behind her. The woman turned to the girl and snapped, "I told you, Alice. Never come to the door. You know it's not safe."

"But Tiddles…" wailed the girl.

The blonde woman handed the cat to the girl and then looked back at me. "Yeah," she said, "He went to the countryside. You won't find him, though. And anyway, I don't think he wants to be found."

So that was that. There was nothing to keep us in London. It seemed to me that London was a city of the young, the desperate and the dying. I was all for leaving, and the sooner the better. But leaving wasn't that simple. We headed back up the Bayswater Road towards Marble Arch. Hyde Park stretched away into the darkness on the right. Faceless Victorian buildings and deserted fast-food shops lined the road to our left.

Then we skirted around Marble Arch itself – a hideous, 19th Century white-marble triumphal arch that's plonked inconveniently in the middle of the road – and we continued on down Oxford Street. Or anyway, we tried to. We didn't get very far. When we got to Selfridges, the road became impassable. It was filled with mounds of stone and concrete. The source of all the rubble was obvious. It looked as though someone had set off a medium-sized bomb in Selfridges. The building was in ruins. Its partially demolished columns rose upwards like some classical ruin – a department-store Parthenon.

"Who'd want to bomb Selfridges?" – Leila was genuinely shocked. More shocked than by the bodies that lay heaped and discarded on the pavements. We were so used to the sight of corpses by now that they had become commonplace and unremarkable.

"I never been to London," Geoff said, "This is the first time."

"It's seen better days," I said.

So then we turned around and took the road leading south. On our left we passed the Dorchester Hotel and then the London Hilton.

"We could see if they have a room free," I quipped, "Would madam care to try the penthouse suite?"

We went down Grosvenor Place and then turned left. A short while later we were in front of Buckingham Palace. You could tell is was Buckingham Palace because there were electric lights illuminating the building. Not only were there lights. There were also guards. Ceremonial guards, wearing red jackets and bearskins. They were standing behind the railings and the gates. They didn't look like they were there to welcome tourists. They had their guns at the ready, aiming through the railings, ready to deal with anyone who came too close. We decided that we'd already come close enough so I veered off up the Mall.

"Looks like the royals are in residence then," Geoff said.

"Electric lights," Leila said, "They must have their own generator. Very posh."

We couldn't go any further because up ahead there were roadblocks. The roadblocks were manned by soldiers. No bearskins this time. Just regular Army uniforms. And guns. Lots of guns. I did a U-turn and soon we were heading back up past the Dorchester.

"I suppose we could stay there," I said, "I mean, is there anyone to stop us?"

"I think there may be," said Leila.

I saw what she meant. The front doors had been smashed in and there were lanterns inside. By their light, it looked as though an orgy was in progress. I guessed that gangs of red-eyes must have broken in and seized the building for their own use. My first thought was: why didn't the Army stop them? We'd seen soldiers in and around Buckingham Palace, which wasn't so far away, after all.

But then again, why would the Army bother to protect a mere hotel? They hadn't protected Selfridges. They hadn't stopped the looting, the rioting and the killing in Hampstead and Bayswater. I thought about the fires I'd seen when we'd walked to the top of Parliament Hill. The anarchy was so widespread that it would have been impossible for the Army to deal with it. Besides which, I couldn't be sure how functional the Army was any longer. Maybe it didn't have the manpower or the organisation?

We drove on.

6

We ended up in a clapped out block of flats in the Elephant and Castle. It was one of those faceless, beige brick buildings that looked as though they might have been designed with Lego some time in the 1960s. It was five storeys high and we found a flat on the fourth floor. We'd planned to stay there overnight. We ended up staying for over week. Maybe it was laziness. Maybe it was because we had nowhere else to go. The flat was furnished, it was unlocked, it had two bedrooms, a kitchen-diner and a bathroom. Amazingly the water was still flowing so the toilet flushed but the shower was icy cold. At least I was able to get a shave at last.

Another bonus of the flat was that there were no dead people in it. It had previously been occupied by an elderly couple. The flat was filled with their emptiness. There were old photographs of a young couple in happier times and of a small, smiling girl who eventually became a tall, smiling woman. There were old vinyl records: Mantovani, Hawaiian Guitar Favourites, Frank Sinatra. There were knickknacks from long-ago holidays – a cuckoo clock from Switzerland, a miniature Eiffel Tower from Paris. There were memories everywhere of hopes and dreams that had faded away to nothing.

The woman who lived in the flat across the hallway (her name was Elvira Simms, she had come from the Caribbean as a teenager, she said, and had lived in the Elephant and Castle ever since) told us about the couple whose flat we were now squatting in.

"They only moved in a couple of years ago," Elvira told us over a cup of herbal tea, of which she was inordinately fond, "Mr and Mrs Craddock. He'd been a school teacher. I don't know what she'd been, she never said. A housewife maybe." – and Elvira laughed so hard that her herbal tea slopped over the edges of her cup. Elvira had a powerful laugh and she wasn't afraid to use it.

Elvira didn't know why Mr and Mrs Craddock had left their flat. "They didn't talk much. Not to me anyway. I think they thought these flats were beneath them. They'd lived in a detached house somewhere before they came here. I got the impression they'd had to sell up. Fallen on hard times, something like that."

Their flat was in immaculate condition. It looked as though they'd cleaned and dusted before they'd left. Elvira thought they might have been frightened by the state of London – the gangs, the violence. Maybe they'd thought that the countryside would be safer than the city. Maybe they'd realised that, just as there were deserted flats in London, there would be deserted houses in the countryside. Maybe they'd gone looking for the good life that they'd thought they had lost. If so, good luck to them. I hope they found it.

We learnt a lot about the downfall of London from Elvira. The basic services – electricity, phones, hospitals, police – had lasted longer in London than they had out in the countryside. But as more old people became sick and more young people lost their inhibitions and turned to violence, things started to fall apart.

"We still got police," Elvira said, "I see the police cars going past, all their sirens going, just like in the old days. But I think they're looking after themselves. There's no damn' way they're looking after us."

The block of flats was two-thirds empty now. Some of the older people had died. In the early days, they were taken to hospital when they got sick. Then later, sick people were left where they were and the bodies were taken away when they died.

"And then, after a while, when someone died, nobody came so we had to get rid of them ourselves. The old woman who lived in the flat next to mine passed over a couple of weeks ago. We managed to get her down the stairs, me and Fred and Bill and Jimmy and some of the other residents. And we buried her in the Kiddies' playground down the road."

"You never got sick?" I said.

She laughed with a thunderous, flesh-wobbling roar, "Me! No damn' flu bug's gonna get rid of me that easy. I put it down to the chillies. Eat plenty of chillies and the bugs don't stand a chance."

It was a theory, I suppose.

On the whole, we got ourselves pretty comfortable in that flat. There was only one way into the block – an arched entrance facing the street – and that had been blocked off by filling it with packing cases and heavy wooden furniture. The entrance was guarded day and night by residents of the building. They took it in shifts. The night we'd arrived, the entrance had been guarded by a youngish, muscular man by the name of Jimmy Jepson. I think he was about my age – late twenties or early thirties. He had the solid, squarish physique that I associate with rugby players. He'd been lounging outside the entrance smoking a cigarette when he'd caught sight of us. We'd been wandering in the area looking for somewhere to stay and the block of flats looked promising. I'd gone and talked to him, he'd decided we were decent, trustworthy people (luckily the night had been dark so he didn't catch sight of Leila's eyes) and then he'd told us about the empty flat.

There's not really too much more to say about our stay in London. We weren't there to see the sights. We stayed indoors most of the time. In the evenings we did some foraging. Most of the shops had been cleared out. But there were plenty of vacant houses that still had stores worth exploring. We made some good finds. In one house we found jars of caviar; the real-stuff, not the cheap lumpfish eggs they sell in supermarkets. In another house we found a cellar full of vintage wines. We went back there a few nights running. I woke up with headaches made of vintage Pouilly-Fumé and Laurent Perrier. We stocked up on tins of dog food for Bobby and a pair of Yves Saint-Laurent dark glasses for Leila. If she wore those, I hoped it might help avoid some awkward questions about her eyes.

A lot of the houses contained bodies. Many of them had been there for some weeks. The rats had got at them, the flies had got at them. Some of them were pretty damned putrid. Often those places had the best pickings. I guess even the red-eyes preferred looting supermarket and pubs to houses that stank of rotting corpses.

You have to remember that I'm talking about the relatively early days. This was maybe a month – five weeks or so, I guess – after the great snow. The red-eyes were heading on the downward slope by then, but there were some, a few, that retained traces of humanity. Some of them had succumbed to the disease. Not all the dead bodies we saw were old people. With others, their bodies had recovered but their minds were gone. But when they formed packs, as they almost invariably did, they were definitely not the kind of people you'd want to socialise with. They were mad, bad and dangerous to know.

Even so, Elvira told us that the red-eyes weren't the ones we needed to be worried about. "It's the vigilantes you want to watch out for," she said. I didn't know what she meant. Then one night we found out.

7

It was gone midnight and we were scavenging from flats down Stockwell way. We were on foot. We went everywhere on foot at night. It was easier to get to places and attracted less attention than driving. It also let us travel underground. It had been Elvira who'd given us that idea. You could go down to the Elephant and Castle tube station, then walk along the tunnels. Take the Bakerloo line and you could go under the Thames and be in Charing Cross in less than an hour. Take the Northern line and it was a fairly short walk south to Kennington and Stockwell. We stuck to the Northern Line. We wanted to stay as far from the centre of town as possible. Our brief experience of everywhere from Hampstead to Oxford Street had persuaded us that south of the river was a better place to be. The red-eye gangs tended to congregate towards what had formerly been the major centres. Were they still going to the cinemas and theatres on Leicester Square and Shaftesbury Avenue, I wonder? There wouldn't have been any point in doing so because the cinematic and theatrical life of the West End was by now a thing of the past. Maybe they just congregated there from habit? Maybe they wanted to be among crowds of their own sort. Maybe their old haunts – the clubs of Mayfair, the pubs of Soho – acted as some sort of irresistible attraction to them?

Kennington and Stockwell held no such attractions. After dark, you could often wander the streets and see nobody. There were occasional small clutches of red-eyes, looking lost, as though they'd booked tickets for a big show but couldn't find the venue.

We were used to the red-eyes by now. We knew they could be violent, we knew they could be irrational. But as long as we kept out of their way, we soon realised that they didn't need to be a threat. Well, not most of the time. Often they just seemed to be out of their heads. As though they were drunk or high on drugs. Or maybe it was more like a sort of dementia. They seemed to move with a purpose that was defined by the group rather than the individual. The way that flocks of starlings seem to fly with purpose even though the movement of each individual bird seems to be unfocussed and without direction.

Only rarely did we see a solitary red-eye. I think those who remained alone were the ones who had entered a more serious stage of the sickness. Sometimes we saw people staggering, lurching, as though they weren't in full control of their limbs. Occasionally, we came across people lying on the ground, looking at first sight like dead bodies. But when you drew closer you would see the limbs twitching. Or sometimes the person's face would turn towards you, skeletal and agonised, the mouth struggling to form words that came out in the form of a drooling mumble. Whether these were really human beings any longer, or whether their loss of reason was so profound that it had robbed them of their humanity, I cannot say. What is certain is that they held for me a pathos and a revulsion that is impossible to put into words. They looked like people, but their minds were gone; their bodies were empty shells whose vacancy was filled with nothing but pain and loss.

On this particular night we'd scored some cans of tinned meat, a decent bottle of malt whisky, some coffee-beans and (the big prize, as far as I was concerned) a hand-cranked coffee grinder. I hadn't had freshly ground coffee since before I'd come down with flu. By the time I'd recovered from that, there had been no power so there was no way to use an electric-coffee grinder. When I found the hand-cranked grinder, I couldn't have been more excited if I'd found a treasure chest filled with Spanish doubloons.

I'd also found a good, high-power LED torch in a shed behind someone's house. We were always on the lookout for torches; and batteries. Most of the torches we found were rechargeable, which made them useless in a world without electricity. The torch I'd pilfered that night was about as good as it got: German made, a high-intensity beam and battery-powered. It must have cost a small fortune. The man who had bought it wouldn't be needing it any more. I guess that had been him, lying in the corner of the shed.

That night we'd walked the underground all the way to Stockwell. We couldn't get any further than Stockwell because there was a train blocking the tunnel. God knows why it had stopped there. Maybe the driver had died? Maybe that's where the train had been when the power went off. There were bodies in the train. You could smell them before you saw them.

On the way back from Stockwell, we passed through Kennington Station and then we carried on towards Elephant and Castle. I was shining my torch to see where we were going and to avoid tripping over the metal tracks. You wouldn't believe how many rats are down there. And mice. Every time the beam of my torch swept across the floor of the tunnels, dozens of little scurrying shapes would go twitching away into the darkness.

There are some places where you can't see far ahead because of the curvature of the tunnels. The tunnels themselves take practice to walk along. The floor beneath the tracks is uneven and has all kinds of metal bolts, sleepers, holes and recesses to trip you up. I often felt myself stumbling and automatically reaching out to steady myself against a wall only to find that the wall wasn't where I thought it was due to the concavity of the tunnel. There a reason why they call it the tube. That's exactly what it is – a long, twisting tube made to pump trains filled with passengers through the manmade cave system of the London Underground. The walls of the tunnels are supported by regularly-spaced reinforcements like ribs. By the light of my torch they made it look as though we were walking through some gigantic intestinal tract – the belly of the beast.

When we were in the tube, we always talked quietly. I'm not sure why because we'd never seen anyone else down there. It just seemed right somehow. The way you talk in whispers when you go into a church. I remember being taken to the Dan Yr Ogof caves in Wales when I was a kid and we talked quietly there too. That's how we heard the gang before we saw them. The first sound we heard was like a distant clanging. Metal on metal. For a horrible moment I imagined that a train was heading towards us, rattling along the tracks. But it was not the sound a train makes. It was the sound a person makes if they happen to be banging a metal bar against the tracks of an underground railway. I didn't know that's what the sound was at the time. But I found out a few minutes later.

As soon as I heard that clanging, I switched off my torch. That made our situation twice as scary. I kept the light off for a while longer even so. Because in the pitch dark, I could see, faintly but certainly, a dim glow shimmering towards us from somewhere beyond the curvature of the tube ahead of us.

"What are we gonna do?" Geoff whispered.

I should probably mention that Bobby wasn't with us. You might think we were slightly mad to go into the tube system late at night but we weren't mad enough to bring a dog with us.

"We are going to back away very quietly and very slowly," I whispered back.

That was pretty much an impossible thing to do with no light, so I turned the torch back on, at its lowest setting, and I tried to shade the beam as much as I could by putting my hand over the top. By keeping the torch pointed at the ground and shining it back down the tunnel in the direction from which we'd come, I was hoping that maybe whoever was around the corner wouldn't be able to see it.

We turned around and tiptoed back down towards Kennington. Tiptoeing down a Northern Line tube tunnel by the dimmed light of a torch is easier said than done. I thought that, on the whole, we were doing pretty well. Until Geoff tripped over something. The tripping wasn't the worst of it. He was wearing a parka and thick woollen pullover so he fell to the ground with no more than a muffled thud that might well have escaped the attention of the people further down the tunnel. His shocked scream in words of one syllable, on the other hand, didn't escape their notice.

That they knew we were there was beyond doubt because in the far distance I heard a voice yell, "There's someone in the tunnel!" That was bad enough. What was even worse was the sound of another voice shouting, "Let's go and find them, my dearest chums!" And then there was the echoing sounds of whooping. It sounded like a tribe of Apaches on the warpath. Not that I've ever heard an actual tribe of Apaches on the warpath but I have seen lots of John Wayne films and that's how they sound in those.

The thing about the London Underground is that once you are in a tunnel there is no way out apart from going forward or going backward. Maybe there are secret exits and side-branches that you could find if you knew your way around. We didn't know our way around and so the only way to get away from the approaching gang was to run like blazes back the way we'd come.

It must have taken about five minutes to get back into the relatively open space of the Kennington Underground station but it seemed like a lifetime. All the time, we could hear the sound of running and banging and whooping as the gang behind narrowed the gap between us and them. Looking back as we emerged into Kennington, we could see half a dozen or so figures, partially illuminated by the lights from their own torches.

We pulled ourselves up from track-level onto the platform. By the light of our torches, the station looked much as it must have looked before the power went off. The walls were covered in advertising posters for shampoo and slimming products. The National Portrait Gallery was advertising an exhibition. Pages from newspapers and fast-food cartons littered the platform.

We dashed down the nearest exit. Then down a walkway. Then we emerged onto another platform. We turned off our torches and flattened ourselves against the wall. In the total darkness the sound of our breathing seemed incredibly loud. Realistically, even in total silence, nobody could have heard us. In fact, our pursuers were making so much racket that they probably wouldn't have heard us even if we'd been talking at normal volume. It was their intention to play cat and mouse with us. They were wandering around the various platforms, stairways and corridors, banging on the walls with that blasted iron bar and shouting taunts – "Come out, come out, wherever you are," and "Don't be shy, chums, we won't hurt you," to which someone else replied, with a laugh, "Oh yes, we will!" then a couple of others shouted, "Oh no, we won't" and so on and on, "Oh yes, we will…."

I'm not brave, I'm not by nature a fighter, I've gone through life doing my level best to avoid confrontation and violence. Finding myself in a pitch dark tube station, being threatened by a gang of maniacs with iron bars and who-knew-what-else for weapons did nothing to calm my nerves. To be blunt, I was more terrified than I had ever been in my life. Geoff was shaking with fear. He grabbed my hand, for the sake of something to hold onto in the darkness. I gave his hand a squeeze and tried to sound reassuring. I tried to keep the tremor from my voice as I told him that we'd be all right.

There was nothing to worry about. And even as I said that, I didn't believe a single word.

I was hoping that the darkness would help us; that if we stayed absolutely still and quiet, the yelling gang wouldn't be able to find us; they'd assume we had got away – made it to the surface or gone down another tube tunnel; they'd get bored of searching for us. My last desperate hope was that, if they did find us, we'd be able to make a dash for it. I wasn't sure where. I'd have to turn my torch on again to see where we were and which was our nearest escape route. It was a desperate plan. No plan at all, really. But it was the only hope I had.

My hope that they might wander off in some other direction was ill-founded. The sound of that iron bar, banging against the walls, came closer and closer. Their shouted taunts got louder and louder. Soon we could see light from their torches as they moved through passages that led onto the platform where we were hiding.

And then, quite suddenly, they were there. A torch was shining into my face, its intense white beam momentarily blinding me. There was no point in running. There was nothing to do but face up to whatever they had in mind for us.

"Looky, looky, chums, see what we have here. Nice little Normals down in our tunnels. What are you doing down in our tunnels, chummy?" – he prodded me in the chest with something pointed. I thought it might be a sword or a spear. But when my eyes started to recover from their torch-blindness, I saw it was an umbrella. The man behind him, however, had a more dangerous-looking weapon. He was carrying the metal bar that we'd been hearing. The bar was about three feet long. I don't know what its original purpose had been but I had a good idea of the purpose it could be put to now if I happened to antagonise the person carrying it. I did my best not to antagonise him.

"We've been to Kennington," I said.

For some reason, that struck the man with the umbrella as funny. He laughed. Then the man holding the iron bar laughed. Soon all half dozen of them were laughing.

"Shut it!" commanded the man with the umbrella and, in an instant, they all stopped laughing.

Geoff said, "We were scavenging, mate. Down Kennington."

"Scavenging?" said the man, "In my manor?"

"We didn't know it was..." – Geoff was opening his rucksack, which he'd put on the ground next to him. The umbrella smashed down on his wrist and Geoff jumped back with a yowl of pain.

Someone in the gang laughed. The man with the umbrella glared at him and he fell silent. "Don't touch that damn' bag, chummy," he said, "How do I know what you got hidden away in there?"

"I ain't got nothing. I was just gonna show you the stuff we..."

"How do I know you haven't got a nice little gun in there, chummy? Or a knife? Or a nice little bottle of acid, 'ey. I wasn't born yesterday, my boy. Back away from the bag, chummy. Go on, further back."

Geoff stepped away from his rucksack and the man with the umbrella stepped towards it. He undid the ties at the top and gently pulled back the flap. There were no guns or knives or acid in there. What there was, however, were several bottles of good booze: whisky, brandy, gin. Some tinned foods. And the coffee-grinder.

"Very tasty, very sweet," said umbrella-man, "We'll take that."

"Hang on," I said, giving a foolish imitation of bravery, "You can't just..."

He poked his umbrella into my chest, "We can do whatever we want to do, chummy. So you can shut your bleedin' chops, 'cos the one thing I can't stand is a loud-mouthed git like you. OK?"

"OK, OK," I said, reverting to my normal state of abject cowardice.

"Consider yourselves lucky," said umbrella man, "For a minute there I was thinking you was red-eyes. And you know what's we does to red-eyes, don't you?"

"I can guess," I said.

"He can guess, chummies!" He turned to look at the rest of the gang, "I don't think he can, do you?"

"We could show him," someone said.

Umbrella-man laughed. "You suggesting we give him a proper bashing, a smashing, a gutting and a mashing like what we'd give the red-eyes? Nah, I wouldn't do that. Just a lesson is what we needs to give him. To make sure he don't try to go scavenging on my manor again. Not without dealing through me, in the proper authorised channels, as you might say."

The man with the iron bar stepped forward then. It was the first time I'd got a really good look at him. He was over six feet tall and he was wearing a ripped denim shirt that showed an impressive mountain-range of muscle protruding through the rips. His nose looked as though it had been broken more than once, there was an old, ragged scar down the left side of his face and hair was cropped close to his skull. He looked like someone who was used to excessive violence and enjoyed it.

He kept thumping the iron bar into the palm of his left hand, the way a more conventional thug might use a blackjack or a baton. "I'll do them over then, shall I boss?"

Umbrella-man smiled. "Be my guest."

I saw the man take a step toward me and raise the iron bar in the air. Then all hell broke loose.

8

The man with the iron bar slammed into the ground, the bar skittering out of his hand, across the platform. The man with the umbrella turned to see what had happened and then he was on the ground too, crying in agony, his left arm stretched out at an unnatural angle as though his shoulder had been smashed or dislocated. Then there was a cry from one of the others as he was whammed against the wall with almighty force. The scene was one of sheer chaos. Umbrella man (no longer holding his umbrella) staggered, with difficulty, to his feet, his left arm dangling uselessly at his side. He shouted an order to someone but it was lost in the hubbub of frantic yelling. The gang, most of whom were holding bars or staves of some kind, were swinging their weapons wildly, but the only damage they did was to one another as bar and baton made contact with arms and shins in the chaotic darkness. Screams of rage mixed with cries of agony. They were running around in total disorder now, flashing their torches this way and that, trying to find their unseen attacker. But to no avail. And then, in desperation, they ran. They retreated back the way they had come. Umbrella man was the last to leave, the pain in his shattered arm was slowing him down. But as he left he shouted curses, promised we wouldn't get away with this, told us he'd hunt us down and kill us.

It was another two or three minutes, I guess, before the sound of the fleeing mob finally died away into the echoing distance of the tunnels. Only then did I muster the courage to turn on my torch and take a good look around. The iron bar was lying at my feet. The man who'd been holding the iron bar was lying a few yards away. He wouldn't be getting up again.

Geoff was standing next to me. I shone the torch towards the other and of the platform. That's when I saw the tall, slim figure, dressed all in black. It was Leila. It wasn't until that moment that I realised that she hadn't been there with me and Geoff all the while.

She must have slipped away before the gang arrived. She was holding her long wooden stick in one hand, the one she always took when she was out walking.

"In case you are wondering," she said, "It's a bo."

"A what?"

"A bo. A Japanese weapon. Oh, dear-heart, you really are so ignorant! Well, actually, any big heavy stick will suffice. Anyway, that lot were all bluster and no skill, which put me as a distinct advantage, I should say. Since I actually know how to use my stick."

"You killed this chap with a walking stick?" I said.

She swung the stick through the air. It made a loud whooshing noise. "If you doubt it, I could try hitting you over the cranium to see how resilient you are."

"No, no, that's OK. I'll take your word for it. Still," I said, "You didn't have to kill him, did you. You could have just scared him."

She snorted with derision. "You heard what they said they'd do to red-eyes, didn't you? They'd give them a bashing, a smashing, a gutting and a mashing. That's what that fellow said. Well, my dear, have you taken a look at my eyes recently? What do you think they'd have done to me?"

I conceded that she had a point. Up until that moment, I'd worked on the assumption that the infected, the red-eyes, were the greatest danger that we faced. Now, I was no longer sure. The gang that had attacked us were all Normals, just like me and Geoff. They were what Elvira called 'vigilantes': gangs that took advantage of the death, destruction and devastation to establish their own little fiefdoms, ruled by greed and terror. And it seemed that one of their greatest pleasures was killing red-eyes. I could see why Leila felt no compunction in killing someone who would gladly have killed her.

Then I recalled the night when we had left the cocktail bar and Leila had deliberately, cold-bloodedly, aimed the Land Rover at an approaching crowd of red-eyes, smashing it straight into them with no sense of reluctance or remorse. And I wondered just how much pleasure she took in killing?

9

The last straw was when the water went off. It was the morning after our encounter with the vigilante gang in the Underground. I went to get a shower, I turned on the tap, there was a rattle, a gurgle, a sputter and a drip and then no more. Running water had been one of the flat's main attractions. Without water, how would we wash, what would we drink? It didn't bear thinking about.

The fact of the matter is that we'd been shacked up in that flat in the Elephant and Castle for too long already. It had never been our intention to stay in London. There was no future for us there. We'd been seduced by the unexpected comfort of the accommodation. But we couldn't stay much longer. We had no reason to do so. And the situation, bad as it already was, could only get worse. The time had come to move on.

There was only one place worth heading for. That's why the Colonel had sought us out, I think. To tell us. If Britain was to be regenerated, it wouldn't begin in London. The seat of power had moved north to Cambridge. It sounded all so easy. A pleasant drive up the M11 and we could be there in a couple of hours. Little did we know!

That night, we headed north. I was driving, Leila sitting next to me while Geoff and Bobby were in the back. As we passed Lords Cricket Ground, a strange shambling creature scurried across the road in front of us. I thought it was a dog. But if so, it was a very misshapen dog with an ugly face and a stiff gait. Leila said, "My God! It's a hyena!"

I was about to comment on the improbability of that when, quite suddenly, a huge animal leapt from the shadows at the side of the road and pounced upon the hyena. As we drove past (I really didn't want to hang around!) Geoff, who was sitting in the back of the Land Rover, glanced out through the rear window. "Wow!" he said, "A tiger!"

I'm not sure if he was correct. The streets round there were dark and, once the animals were out of our headlights, I'm not sure if we would have been able to identify them reliably. That's splitting hairs, however. Whether it was a tiger or a panther, a leopard or a lioness, one thing was for sure – it was some kind of cat. And not your average tabby. It was the sort of cat you really wouldn't want to meet unless you happened to be inside a Land Rover at the time. And even then, it scared the living daylights out of me.

We weren't far from London Zoo. Somebody must have let the animals loose. On the one hand, I could see that might make sense. If the zoo was no longer functioning, if food wasn't being delivered and the zoo keepers were no longer at work, the animals would die. At least, let loose in the city, they stood a chance. They would fend for themselves. Survival of the fittest. Maybe the local residents might not have been so keen. Then again, they had plenty of other problems to worry about. On the plus side, maybe a few lions and tigers might help to keep the streets clear of the mobs, the looters and the rioters. Maybe the big carnivores would hunt down the sick, the dying, the infected while the scavengers, the buzzards, jackals and hyenas, might help to pick clean the bodies of the dead.

The first sign of major trouble came when we arrived in Chalk Farm. We'd gone up Adelaide Road and arrived at the T junction. The entrance to the underground station was on our left. We were planning to turn right towards Camden Town when suddenly a crowd of people came running from that direction. My first thought was that they were running towards us, that they were planning to attack us. But I quickly realised that they were running wildly, panicked, without any well-defined direction. Some of them ran off to our left, up Haverstock Hill, some ran right past us along Adelaide Road. Most of them, however, were heading into the underground station. In the darkness it was impossible to be sure if the running people were red-eyes or Normals.

We heard machinegun-fire. Some of the people dropped to the ground. There was a light shining on them, panning across them like a spotlight. And then I saw the tank. Don't ask me what sort it was. I'd only seen them on TV before. It was one of those huge, lumbering machines – much bigger than I'd imagined, in fact – with caterpillar tracks running over a long array of metal wheels, and a big gun sticking out at the front.

Behind the gun, with their heads and upper bodies poking up through trapdoors in the upper surface of the tank, two soldiers stood. One soldier held the spotlight, which he used to illuminate the crowd trying to get away from the tank. The other soldier had a machine gun mounted on some sort of swivelling pedestal from which he raked an arc of bullets into the fleeing crowd. They didn't stand a chance. The bullets tore through them and they fell to the ground. As they fell, the people behind them ran into them and climbed over them until they too were cut down by bullets.

To say that I was freaking out would be an understatement. I tried to reverse the Land Rover but I must have been in the wrong gear or something because it made a grinding noise and didn't move. I wished I'd let Geoff do the driving. He operated the Land Rover much better than I did. Geoff was screaming at me – "Go back! Back! Hurry up! For God's sake, hurry up!". Leila was screaming too. Mostly obscenities of no more than two syllables. Bobby started running around and woofing. I was trying to stay calm. The screaming and woofing didn't help. But eventually I got the damn' thing into gear and we backed up a way until I went past the entrance to a street on my left. I nosed the Land Rover into that street and went down it as fast as I could, thinking to get away from all the shooting.

That's not what happened. The road led towards a bridge that goes over the Camden canal. Someone in their wisdom had banned cars from the bridge. There was a pedestrian walkway but the road had been reserved for bicyclists and a line of big metal bollards had been placed right across the entrance to the bridge, so there was no possibility of taking the Land Rover that way. The only way out was to follow the road to the left, which is what I did. Seconds later we were back where we'd started. Or anyway, very close. We came to another junction. The tank we'd seen was now on our left, pointing its guns directly at the Chalk Farm underground station. From this angle I could see that a second tank had come down Haverstock Hill. The two tanks had converged on the tube station, forcing the crowds of fleeing people to go into it.

Machine-guns were mounted on both tanks and the soldiers manning them were firing directly into the crowd. It was shocking to see so many people killed so quickly, efficiently and thoughtlessly. Even if they were infected (and of that I still wasn't sure), even if their condition would inevitably have continued to degenerate as the disease ravaged them, even so, they had all been human beings. Who knew what they once had been? Artists, scientists, road-sweepers, writers, petty-criminals, opera singers. Each and every one of them had been a child once with hopes and fears, loves, hates and ambitions. And then, in mere seconds, they were dead meat on a street corner.

Then the big guns started firing: the main guns mounted at the front of the tanks. They fired shells into the entrance of the Underground station. There were massive explosions. The pounding made the air vibrate. The familiar edifice of the station, the glossy brick-red tiles, its elegant Edwardian arches, crumbled under the onslaught. I thought of the people trapped inside, who had run into the station. They had expected to find safety only to be trapped like rats. I wondered if any of them had managed to make it down to the lower levels, and whether that would have saved them?

And then another thought came to me and it only added to the bleak desperation of the scene. The tanks had destroyed the tube station. They hadn't hesitated to do so. Which meant that there were no plans to get the underground running again. Which meant that the military – and the Government – had given up on London. I wondered how many people would be killed before London was regained?

10

We headed down towards Camden Town but soon we spotted some armoured cars at the far end of Camden High Street so we turned up towards Kentish Town. Then we wandered around through a maze of streets until we lost track of where we were. Eventually, we found ourselves on Abbey Road and then we arrived on the Finchley Road and after that we just kept on going. Once we were north of Edgware, the roads became pretty empty again. It was a huge relief to escape from London.

We took the B roads, moving out into the countryside. We decided to head out west, towards the Chilterns. Some time in the early hours of the morning we stopped in a lane next to a field with a small wooden gate. We unfurled our sleeping bags in the back of the Land Rover and we slept soundly throughout what little remained of the night. We were awakened by the sound of church bells.

On glancing outside, we discovered that what we had taken to be a field was, in fact, a cemetery. At the far end of the cemetery stood a small church. To my unecclesiastical eye, it looked like a typical English church by which I mean it was made of grey stone, had a bell tower sticking up at one corner and was studded with a suitable number of stained glass windows. Beyond that, I couldn't have told you a single thing about it. All I was interested in was the bells. I knew that church bells were put at the top of a tower and had ropes hanging down. To ring bells, people had to pull ropes. Since I could hear the sound of several bells being rung, I assumed that meant there must be several bell ringers. I didn't think that the red-eyes were likely to choose bell ringing as their favoured pastime. So whoever was inside that church was, I assumed, sound of mind and body and just the sort of people we most wanted to make contact with.

After a short discussion, Geoff, Leila and I agreed that a morning visit to an idyllic English country church would be the perfect way to start the day. None of us were religious (though Leila claimed she believed in ghosts, mainly because she'd met a few and had held long and interesting conversations with them). So off we strolled through the cemetery with Bobby trailing along behind.

The moment I entered the church, I was almost struck senseless by the stench of burning incense. "Must be High Church," Leila commented approvingly. I remarked that I had no idea what the height of the church had to do with anything, to which she replied that I was invincibly ignorant. She explained that High Church is a concept defined by the abundance and gaudiness of the statuary and the density of the incense smoke. Judged purely on the density of the fumes, the Church of St Cumberbatch in the Wold (for that is what this one was called) was eight miles high and rising.

Of human occupants, parishioners, worshippers and clergy, however, the building was devoid. Or so it seemed. However, our chatter (not to mention Bobby's woofing) eventually attracted the attention of a man whose head popped out from behind an ornately carved wooden screen at the far end of the church. The head was immediately followed by the body, at which point I could see that the man was dressed in long flowing, black robes of the sort which generally characterise those people of a clerical disposition: vicars, priests, vergers and the like. The fact that he was also wearing a white dog collar confirmed me in my supposition.

"Good morning, good morning!" cried the man.

"Good morning," I mumbled in reply, adding, just to test the water, so to speak, "Vicar?"

He didn't correct my use of this title so I congratulated myself on determining his identity and carried on – "Lovely bells you have here."

"Yes, aren't they!"

"I don't see any bell ringers though."

"There aren't any."

The bells were pealing loudly. "Then who…?"

He smiled. "Electronic."

"The bells are electronic?"

He smiled again, "Marvellous, isn't it? Modern technology."

"You've got power here?" Geoff asked.

"A small generator. Petrol powered. You haven't got any spare petrol, I suppose?"

"Only some diesel," I said.

"And you aren't getting your filthy little paws on it!" Leila added menacingly.

The vicar, looking suitably menaced, drew back. Then, smiling, he asked: "Have you come for Holy Communion, Morning Prayer or the Sung Eucharist?"

"Which do you recommend?"

"Well, I'm rather fond of the Sung Eucharist myself. But I could run to a Holy Communion if you'd prefer?"

"You couldn't run to a cup of tea and some Eccles Cakes, could you?" Geoff said.

A look of nostalgic bliss momentarily flitted across the vicar's face. "Ah, Eccles Cakes! Those were the days, what? Tea, I can run to. Possibly a desiccated Marie Biscuit. Sadly the delights of an Eccles Cake must remain no more than a distant dream. I take it the tea is of more interest to you than the Sung Eucharist then?"

I was trying to think of a diplomatic answer but Geoff and Leila, less concerned with the niceties of diplomacy, had already made their preferences abundantly known. The Sung Eucharist had lost. Tea and biscuits it was.

The vicar took us into a small side room which he called the chasuble. Apparently it is where he went to put on his vicarly clothes. Leila said, "I thought a chasuble was something priests wore."

He glared at her but regained his composure quickly. "Silly me. I'm always making that mistake. I meant the sacristy."

Leila, determined to be perverse, said, "This looks more like a vestry to me."

The vicar had to think about that. "It all depends on the denomination".

Whatever it was, sacristy, vestry or chasuble, the only thing I was interested in was the small electric kettle that the vicar kept in there. He filled it with water, plugged it into a wall socket and used it to boil the water for tea. Electricity! It was like a miracle. I thought briefly of uttering a little cry of "Praise God!" but wasn't sure if that would be considered indecorous, or maybe even blasphemous, so I just said, "Milk but no sugar for me, please." I resolved to go and take a look at the miraculous generator as soon as the chance presented itself.

As we sat there, chummily nattering, we introduced ourselves to the vicar and he introduced himself to us. "Father O'Brien but you can call me Pat."

"Irish?" said Leila.

"Donegal."

"You've got a Welsh accent," I said.

"I do missionary work," he replied.

"Do you still get people coming here?" I asked, "A congregation, I mean."

"Attendance has been falling off of late. I would be the first to admit that. In fact, just between you and me, you're my first customers all week. Would you care for something a bit stronger with your tea?"

He produced a bottle of Johnnie Walker Black Label whisky from a drawer under the table and sploshed a good measure into four mugs without waiting for a reply. Then he topped them up with some dark-brown, muddy-smelling tea which had been brewing in a brown, ceramic pot. It tasted surprisingly good. To be honest, I would have preferred the whisky without the tea. But the tea without the whisky wouldn't have been a tempting option.

We engaged in a bit of light conversation for a while, mostly about how many people had died in the villages round about, how one old lady's son had shot the cat, himself and the old lady "though not, I think, in that order", how the decline in religious belief was surely responsible for the calamity that had been visited on mankind: "Cursed shalt thou be in the city, and cursed shalt thou be in the field. Cursed shall be thy basket and thy store. Cursed shall be the fruit of thy body, and the fruit of thy land, the increase of thy kine, and the flocks of thy sheep. Cursed shalt thou be when thou comest in, and cursed shalt thou be when thou goest out.' Leviticus: 24:16."

"You're a cheerful sod," mumbled Leila.

For myself, I was impressed that he'd been able to quote Leviticus from memory until I noticed that the verse hung on the far wall, embroidered in pink wool on black tapestry. The gift, no doubt, of some devoted parishioner with a taste for the macabre.

"More tea?" said Father O'Brien, topping up our mugs with Johnnie Walker.

All in all, we had found what seemed to us to be the perfect spot to spend a few days while we came to a decision about what to do next. I was all for going on to Cambridge as quickly as possible. Leila wasn't so keen. She reasoned that if the Government had relocated to Cambridge, security was likely to be tight around the city. That meant that it would be guarded by the military. And the military might not take kindly to the unannounced arrival of three misfits like us, plus a mongrel dog. We'd seen, in London, how the Army dealt with people of whom it didn't approve. We didn't want to be next in the line of fire.

So we idled away the rest of the morning like tourists. Father O'Brien gushed on about the magnificent rood screen which dated from 1450 and was one of the finest in Britain. I discovered that the church bells which we had heard and which the vicar had mysteriously told us were operated 'electronically' were not, as I had imagined, operated by an elaborate robotic system of cogs and pulleys. They were nothing more than a recording, played through loudspeakers mounted in the bell tower. That, I admit, was a bit of a disappointment. Still, at least he had a generator. It was a rusty old device that chugged away at the back of the church, producing a nasty burning smell.

Then we whiled away some time reading the inscriptions on the headstones. It was disturbing to see how many children had been buried there in the 19th and early 20th centuries. The graves went back several centuries. The older ones were leaning at strange angles. Some of them were even lying flat on the ground, hidden beneath mounds of rough grass and moss.

In the afternoon, the vicar made some sandwiches with real bread and tinned salmon. It was a huge treat. Better than dining at the Savoy. I asked him who had baked the bread but he was coy in answering, saying merely, "Oh, a parishioner". I didn't know it at the time but we were soon to make the acquaintance of that parishioner and it would have a profound effect on our lives for some time to come.

At the end of the day, we sat all together on the hard pews in the church. The vicar had lit some huge candles in tall sconces. Presumably these were normally kept for special occasions – requiem masses, maybe, and Christmas carol services. The golden, flickering candlelight gave the place a welcoming, almost magical, air. If I were religious, I suppose I'd say that the candlelight made the church look sacred, holy, or whatever the right word might be. All it needed to complete the illusion was a choir singing and an organ playing. It had neither, so we listened to golden oldies on an old battery-powered cassette-tape recorder – Neil Diamond, Fleetwood Mac, ABBA – while drinking whisky and eating pork scratchings, all of which had been provided by the vicar.

When the whisky bottle was empty, the vicar declared that it was time to turn in for the night. He was terribly sorry that couldn't offer us a room at the vicarage (he didn't say why not and I assumed it was because he didn't trust us enough) but we were welcome to bed down on a pew.

Leila wanted to know if there was a crypt as she'd always wanted to spend the night in one of them. The vicar was terribly sorry about that too, as there wasn't one. So finally the vicar swanned off to the vicarage while we got out our sleeping bags. In spite of the vicar's assurance that the pews were comfortable, they weren't, so we bedded down for the night on the floor. Geoff went to sleep right away. He snored quite loudly. Bobby snuggled up to Geoff and he snored even more loudly. Listening to the stereophonic snoring of a teenager and a dog in a church at midnight is a memorable experience but not, on the whole, one I wish to repeat.

We put out all the candles except for one in an elaborate brass candlestick, which Leila placed alongside her sleeping bag. She had found some church magazines which gave long and uplifting accounts of the missionary work being done by nuns in the Congo and she lay there, reading them by candlelight, thoroughly engrossed.

I was just dozing off when Leila said, "There's something not quite right about that vicar?"

I'd been thinking the same thing. "All the boozing?"

"No. He's a vicar. Boozing comes with the job. There are other things though. I mean, what vicar doesn't know his chasuble from his sacristy?"

"After a few hefty slugs of Johnnie Walker, I can understand how he might get a bit confused on the finer details."

"Then there's the Welsh accent, if that's what it is. And – the real clincher – he can't tell his Deuteronomy from his Leviticus."

"What? What are you talking about?"

"The verse he quoted. 'Cursed shalt thou be in the city, and cursed shalt thou be in the field,' and so on and so forth. He said it was Leviticus 24:16. It isn't. It's Deuteronomy 28:16."

"You sure?"

"Of course I'm sure."

"How do you know that?"

"Because Leviticus 24:16 is 'And he that blasphemeth the name of the Lord, he shall surely be put to death, and all the congregation shall certainly stone him: as well the stranger, as he that is born in the land, when he blasphemeth the name of the Lord, shall be put to death.'"

"That doesn't answer my question."

"What?"

"What I meant was, how do you know the number of *any* verse in Deuteronomy? Or Leviticus, for that matter?"

She looked at me as though I was mad. "I went to a Catholic girls' school."

I told her that I'd noticed that the verse that the vicar had recited had been embroidered and framed on the wall. He hadn't been quoting it from memory. He'd read it from the embroidery.

"And then there's the name," Leila said.

"The name?"

"Pat O'Brien. Doesn't it sound too twee somehow? The perfect name for an Irish Catholic priest."

"You can't blame him for his name."

"Except this is an Anglican church."

"I don't think Irish vicars are banned, as far as I am aware."

"It's like an actor's name, don't you think? In fact, it was an actor's name. Pat O'Brien. He played the priest in old Hollywood films. Did you ever see 'Angels With Dirty Faces' with James Cagney?"

"Don't think so."

"Well, if you had seen it, you'd know that the priest had been played by Pat O'Brien."

"I'm sure it's a common enough name in Ireland. Like John Smith in England. Or Tom Jones in Wales."

"There's another Pat O'Brien too. Musician. Heavy metal guitarist."

"There you are, then," I said. I didn't mind Leila showing off with her knowledge of the Bible. I was a bit miffed that she knew of a guitarist that I didn't. I am, or was, a guitar teacher, after all. If things had gone a bit differently in my life, I might even have become a rock guitarist myself.

"Pat O'Brien is obviously a very common name," I said, "Which group does the guitarist Pat O'Brien play with out of interest?"

"Cannibal Corpse," she said, "One of my favourites. Oh well, nighty-night then."

And she blew out the candle.

11

The next day, we ate pineapple for breakfast. Well, actually, we had coffee (proper freshly-ground coffee), bread, butter and marmalade and finally – the pièce de résistance – an actual fresh pineapple. Not tinned. Not dried. The real thing! If the vicar had turned water into wine I could hardly have been more amazed.

We ate in the sacristy. He had thrown a white table cloth over a big wooden chest which, I think, is where his vestments were kept. When we went in, places had been set for us, with white china plates, knives, forks, spoons and coffee cups. The first thing that hit us was the smell of the coffee. The second thing that hit us was the pineapple. I mean, it didn't literally hit us but I wouldn't have been much more shocked even if it had done. The sight of that incredible, impossible, exotic fruit standing with its spiky leaves in the air, like a showgirl at the Moulin Rouge, stopped us in our tracks. It was just so incongruous. So unbelievable. Nobody was importing pineapples. Not these days. It just didn't happen.

The effect on us must have been obvious but Pat, the vicar, pretended he hadn't noticed. He told us to sit down, help ourselves to bread and marmalade, apologised that he couldn't quite run to bacon and eggs at the moment. And then, casually, he added: "Oh, and if you'd like a slice of pineapple, help yourselves."

We didn't need to be told twice. There was a big serrated knife lying on the tablecloth and Leila used it to slice the pineapple into neat rounds from which she cut the knobbly skin before handing pieces to each of us, the vicar included. Even Bobby had some which, surprisingly, he appeared to enjoy greatly.

"Where the Hell…" I said – the vicar's eyebrows shot half way up his forehead, so I started again, "Where the heck did you get this pineapple?"

"Oh, one of my…"

"One of your parishioners?"

He smiled.

"Not, by any chance, the same parishioner who made the bread?"

He said that it was.

"And are you going to tell us who this parishioner is? And how exactly he got hold of a pineapple?" Leila said.

"There are certain things… I, er, must be discreet about. A vicar has responsibilities, you see. Like a doctor."

"The secrets of the confessional?" said Leila.

"You are perhaps mistaking me for a Catholic priest?" said Pat O'Brien.

The vicar scored a few points there, I thought. Leila was convinced that there was something not 'quite right' about Pat O'Brien and she had been deliberately trying to catch him out.

"In fact," O'Brien continued, "It is a common misapprehension that confessions are the exclusive preserve of the Roman Catholic Church. We may not indulge in the same formalities, but it is not at all uncommon for an Anglican priest to hear a confession."

"Yeah, yeah, OK…" – Leila was being politely told off and she didn't like the experience, "You still haven't told us where you got the bloody pineapple!"

"More coffee?" said the vicar, smiling beatifically.

The next day we met our benefactors. They attended Sunday Evensong. They seemed suspiciously pleased to see us. At least, their pleasure struck me as suspicious at the time. I think they were simply pleased to see anyone who wasn't sick, mad or trying to kill them. They invited us back to their manor. It was a real manor. A rambling, stone-built, turreted and moated house which, Lady Degris informed us, dated from the 14th Century "so this isn't the first plague it's lived through." Lord and Lady Degris proved to be charming in the old-school way. I found myself liking them a great deal. But I found myself liking Mrs Clompton a great deal more.

12

Mrs Clompton reigned over the kitchen like a monarch. She remembered a time when the house, and in particular the kitchen, would have been filled with teams of servants: the cook, a first and second kitchen maid, a scullery maid, not to mention the housekeeper, butler, valet and parlour maid. "And even then, her Ladyship was forever complaining about the lack of help about the house. By her Ladyship, I don't mean Lady Degris as is here now but Lord Degris's mother who was of a much grander and forbidding sort. Of course, in her mother's day, all these grand old houses would have had a couple of dozen servants."

We were sitting in her kitchen, a vast cave of a room with two huge ceramic sinks beneath the only window and two walls lined with work benches, cupboards and shelves. Dominating one side of the kitchen was a big old cast-iron Aga cooker, squat, solid and gleaming. Before the catastrophe, Mrs Clompton had been the only servant to 'live in' (she had rooms on the top floor of the house) but there had also been a maid who came in every day, plus a gardener and a chauffeur. I didn't ask what had become of them all. If she had wanted to tell me she would have done so.

It was Mrs Clompton who explained the mystery of Pat O'Brien, the vicar who had only a tenuous grasp of the ways of the Anglican Church. Until quite recently, he had been the verger which, as far as I could make out, was not much more than a fancy name for a handyman and general dogsbody with the added benefit of robes and vestments.

"Oh, he was never much on the religion, though," Mrs Clompton laughed so hard that her bosom quaked, "I'm not sure if he even believes in God. Oh, we used to have a very godly vicar before. Not that his God did him much good. Though, by rights, I shouldn't be questioning His works," she crossed herself, "But when the vicar died there was no one else so we asked Pat if he would take it on. He's not too hot on the finer points of doctrine but his heart's in the right place."

In spite of Leila's doubts, it turned out that his name really was Pat O'Brien. His father came from Donegal. His mother came from Betws y Coed. Which also explained the lilting Welsh accent.

During our time in London, our life in the Elephant and Castle flat had been moderately comfortable. By comparison, however, life in Degris Manor was like paradise regained. We each had our own room (Bobby shared mine) and we ate regular meals. Mrs Clompton was a fabulous cook. She made cooked breakfasts whenever possible (the Degris's kept a few pigs and sheep so bacon and lamb chops were often on the menu). She baked bread every other day in the oil-powered Aga. And when I told her that Pat O'Brien had claimed that Eccles Cakes couldn't be had for love or money, she baked some of those too – and jolly good they were!

She cooked gargantuan dinners that ranged from roast beef and Yorkshire Pud to Indian curries (of which Lord Degris was inordinately fond) not to mention a superb Lasagna and an unparalleled Paella. The manor had two petrol-powered generators and there was a big walk-in cold-room where most of the larger cuts of meat were kept.

The walls were covered with innumerable oil paintings of stern-looking bewigged gentlemen and bonneted ladies with tight-lipped expressions that suggested they suffered simultaneously from piles and constipation. One day, I asked Lady Degris who they all were – "Oh," she said, "ancestors". In my family, we had relatives. The Degris family had ancestors.

There was also a very striking photograph of a young man which stood prominently upon the grand piano in the Morning Room. The young man had dark, curly hair and what I think is called a 'brooding' expression. In the photograph, he was sitting at the same piano upon which the photograph now stood. I asked Lady Degris who it was. "My son," she said, "Percival."

"A musician?" I said.

She smiled. "Yes. A very fine musician."

"That's interesting," I said, "So am I."

She gave me a suspicious look as though she thought I was lying. "I play the guitar," I explained, "I'm a guitar teacher."

"Ah? My son Percival was a composer."

Oh well, I thought, that puts me in my place!

"Though he did play the guitar. Very well."

I noticed the past tense – "he was, he did…"

I wasn't sure if it was the right thing to ask what had become of him. So many people had died recently. I assumed he may have been among them. Perhaps it would have been better if I had asked. But I didn't. I just said, "He was a handsome chap."

"Oh , yes," she said, "He was."

When Lord Degris asked us if we'd like to "stay on for a while," we didn't hesitate. Of course, we would like to! It wasn't a purely charitable offer of accommodation, however. Maintaining the manor and its gardens required a great deal of labour and, before our arrival, that labour had been notably thin on the ground. Lord and Lady Degris (who insisted that we call them Tommy and Gladys but somehow they seemed far too grand for such commonplace names) did their best to "muck in" as His Lordship put it. But they were both quite old and not really up to the task of maintaining a property on that scale. Lord Degris enjoyed pottering around in the glasshouse and I found that I enjoyed that too. The two of us would spend hours in there, sowing seeds, pruning back the passionflowers, digging, spraying and mulching.

It was in the glasshouse that the pineapples were grown. It would have seemed remarkable to me to have seen a pineapple growing anywhere in England. But to see a row of plants thriving in early March and in the middle of the greatest chaos to have hit Britain since the last War, was nothing short of gobsmacking.

For some reason, I'd always assumed that pineapples grew on trees. They don't. They are more like a low-growing cactus or succulent with a big spikey crown of leaves like an agave, from the centre of which protrudes a thick stalk. Sitting right at the top of this stalk is the big, knobbly pineapple fruit.

The atmosphere inside the glasshouse was warm and humid. Although there were a couple of old, cast-iron radiators in there (powered by a generator), it turned out that much of the heat was provided by a much more unusual source: horse dung. This had been placed in huge quantities into a trough running the length of the glasshouse where it steamed gently as it decomposed.

A side product of its decomposition (apart from the smell!) was heat. Apparently, pineapples were a passion of the Victorians and horse-dung heating was one of the more improbable methods that was used to cultivate them.

"It is my belief that we have the only privately-owned pineapple pit in Britain," his Lordship boasted, "Though it takes so much damn' horse shit, I doubt if it will serve us another season." Lord Degris is the only person I've ever heard say "horse shit" and make it sound posh. That's breeding for you!

13

Early one morning I was awakened by a loud bang. At first I wasn't sure if I'd dreamed it. I lay in bed, with Bobby curled up on the eiderdown next to me and I listened but all I could hear was an owl hooting and, in the far distance, some sheep bleating. I looked at the clock next to my bed whose luminous dial faintly claimed that it was 6:45, but I only had its word for that. Time had ceased to have much meaning; most of the clocks I looked at had different opinions on the matter.

I got out of bed, stretched, and walked blearily over to the curtains. I pulled them back and glanced outside. There wasn't much to see as it was dark apart from the slightest glimmer of approaching dawn. So I went back to bed and forgot all about it.

Then a few days later, I heard it again. I was awake immediately this time. Right away there was another bang. And another. It was a gun. It sounded like a powerful gun. It made one heck of a noise. It scared me. I thought that maybe we were under attack. Maybe an armed posse had arrived, determined to seize the manor by force and ransack it for the treasures it contained. And do what with its occupants? Torture? Rape? Kill? The most lurid scenes of violence and death played themselves out in my mind before I finally drifted back to sleep.

Geoff told me later that he'd heard the gunshots too. Leila, however, had slept through it all, oblivious.

Pat O'Brien came along later, to help around the house (I wasn't sure what he was supposed to be doing, precisely; his idea of help tended to involve standing around chatting and drinking cups of tea). I asked him about the gunfire.

"Gunfire?" he said, as though the word was unfamiliar to him.

"Yes, gunfire. Bangs. In the night."

"You sure it was gunfire?"

"What else could it be?"

"Foxes," he said.

My first thought was that Pat had been on the whisky again.

"Foxes don't go bang," I said.

"No, but people shooting them do."

"What people? I haven't seen any other people around here."

"They can be a damn' nuisance, foxes can," Pat persisted, "They creep into the chicken sheds at night and eat the chickens."

"What chickens? Whose got any chickens around here?"

"And ducks. A fox will take a duck as well as a chicken."

I supposed it might be possible that there were still some working farms in the area. I asked Mrs Clompton if she ever managed to get any chickens, thinking that she might know someone who kept them. But she just smiled and said wistfully, "If only I could get a chicken, lad! If only I could…"

Sometimes, late at night, Leila and Geoff would come to my room. We used candles after dark because the generator was turned off and, in any case, it wasn't powerful enough to keep all the lights in the entire manor running. We'd sit on the bed or sometimes we'd sit cross-legged on the floor. And we'd talk. Geoff said he'd heard another gunshot during the night. Geoff thought it might be the Army. But I didn't think the Army would send in a lone soldier. They'd come in force with armoured trucks and tanks as they had in London. Leila said it was probably someone out hunting, which sounded more likely.

Sometimes we listened to the radio. We couldn't get shortwave reception, not in my room at any rate, without the benefit of the long-wire antenna. But medium and longwave reception was OK. The BBC was still broadcasting repeats punctuated with occasional 'news bulletins' which always said more or less the same thing which could be paraphrased as "Don't worry. Everything is OK."

But it wasn't the BBC we wanted to hear. The only station we were interested in was Radio True Britain. It didn't have reliable or predictable broadcasting times so it was always pot-luck as to whether or not we'd be able to tune into it. Even when we did manage to tune in, we could never be sure if what they were broadcasting was true. Still, it was our only real source of news and we clung to every word…

"This is the news from Radio True Britain. People Of Britain. The time for Resistance has arrived. We are hearing reports that Infected groups have taken control of Leeds, Manchester, Birmingham, Glasgow, Cardiff, Plymouth. The Government claims that the situation in London is under control. However, we have received reports that significant bombing operations have been undertaken across central London resulting in mass casualties. It is not known whether the majority of the casualties are among the Infected or the Resistant. We advise you to stay clear of the cities. We repeat: stay clear of the cities. We also advise you to make contact with other Resistants. How can you tell who is Resistant and who is Infected? If you are listening to this, you are Resistant. The Infected are no longer rational. To all intents and purposes, the Infected are no longer human. They are not sane. They are animals. Do not trust them. Please keep listening to Radio True Britain. We hope to bring you more news shortly. And now over to Peter Quinn for the All 80s Radio Hour…"

14

One day we heard a huge explosion. At first I thought it was thunder. It seemed to come from over the hills to the North west. Then there was another explosion. It wasn't thunder. The explosions were happening in rapid succession now. It sounded like a distant firework display: *bam! bam, ba-ba-bam! bam!*

I'd never heard bombs falling in real life. I'd only heard sounds like this on the TV news. Coming from war-zones: Baghdad, Gaza, Afghanistan. I can't begin to tell you how chilling it was to hear those sounds echoing across the Chiltern Hills. Then we saw fighter jets, streaking across the sky. They were leaving the bombing zone to return, I presumed, to wherever they had set off.

Leila and I were out in the garden at the time, trimming back a beech hedge. "Ours?" I said.

"The RAF?" She shrugged. "Could be the Americans."

The idea that the Americans, our long-term, trusted allies, would sent fighter planes to bomb us as though we were the enemy filled me with dread.

"What?" said Leila, smiling broadly, "You'd rather it was our own air force bombing us than a foreign air force?"

"If it's the RAF, they must have a good reason," I said.

Leila laughed. "Personally, if it was me they were bombing, I wouldn't care whose bombs they were. American bombs? British bombs? The end result is the same."

The air was clear that day and when we glanced back in the direction from which we'd heard the bombing, we saw smoke drifting lazily into the sky.

"What's over there?" I asked, "Is it a town? A military base?"

"How do you expect me to know? I have only the vaguest idea of which bit of the country we are in anyway. Somewhere to the North and West of London. It could be anywhere from Norwich to Newcastle, as far as I know."

"Norwich is North-east of London," I said.

Leila pruned back an innocent beech branch with unnecessary violence and gave me a look which indicated that if I didn't tread very carefully, I'd be next.

"Could be Bristol," I said.

"Are we near Bristol?"

I didn't know. My knowledge of British geography is sketchy at the best of times. Since I wasn't ensure exactly in which bit of the English countryside Degris Manor was located, I could only guess wildly as to what town might lie on the other side of the ridge of hills. Later on, I asked Mrs Clompton if she'd heard the bombing and what she made of it.

"The Russians. That's what I reckon. Bombing Cheltenham. They've always had their eyes set on Cheltenham, the Russians have."

The idea that the Russians would want to bomb Cheltenham struck me as hilariously preposterous. All I knew about Cheltenham was that it was a quiet, quaint little town that was the home of the famous Cheltenham Ladies' College. That didn't seem like the sort of place the Russians would seek out as a particular target for aerial bombardment. Then again, I wouldn't have thought that Russian spies would have sought out the little town of Salisbury with its cathedral "famous for its 123-metre spire". So who can tell?

I asked Lord Degris later. He said he was of the opinion that the target of the bombing had been rather further away than we supposed. Bristol perhaps? Or even Birmingham."

I told him that Mrs Clompton believed the Russians had been bombing Cheltenham.

"Ha! She believes that, does she? Well, if it were the Russians, it would be a damn' good target. After all, that's where all the intelligence chaps are based, isn't it. GCHQ, I mean."

I'd forgotten that GCHQ was based in Cheltenham. Suddenly, Mrs Clompton's theory didn't sound so farfetched.

"But I don't believe that for a moment," Lord Degris added, "Oh no, take my word for it – that was the RAF we saw this morning. Restoring order and so forth. I'm sure they'll have things under control soon. Yes, no doubt at all about that."

15

"This is the news from Radio True Britain. People Of Britain. America has fallen. Repeat. America has fallen. We have received credible reports from our contacts in America that the American Government has been suspended and that the USA is now under Martial Law. I repeat, the USA is now under Martial Law.

"Over the past couple of weeks we have been hearing conflicting reports about the current situation in the USA. We have heard that the President is dead, that he fled the country, that he was imprisoned by the military, and all kinds of other unsubstantiated reports. Since most commercial American TV and radio stations are now off the air, it is hard to piece together the truth of the matter. We are in contact with several independent broadcasters in the States and as far as we can ascertain, it seems that the first case of the sickness in North America was identified in Colorado about four weeks ago. This was not associated with any major weather event to compare with the Great Snow in Britain and the supposition is that an infected person brought the pathogen back from Europe. At first, the US authorities believed they had the disease contained. But soon the sickness began breaking out in other areas – Washington State, Alabama, Arkansas, New York…

"As we reported some weeks ago, the Americans initially considered the disease to be a purely European problem. High-level discussions were taking place on how to deal with it. No plans were formally announced, but when asked what the solution to the European problem might be, the President repeatedly used the expression 'nothing is off the table'. This was widely interpreted to mean that military action against Europe was being contemplated.

"The spread of the disease in the USA began much more slowly than in Britain and Europe. We believe this may be due to the fact that the agent was not dispersed atmospherically over a huge landmass as seems to have been the case here. It appears that the means of transmission must therefore have been person-to-person contact.

"This raises the question of why a second wave of the disease has not affected Britain. According to the Government's Chief Scientific Advisor, it is conceivable that those who have not been infected may already have an acquired immunity. He warned, however, that a mutation of the pathogen cannot be ruled out in which case a second wave of the pandemic is to be expected.

"Two days ago we are told that the American Government was, in effect, taken over in a military coup. The whereabouts of the President are still not known. And now back to Peter Quinn for another scintillating selection of hits from the 1980s…"

The strange electronic-percussive opening of the Tears For Fears song, 'Mad World' wavered in and out thanks to the uncertain reception of our little radio. We were sitting cross-legged on the floor of my bedroom. A couple of candles in saucers resting on the floor provided a flickering illumination.

"It's a very, very mad world… mad world… mad world…"

"America's gone down the tubes then," Geoff said.

"Looks like it," I said.

"Oh well," he said, "No chance the yanks will come and rescue us then."

"Did you really think they would?"

"Don't know. You can only hope, can't you."

"Oh, you two crack me up!" Leila said, "The Americans never had the slightest intention of coming to the rescue. If they came at all, they would be bearing gifts of atom bombs and poison gas."

"Don't be daft," Geoff said, "The Americans are on our side."

"How sweet to be naïve! When it's a case of life or death, they are on whatever side will keep them alive. However if they are in as bad a state as we are, I don't think they'll be wasting their time and money by sending their bombers over here."

"That's good news, then," I said.

"Of course," Leila added, casually, "I could be wrong. I often am."

16

The time we spent at Degris Manor was one of the most pleasant periods of my entire life. It was a little world unto itself. Time passed there as though time was in plentiful supply and nobody much bothered to economise on it. Walking through the extensive woodlands on the estate, I watched the primroses bloom and the wild daffodils and early purple orchids. March began cold and wet and everywhere I went was muddy. But towards the end of the month the weather changed for the better. It grew warmer, the sun shone more frequently and some days were so unseasonably warm that I was able to go about wearing a T-shirt.

In the evenings we would gather together in what Lord and Lady Degris referred to as 'the sitting room'. It looked like a cross between the lounge at a country house hotel and the library of a small university. It was a huge room by the standards of any normal house but quite small and cosy by the standards of Degris Manor.

Sometimes I sat there and read – the walls were lined with shelves of books by authors ranging from Aristotle to Agatha Christie (I skipped 'The Metaphysics' and went straight for 'Murder At The Vicarage'). Sometimes we drank wine (Lord Degris had a well-stocked cellar and I tried to give the impression that I could tell a good Chablis from an indifferent Chateauneuf du Pape but I don't think he was fooled). And then one night he brought out the Beast. That's what he called it. In fact, it was beautiful and magnificent. The Beast was a guitar. A hand-made classical guitar. Its body was made of light, golden spruce with a Rosewood fretboard and a Spanish Cedar neck. The sound-hole was surrounded by a decorative inlay of mixed-colour woods. This was not the sort of guitar you walk into a shop and buy. This was a one-off, custom-made by a skilled luthier.

"Percy's guitar," he said, handing it over to me, "If you'd like to play it…"

Of course I wanted to play it! I loved my old Harald Peterson guitar, the one that had been smashed to pieces by vandals. But The Beast was altogether an instrument of a different calibre. It was, in fact, by far the finest guitar I had ever seen, let alone played.

I held it as gently as a new-born kitten. I tuned it and even in the tuning of the strings, the tone was exquisite. It could have done with a new set of strings, but that was a minor matter and not something I would have been so impolite as to mention.

That first evening, I sat in front of the fire but not so close that the heat would detune the strings – the Sitting Room boasted a huge open hearth that blazed with logs – and I played the Bourrée in E minor by Bach, the Romance del Pescador by Manuel de Falla and a couple of pieces by Dowland. I played for the pleasure of playing but the others treated it as a concert. They clapped after I finished each piece. I got the impression that my repertoire was a bit too classical for Lord Degris's taste so I branched out into a few lighter pieces – I remember I played Maple Leaf Rag by Scott Joplin and Yesterday by The Beatles. Half way through that one, Leila began singing the words. Once again, I was astonished by the diversity of her talents. She had a glorious soprano voice. Here was a young woman who could ram a car into a crowd of people, calmly work out the best way to kill a cow with a knife and yet could reduce people to tears with the beauty of her singing voice!

Then Lady Degris asked me if I knew the Concierto de Aranjuez by Rodrigo. Fortunately, I did. It was one of the examination pieces I had studied at college. I played the famous and beautiful Adagio. When I finished, I looked up and was surprised to see Lady Degris walking out of the room. I was horrified. I assumed that the quality of my playing had disappointed her.

After a short pause, Lord Degris looked at me and said "Percy used to play that. It was my wife's favourite."

Leila told me later that tears had been running down Lady Degris's face while I had been playing. She had been remembering her son. I played the guitar on many other evenings after that. But never again did I play the Concierto de Aranjuez by Rodrigo.

Apart from working in the greenhouses, I also did a bit of gardening. At that time of year, there wasn't much to do. I did some digging and I cut back some of the more egregious brambles. But mostly I either worked in the glasshouse or else I helped Geoff with the fortifications. Ah, yes, the fortifications: they are worth explaining.

As I mentioned, the manor house was moated. The house itself was a huge square construction whose walls rose straight up from the water of the moat. The only access to the house was over a narrow stone bridge across the moat. Sadly, there was no drawbridge but even so the house would not have been easy to launch a sneak attack upon. The moat was surrounded by gardens. And the gardens, which must have taken up four of five acres, were surrounded by a high stone wall. The wall would have been difficult to climb but certainly not impossible with the aid of a ladder.

Lord Degris had the idea of adding rolls of barbed wire to the tops of the walls. Which would have been fine if we'd had some rolls of barbed wire. As we hadn't, we had to come up with other ideas. Geoff spent some time scouting around the locality in the Land Rover looking for something suitable. My first idea was to cement pieces of broken glass into the tops of the walls. Going around the houses and pubs it was easy to find plenty of glass. The cement came from a local builders' yard. Geoff and I mixed up the cement, smashed some bottles and stuck the glass on top of a wall. It was a lovely job and we were proud of it. It took us about four hours to do two yards of wall. As I said, the wall surrounded four or five acres. In other words, there was a heck of a lot of wall. At the rate we were working, we'd be lucky to have it finished within Lord Degris's lifetime. So we went back to the barbed wire approach. Luckily there was a farmers' merchant about ten miles away. They had plenty of barbed wire. We ferried back as much as we could in the Land Rover and gave that a try. Geoff and I managed to do about four yards of wall in about four hours this time. Twice the speed of the broken glass. Even so, it was still going to take us years to finish the job.

Lord Degris surveyed our work, strode along beneath the two yards of wall studded with glass and the four yards of wall topped with barbed wire. He hummed and he hawed and he scratched his chin and he bounced up and down on his toes (activities which, I gathered, were necessary to his intellectual analysis of the problem) and then he declared, "It'll never work! Just have to rely on Old Dooley then."

I didn't know what he was talking about until he went and fetched Old Dooley. It turned out that Old Dooley was not, as I'd supposed, some elderly gent who specialised in the fortification of mediaeval manor houses. Old Dooley was a gun. A rather fine gun at that. It's what I, in my ignorance, would have called a rifle because it had long barrels and a big wooden stock – in other words, it wasn't a revolver and, in my limited knowledge of guns, if a gun is not a revolver and it's not a machine gun then it must be a rifle. But Lord Degris insisted that it was a sporting gun – a 16-bore percussion double-barrelled sporting gun at that. It was a wonderful looking thing but it looked more like an antique than a workable weapon.

"You plan to shoot people with it?" I asked.

"If necessary."

I laughed. Geoff glared at me. The idea of being shot by Old Dooley wasn't as funny for him as it was for me. I'd never been shot in my life. Geoff had. Luckily he'd only been shot with some clapped-out old pheasant gun. Looking at Old Dooley, I had the feeling that anyone who got shot by that wouldn't be in any state to talk about it later on.

"Have you ever shot anyone? Killed anyone, I mean?" I asked.

Lord Degris paused before answering. "Once."

His grim expression didn't encourage further enquiry so I left it at that.

Lord Degris had quite a collection of guns. He kept them all locked away in an oak cabinet. He had deer guns and pigeon guns. He had modern guns and antique guns. He had an old Webley revolver and a newer SIG Sauer semi-automatic pistol.

"Is this all legal?" I said, "I mean, was it all legal when we still had laws about that sort of thing?"

He raised an aristocratic eyebrow. "Do I look like an East End gangland thug, dear boy?"

He had elegantly avoided my question. I suspected he had spent his lifetime elegantly avoiding awkward questions and he was very good at it.

"Suffice to say," he continued, "that we have a great many pigeons around the manor and I am a very good shot."

"That explains," I said.

"You speak in riddles, dear boy. What does it explain?"

"The gunshots we hear sometimes. In the mornings and evenings mostly."

"Ah, indeed so. The morning and the evening is when the pigeon is at his most troublesome."

Later that evening, while I was in the kitchen helping with the washing up, I asked Mrs Clompton about Lord Degris's claim to have shot someone dead. "I wasn't sure if he was joking," I said.

She shook her head. "No, lad, he wasn't joking. He killed someone just a couple of weeks back. But don't you mention it to him. And don't say I told you."

"You are serious?" I said, "Who did he kill?"

"His son, Percy."

I thought of the photograph on the piano. The good-looking young man with dark, curly hair. The musician, the composer, the young man whose guitar I had been playing when his mother had left the room in tears. At any other time, it would have been impossible to imagine what could have happened to cause a father to shoot his beloved son. Mrs Clompton didn't relate the full circumstances of the event. There were tears in her eyes and I could tell that she didn't want to talk about it. All she would say was, "It was for his own good. As well as ours. He's better off out of it, if you want my opinion."

17

Since Old Dooley had now been recruited to the task of repelling invaders, Geoff and I were no longer needed to add defences to the battlements. Which meant that Lord Degris had to find something else for us to do. There was plenty of choice. He needed petrol for the generators and oil for Mrs Clompton's Aga stove. Geoff and I went and syphoned fuel from tanks we found in houses and farms round about. Lord Degris needed tiles on the roof fixed. We fixed them (after a fashion – though I'm not sure I'd trust them in a downpour). He needed his pigs' sties cleaned; we cleaned them. He needed his sheep treated for the innumerable parasites to which sheep are prone; we treated them. He needed the horses (he owned three), fed, groomed and exercised. I didn't mind the feeding and grooming but there was no way anyone was going to get to ride them (those horses were incredibly tall – if you came off them, you'd land with one heck of a thump). Both Geoff and Leila knew how to ride horses and I was happy to leave that task to them.

Leila spent most of her time in the kitchen. It turned out she was a fantastic cook. Not quite as good as Mrs Clompton, but not far behind. Between the two of them they managed to make some of the best meals I've ever eaten. There was no longer much that surprised me about Leila but her culinary skills did. I knew she was good at killing things. It hadn't occurred to me that she'd be equally good at cooking them afterwards.

One day, Geoff teased her about it. "Ah well," he said, "I've always reckoned a woman's place was in the kitchen."

Without a moment's hesitation, Leila floored him with a forearm jab to the throat. Nothing more was said on the matter. Leila had made her point and Geoff had learnt an important lesson in life. If you want to eat the food, don't piss off the cook.

In many ways, our life at Degris Manor was idyllic. But it couldn't last. For a while, I think we deluded ourselves into thinking that this would be how we would live for the foreseeable future. Lord and Lady Degris treated us as members of the family. As for Mrs Clompton – if you hadn't known better, you might have thought that Leila was her daughter, she mothered her so much. Even Pat O'Brien turned out to be a decent bloke, in spite of our initial mistrust, as long as you didn't make the mistake in drinking with him. He had a prodigious intake of whisky. If you tried to keep up with him, glass for glass, it was touch and go whether you'd be sober enough to get out of bed the next day.

Some time in early April, I was walking in the woods when I noticed the first few bluebells beginning to uncurl. That's when it struck home to me how long we had been at Degris Manor. It must have been more than a month. I was getting the itch to move on. Much as I loved it there, fond as I had grown of Lord and Lady Degris, Mrs Clompton and Pat O'Brien, this was not where I needed to be. It was a false life. A fake life. Degris Manor was remote, cut off from the rest of the world, the 'real' world. I couldn't imagine myself growing old there, cloistered away like a monk. I needed people. I needed the world. No matter how dangerous that world might be.

Geoff and Leila felt the same way. There was something stultifying about life at the manor and they were eager to be off again. When I broke the news to Lord Degris, he took it in his stride, barely batting an eyelid. Lady Degris, however, seemed genuinely quite shocked. It only then occurred to me that she too might have felt cut off – lonely. The morning we left, she called me into the Sitting Room and told me she had something for me, "a little keepsake". I couldn't believe it when she handed me a beautifully made leather case containing her son's guitar. It was such a wonderful instrument and clearly meant so much to her that I was reluctant to take it. But she was insistent. "My son will never play it again," she said, "But it deserves to be played. Don't you think?"

What could I say? Of course it deserved to be played. Nevertheless, I was overwhelmed with emotion. I actually flung my arms around Lady Degris's neck and kissed her. This, I am quite sure, was a gross violation of etiquette. But she didn't seem to object. I knew I would miss her. I would miss them all – Lord and

Lady Degris, Mrs Clompton, even Pat O'Brien and his endless bottles of whisky.

But once we'd decided to leave, there was no going back. On a warm, sunny morning in mid-April we packed our things into the back of the Land Rover (I wrapped my sleeping bag carefully around the guitar case to try to cushion it against the bumpy ride it was about to have) and we waved goodbye for the last time. We drove down the gravel-covered drive towards the great iron gates set into the high walls around the grounds of the manor. Pat O'Brien was waiting there to open the gates which were held tightly shut by a heavy, padlocked chain. My initial fear was that our exit might be blocked by red-eyes. We had often seen small groups of them roaming around but they generally seemed slow and sickly and I wasn't sure how much of a danger they really were. But, in any case, I needn't have worried. The road beyond the gate was clear.

Occasionally there were some bodies on the verges at either side of the road, though. I'd seen them before on our scavenging trips around the countryside. They were all neatly arranged in heaps, as though someone had moved them there to keep the road free.

The road ran alongside the manor wall, leading down towards Pat O'Brien's Church. There were half a dozen or so more bodies lying at the base of the wall. When we were out of sight of the gate, I decided to get out and take a look. I'd never bothered to examine the bodies before. But now that we were leaving, my curiosity got the better of me. The fact that the bodies lay only on the roadside next to the manor wall intrigued me. I can't say I was greatly surprised to see that each body had been shot through the head. I imagined them trying to climb over the gate or scale the walls.

I remembered all the gunfire we'd heard in the mornings and evenings. I realised then that Lord Degris must be every bit as good a shot as he claimed to be.

I recalled asking him if he'd ever shot a person and he had replied "Once". Cleary he didn't think of the red-eyes as people. What did he think they were, then? Subhuman? Animals? Once upon a time they had been his near neighbours, living, working and growing up in the small hamlets and remote farms dotted around the countryside. They had been mothers and fathers, sons, daughters, friends and lovers. Maybe some of them had worked for

Lord Degris – fixing his roof tiles, pointing his walls, tending his gardens. But now they were less than human. He could shoot them with as easy a conscience as he might shoot a pigeon.

Yes, he was a good shot, right enough. But I felt sure that one day his luck would run out. I felt equally sure that he knew it would. And he didn't care.

18

"Are you sure it's safe?"

"Nowhere's safe," I said, "Just keep your eyes open."

"Why don't we just keep on driving?" Geoff said.

"Because I'm tired, you're tired, Leila's tired..."

"No I'm not!"

"...and Bobby needs to have a pee."

The dog had been scurrying around in the back of the Land Rover for the past twenty minutes. Since I was in the back of the Land Rover with him, if he decided to have a pee, I'd be the one to know about it first. That wasn't the main reason I was keen to have a break, though. If you've ever travelled in the back of a long wheelbase Land Rover with no seats and no upholstery, you will appreciate why my heart skipped with joy when I saw a service station at the side of the motorway. It would give us the chance to pull in, stretch our legs and let the bruises which I'd acquired from being thrown about in the back of the Land Rover recover a bit before they took their next battering.

Geoff was, as usual, driving. He pulled over towards the slip-road that led up towards the service station. We'd seen very little moving traffic on the motorway that day. There were the usual dead cars, of course, slewed inconveniently across the lanes, crashed or burnt out. Who knew the stories behind those? Left-over wrecks from joyriders? Vehicles that had been driven by old, sick people at the moment of death? We had started to take the wrecks for granted. We barely even noticed them.

The sun was shining and, for early April, the weather was warm. It would have been wonderful to go into a café and order a cold drink or an ice cream. But there was no chance of that. Everything was quiet and still. No sound of traffic roaring past. Just the whispering of the wind through the bare branches of the trees and the ever-present twittering of birds.

When I opened the back door of the Land Rover, Bobby leapt out and immediately went off in search of a convenient lamp post. I made my way, almost by instinct, towards the foyer of the service station. I don't know why I did that, really. Force of habit, I suppose. You stop at a motorway service station and the first thing you do is walk over to the foyer. Go to the toilet. Have a look around the newsagent's. Maybe grab a coffee and a sticky bun.

Leila called out that she was taking Bobby for a walk. There was a weed-infested grassy area and a small copse of straggly trees behind the service station. Geoff went with Leila and Bobby. They had no sense of adventure.

The glass doors leading to the foyer would, once upon a time, have slid open thanks to the magic of cutting-edge-glass-door-sliding-open technology. In the absence of electricity, that technology had gone the way of all other cutting-edge technology. It made you realise why wooden doors with handles that you had to turn were such a good idea; they continued to work whether or not modern civilisation happened to have crumbled all around them.

The glass foyer doors must have been closed when the power gave out because they were closed now. They might have been a barrier to me but for the fact that some considerate vandals had smashed the glass so I could step through the metal frames unimpeded.

The place stank. It smelled of decay and dampness, piss and putrefaction. The newsagent's shop had been wrecked. Magazines and paperback books had been scattered everywhere. The coffee shop had been wrecked too. There were broken plates and cups all over the floor. There were a few mouldy buns in one of the display units but I wasn't that hungry.

There were no electric lights, of course, but there were so many windows that it barely made any difference. I was desperate for a pee so I headed for the toilet. Like I said: force of habit.

The toilet stank worse than the rest of the place. I'm not going to try to describe the smell. You'll have to imagine it. All I'll say is that a heady blend of human excrement and ammonia were the dominant themes. The toilets had no windows and when I went inside the door closed behind me, leaving me in total darkness. That's how I came to notice the light shining in one of the toilet stalls. It was just a faint glimmer visible in the gap under the door. If there had been any other light in the place I wouldn't have seen it.

I went back into the foyer. I needed something to keep the door to the gentlemen's toilets wedged open. I tried to pick up a rubbish bin but it was fixed to the floor. Why had they fixed the rubbish bins to the floor, I wondered? Had they really been afraid that people would steal them? I went into the café. I thought I might be able to grab a chair. But there weren't any chairs. The only seats were benches fixed to a metal frame that also supported the tables. Maybe their customers had tried to pinch the furniture too?

Eventually I found something suitable in the newsagent's. It was a huge pink teddy bear about the size of a small St Bernard dog. The teddy bear wasn't fixed to anything. Clearly not even the most kleptomaniac of customers would have been mad enough to bother nicking it.

I went back to the gents, opened the door and shoved the teddy into the gap so that the door stayed half-way open, letting in enough light for me to navigate my way between the basins and urinals. I glanced again at the lines of stalls where the light had been. There was nothing. I pulled teddy out of the gap and let the door swing fully shut. Even in total darkness, there was no light showing through the gap under the stall. I opened the door again and put teddy back into the gap.

I still needed a pee so I went to one of the urinals and used it for its intended purpose. I would have washed my hands but no water came out of the taps so I wiped my hands on my jeans and returned to the problem of the mysterious light I'd seen emanating from the toilet stall. There were ten toilet cubicles (and therefore ten toilet doors) arranged in a line opposite the urinals. I tried to calculate which one had been the one from which the light had shone. It had been towards the far end of the line of cubicles. It hadn't been the last one of all, though. So I reckoned it must either have been the eighth or the ninth one.

I strode up to stall number nine. According to the dial on the door it was vacant. I gently pushed the door and peeked inside. It was too dark to see much so I went inside and kicked my legs around a bit. All they hit was the ceramic toilet bowl. Then I went to its neighbour, stall number eight. Aha! The dial said that one was engaged. I pushed the door. It didn't budge. I stepped back a few feet and bent down. The bottom edge of the door was several inches above the floor. In the dim light, I could just about make out two feet. I had my own torch in my pocket. I took it out and shone it through the gap under the door. There were definitely two feet. They were wearing bedroom slippers with woolly pompoms on the top. I shone the torch up a bit further. It showed that the feet were attached to two legs wearing stripy pyjama bottoms. I stood up and rapped soundly upon the cubicle door.

"How long are you going to be?" I said.

Silence.

I banged again, more loudly. "I know you're in there. It's no good pretending. I can see your feet."

"Use another one."

"What are you doing in there?"

"What do you think?"

"How long have you been in there?"

"None of your business."

"This is a public convenience," I said, "You can't take up full time residence."

"I'm an old man," the voice said, quavering with emotion, "It's my bunions. They play me up. I have to sit down a lot."

"Are you the only person here? Or are there others?"

"Others? In this cubicle? Are you suggesting I am here for immoral purposes?"

"You can't live in that cubicle."

"Why not?"

"Why would anyone want to live in a toilet?"

The door to the stall suddenly flew open. "You ask too many questions. What are you? A Jehovah's Witness?"

"Do I look like a Jehovah's Witness?"

The man standing before me must have been about seventy or so. He was wearing a beige duffel coat over a pair of striped pyjamas, and a greasy woolly hat with a bobble on the top. He looked me up and down for a few seconds. "What does a Jehovah's Witness look like?" he said.

"I'm not sure."

"Well then. You could be one. Not that I'm bothered. I'm devout Catholic. Lapsed. You haven't got any sardines, I suppose?"

"No. Why?"

"What do you mean 'why?' You think I want to play cricket with them? Or grout a wall? What sort of bloody question is that, 'ey? Why do I want sardines? To eat. That's what I want sardines for."

"I haven't got any sardines."

"Well, then, why didn't you say? Anyone else with you?"

"That's what I asked *you*."

Just at that point, Bobby arrived. He leapt over the pink teddy bear that I'd jammed into the gap in the door, ran straight up to the man in the duffel coat and barked. The man immediately backed into the toilet stall and shut the door.

"It's all right," I said, "The dog's friendly."

"How do I know that? I've only got your word for it and you've done nothing but lie to me so far."

"If there are any sardines in the place, maybe he could sniff them out."

The door to the toilet stall flew open again. "You think I'm soft in the head, do you? How'd he sniff out sardines? They are in tins. He can't sniff through tins, can he? What's his name?"

"Bobby."

Bobby barked. The man patted him on the head. "I like dogs. Dogs like me. I had a dog once. I called him Aristotle."

"Why did you call him that?"

"Because it was his name." The man gave me a look of withering scorn. "Are you a bit simple, son? You haven't taken in half I've been telling you."

"Come outside and we can talk things over at our leisure. The smell in here's a bit overpowering."

"I hope you are not criticising my personal hygiene. That's something I'm very sensitive about. Personal hygiene. And there's nothing wrong with mine. What's that pink teddy bear doing there?"

"Keeping the door open."

He stuck out his bottom lip and scrunched up his thick grey eyebrows in an expression that showed he didn't believe a word I'd said.

"In case it has escaped your attention, son, this is a gentleman's public convenience."

"I had noticed."

"Pink teddy bears are not what you would call common fixtures in gentlemen's public conveniences."

"There aren't any chairs in the restaurant," I explained, "They are fixed to the tables."

He grunted. "I fail to see the relevance. I'll ignore the teddy bear for now, but if you try to put one over on me again I may not be so forgiving."

I stepped out into the foyer and the man in the duffel coat followed me.

"Nice weather we're having," he said.

The weather was, as a matter of fact, not at all bad. It was one of those mild, sunny early spring days when the sky seems to have painted itself in a shade of steely incandescent blue. Not that you could see much of that from where we were standing, in the gloomy, rubbish-strewn foyer with the gents to one side and the wrecked remains of Martha's Coffee & Muffins to the other side.

Suddenly the old man put out his right hand, which was wearing a dirty blue woollen glove. "Smith, art historian, MA, PhD etcetera, etcetera, at your service."

Trying not to show any obvious reluctance, I shook the filthy outstretched hand, "Jonathan Richards."

He looked at me quizzically, raising one of his shaggy eyebrows to indicate that he was expecting something more. "Guitar teacher," I added.

"Musician? Hmm. That's something, I suppose."

"Are you really an art historian, MA, PhD etcetera, etcetera?" I asked.

"What d'you mean? Are you suggesting that I am living under false pretences?"

"No… But…" I glanced at the gentleman's toilet with what I hoped was a meaningful stare.

He coughed gently into his hand. I got the impression that this was his way of showing that I had raised a topic of some delicacy.

"The fact of the matter is that I am living in reduced circumstances at the moment. My stipend has been cut."

"Your stipend?"

"My remunerations. From the university."

"You teach at a university?"

"Taught. Work seems to have dried up a bit lately."

"How did you end up here?"

"I can't talk about it."

"Why not?"

"I like to preserve my privacy. You haven't got any sardines, have you? Did I ask you that before?"

"You did."

"Pilchards would do at a pinch."

"What sort of thing did you teach?" I asked.

"Did I mention I was an art historian?"

"You did."

"Would it surprise you, then, to learn that I taught art? The history of art, to be specific."

"I suppose not."

"What do you think of Velázquez?"

"The painter?"

"You've heard of him, then?"

"Is he the one who paints butlers on beaches dancing under umbrellas?"

"Butlers on beaches? I think you might be getting him, confused, son. With someone else."

"Then, sorry, I don't have an opinion."

"You play the guitar, you say? I like a bit of guitar music every once in a while. Soothing."

"Why did you leave?"

"Leave?"

"The university."

"Other opportunities presented themselves."

"You'll have had rooms in college, I suppose?"

"I had a suite of rooms. Very nice they were. Flock wallpaper. Rugs. The lot."

"And now you are here?"

"I value my freedom. Besides which, there was a bit of a nasty business, you see. The undergraduates, they developed some very antisocial habits. Which is why I took my leave, departed, got away, scarpered, skedaddled and ended up here. I took a room in the motel at the back of this place. TV, minibar, air conditioning. None of it works but it's better than nothing."

"You don't live in the gentlemen's toilets, then?"

"What! Me! Live in a public convenience! What do you take me for? I like my creature comforts. I am, as you might say, used to comfortable living. I had my own rooms, as I may have mentioned, when I was a fellow. All mod cons. Fridge, bathroom, cocktail cabinet. You wouldn't believe the luxury we fellows live in."

"Then why were you…?"

"In the gentleman's convenience?"

"Yes."

"What do you *think* I was in there for? Do I have to spell it out? I happened to be passing and I was caught short. So I popped in. The flush is a bit haphazard, the water supply being not what it once was, and the soap's gone hard. But it's better than using the facilities in the motel. Keeps the odours away. At a remote distance, as you might say. You haven't got a Mars bar about your person, I suppose? No, I didn't think you would. What with the distance you've travelled. It would have melted. How far have you travelled? You didn't mention."

"A fair way."

"That's what I thought. You look a bit… you know…"

"Dishevelled?"

"Unkempt."

"It's been a while since I had a haircut."

"I can see that. What did you say your name was…?"

"Jonathan."

"I had a dog once called Jonathan. Or was it a cat? One or the other. So what brings you to these parts, Jonathan?"

"Oh, I'm just passing through. En route to my final destination."

"Going somewhere, are you? Good idea. Travel broadens the mind. I used to travel. Been all over the place. Scarborough, Bognor Regis, Grimsby. You got anywhere special in mind, son?"

"Cambridge."

His eyebrows descended again, shrouding his eyes. "Cambridge. You don't want to be going to Cambridge, boy."

"Really? Why?"

"That's where I came from. Things are bad. Very bad."

"Things are bad everywhere. Which college were you at?"

"What?"

"In Cambridge. I wondered which college you were attached to?"

"I moved around."

There was the sound of a foot scrunching on broken glass immediately behind us. Smith, art historian, MA, PhD etcetera, etcetera, spun around. It was Geoff, followed closely by Leila. Bobby woofed and ran up to them. Geoff hugged the dog – "So that's where you got to, Bobby. We've been looking for you every…" The words choked away into silence when Geoff caught sight of the gun. It looked like a Glock semiautomatic and Smith, art historian, MA, PhD etcetera, etcetera, was holding it.

19

"Bang! Bang! Bang!"

Geoff staggered back. "Yow! That hurts!"

"Bang! Bang! Bang!" Smith shouted again, pulling the trigger with each "Bang!"

A cascade of tiny yellow plastic balls shot from the gun and gave every appearance of irritating Geoff more than they hurt him. Smith blew across the muzzle of the gun, the way cowboys do in films, then reached inside his duffel coat to put it back into the holster which was attached to his belt.

I didn't say anything for a while. I was too shocked. I'd thought the old man had a real gun, with real bullets. It had certainly looked like a Glock. Though, on mature consideration, I had a feeling that Glock semiautomatics favoured a grey-to-black colour scheme rather than the shiny metallic sapphire-blue of the gun that Smith had used. "I was just checking," he said.

"Checking what?"

"That you weren't one of them. Nasty buggers, they can be."

"I think he means red-eyes," I said.

"Do I look like a red-eye?" said Geoff, sounding miffed.

"You're young. It pays to be sure. They don't like being shot, you see."

"Yeah, well," said Geoff, "I'm not so keen myself. And believe me, I've been shot by better than you."

"You've shot some red-eyes with a toy gun?" – Leila looked impressed.

"If I'd had a real gun, I'd have shot them with that," said Smith, "But this was the only gun I could find. It was in the toy section of the newsagent."

"You shot them with a toy gun – and your *survived*?" – Leila wasn't just impressed; she was incredulous.

"They scare very easy. Toy gun, real gun, I don't think they can tell the difference. Like children is what they are."

"No," said Leila, "Not like children. I'd say they are more like people tripping."

"Ah…" Smith considered this for a moment – "Drugs, you mean? I've never had anything to do with drugs myself so I'll have to take your word for that. I knew a student once, though, an undergrad, who wouldn't go anywhere near a certain rose bush in the fellows' garden. He said there were faces in the roses and they were watching him."

"Acid?" I said.

"Mushrooms. That's what I was told, anyway. Betty Miller, she was the bedder who cleaned his rooms, told me it was mushrooms. I don't entirely see how that explains it though. I've had many mushrooms over the years and I've never seen faces in rose bushes."

"Psilocybe semilanceata," Leila said.

"I beg your pardon?"

"Magic mushrooms. Hallucinogenic. Psilocybe semilanceata is the most common species. There are others, of course, but in all probability…"

"OK, OK," I interrupted, "All very interesting, I'm sure. But getting back to the red-eyes. Are there any in the vicinity now?"

"About a week ago was the last I saw any. I thought they'd come back again when I heard your truck. That's what my assumption was. Which is why I hid in the gentlemen's conveniences."

"You told me you went in there for a…"

Smith blushed slightly. "Please. Not in front of a lady. The two activities are not what you'd call mutually exclusive. What began as a call of nature ended up as an act of self-preservation. The magic mushrooms you were discussing remind me of something someone said, a colleague as you might say, a professor of neuro-something, he happened to mention it at High Table one night."

"High Table?" Leila raised an eyebrow. She'd missed out the old man's account of his illustrious academic career. I filled in the details. Leila looked sceptical. Smith continued: "This was back when the troubles were beginning, you see. The undergrads weren't as bad then as they got later on. My friend, the professor of neuro-wotsit, he thought it was some form of mental thing. Like they were going bonkers, as you might say."

"Schizophrenia?" I suggested.

"No, the other thing. Going gaga."

"Dementia?"

"That's the thing. But I said, they're teenagers. Well, so they are, mostly. Eighteen, nineteen, something like that. Too young to be going gaga. How'd you fancy a biscuit?"

"What?" Geoff and Leila exclaimed in unison. They were not as accustomed as I was to Smith's grasshopper leaps from one topic to another.

"Chocolate digestives. Only milk chocolate. If dark chocolate is your craving it must remain unconsummated."

We followed the old man back to the restaurant. He went into a storeroom at the back where he found some warm cans of Coke and a packet of McVitie's chocolate digestive biscuits. We ate and drank as we sat at a table by a window overlooking the carpark and the empty motorway beyond.

"Teenagers. Two of them. Eighteen or nineteen years of age I'd say. The ones who came here, I mean. Let's see. About a week ago, that was. Ten days maybe. A boy and a girl. A little lemon-yellow mini is what they were driving. I thought they can't be wild ones, the red-eyes that is. Because red-eyes wouldn't be able to drive a car. That's what I thought. But I was wrong."

"Quite a few of them can drive," I said, "We've seen them."

"It must be some sort of remembered behaviour," Leila said, "Like walking or eating. Things that they've always done, they continue to do. But new or unexpected things, things that have to be thought about, problems that have to be worked out… that's what baffles them."

Smith, I noticed, had been staring intently into Leila's eyes while she'd been speaking. "If you don't mind my asking…" he slowly crumbled a piece of chocolate digestive biscuit and watched the crumbs fall into a little heap on the Formica table top, "I mean, don't get me wrong, politeness is my watchword. Especially where ladies are concerned. But…"

"My eyes?" said Leila.

"Well…"

"Bloodshot. Which means I'm Infected?"

"Well…"

"There are other reasons for bloodshot eyes, you know."

"And in your case…?"

"Lack of sleep," Leila said, "Due to a bad case of haemorrhoids."

"Ah. Say no more. You speak to a fellow martyr."

"In fact," Laila went on, "You were right the first time. I am infected. Or, anyway, I was. But I recovered. I think. Don't ask me how. I just did."

"The man and the woman who drove here. In the lime-green mini…"

He had said the mini was lemon-yellow before. I was about to point this out but I thought better of it.

"They had bloodshot eyes. Red and raw they looked. And they were thin. Very thin. Gaunt. There was dried blood around their noses. And their mouths. It made me wonder where it came from. It might have been their own blood or… well, I couldn't say where the blood came from. It made them look like animals. Not that I have anything against animals. I've always liked dogs." To prove the statement he popped a chocolate digestive biscuit into Bobby's mouth and the dog gobbled it down in a moment.

"A slouching gait is what they had, those two. They didn't say anything. Not at all talkative, they weren't. I had the impression they had breathing problems. Like the coal miners used to have in the old days. Do you remember coal miners? No? Before your day, I suppose. Wheezy, chesty sounds, they made. I'm not sure if they even talked to each other. The red-eyes, I mean. Coal miners could, I believe, be quite loquacious. They grunted, though. The red-eyes, I mean. Is everyone that far gone now, I wonder?"

"Some are worse," I said.

"When I was in Cambridge, I could see it was getting bad. There were gangs roaming around town. Undergraduates. Town lads too. The things they got up to! I mean, undergrads are a bad lot at the best of times. But not like that. Dirty, they were. Like wild beasts. The beasts of the field that come to devour and, like dumb dogs, cannot bark. As it says somewhere in the Bible."

"Isiah 56:9," said Leila, annoyingly.

"But at least," said Smith, "in the old days, even the most ignorant undergraduates talked, not just grunted."

"You were telling us about the two red-eyes who came here," I reminded him.

"Was I? Here? Oh yes. A little blue mini they were driving. Or it may have been a Volkswagen Beetle. Something of that sort. It wasn't a Ferrari, that I do know. Terrible posture, they had. Slouched. I thought they were going to attack me. I was walking around outside at the time, taking the air, and when they saw me they started running towards me. Lucky for me, I had this," – he indicated the imitation Glock in its belt holster – "I waved it at them. 'Don't come any closer,' says I, 'I'm armed and I'm not afraid to use it'. When they heard that, they started running towards me even faster.

"Then, when they were a few yards away, I shot them. Of course, this gun doesn't fire proper bullets. Just yellow plastic balls. But from the fuss they made, you'd think I'd shot them with a machine gun. The young chap, from the screaming he made you'd think I'd shot him through the guts. Sounded like the squealing of a stuck pig – from descriptions I've read, at any rate, though I've never actually heard a pig being stuck so I cannot confirm the accuracy of that description. The woman ran up to him and flung her arms around him. She looked at me and there was pure hatred in her dead, fishy, blood-red eyes. Then the two of them turned tail, hotfooted it back to their car and drove off into the wild blue yonder."

"You had a lucky escape," I said.

"Not lucky. I used my noddle. Asserted my authority is what I did."

"Lucky even so. When you think how it might have turned out."

"I tell you, they were like frightened children. What could they have done to me?"

"If they'd been minded to, they could have ripped you apart."

Smith was silent for a while. Then he said: "Yes, you might be right. That's why I laid some booby traps. Just in case they happened to come back."

20

We stayed at the motel that night. Smith somehow managed to find three tins of baked beans, a tin of pears and a tin of evaporate milk. We feasted like royalty.

The motel itself was dark and damp and dirty. It was on two levels and we took rooms in the upper level. Many of the rooms had been wrecked, probably in the early days of the infection when people still inhabited the motel, but a few rooms were in good condition. Smith lived in the corner room at the far end. I took the room next to his. Leila and Geoff took rooms across the corridor from us. We had brought some bottles of whisky with us and we shared one of these with Smith that evening. We sat around in his room drinking from tooth glasses and telling tales of the old times.

I was by no means certain if Smith's account of his academic life bore any resemblance to the truth. In his wrinkled pyjamas, grubby duffel coat and bobble hat, he looked (and smelled) like a tramp. But you never can tell with academics. The great universities are filled with people who, in other walks of life, would be considered unemployable. After a few glasses of whisky, he started waffling on at great length about the aesthetic failure of analytic cubism. So he was either telling the truth or he was one of the world's great con-men. What did it really matter, anyway? Art was one of those things we used to have in the old world. People have too many other things to worry about these days.

The following day I woke up late – about ten o'clock. Bobby was lying on the bed snoring. I staggered across to the shower and turned the tap hopefully but nothing came out. At this rate I reckoned it wouldn't be too long before I smelled as ripe as Smith. Maybe that would be all our fates in this dirty, unwashed world. We'd rot away like lumps of old Stilton.

I knocked on the doors to Geoff's and Leila's rooms but there was no answer so I looked inside. The rooms were empty. Smith's room was empty too. For an irrational moment I thought they might have left without me – left, departed, got away, scarpered, skedaddled, as Smith might have said.

In fact, they were downstairs, stuffing their faces in the restaurant. On the menu this morning were bowls of Cornflakes topped off with lashings of tinned evaporated milk. Once upon a time I would have found it disgusting. That morning, it was delicious.

We sat by the big windows and watched the almost-empty motorway. I say "almost empty" because there were a few vehicles that went past. There were one or two cars and even one big lorry – the sort that once upon a time carried freight to and from countries all over Europe. I tried to imagine what sort of person would be driving one of those now. I was pretty certain that no cross-channel ferries were in operation and I doubted whether the Channel Tunnel could have been operational. Maybe the Government, if there really was still a Government, had commandeered lorries to mobilise the great recovery operation? The thought was comforting even if improbable.

I still hoped that there would be a chance of making contact with other people – people like us – that we might, one day, be able to get together and form a bigger group. Find a small town to inhabit, get things working again. But most people were suspicious of us. And we were suspicious of them. So, for the time being, it was just me, Geoff, Leila and Bobby.

"You are still set on Cambridge, son?" Smith asked.

"We have to aim for somewhere," I said, "Cambridge seems as good as anywhere."

"You can come with us if you like," Leila said. I could have throttled her. The Land Rover was overcrowded as it was. I didn't fancy trying to cram in another person. Especially not one who smelled the way Smith smelled.

"I am most grateful for the offer," he replied grandly, "But I must decline. Cambridge is a place which I particularly wish to avoid. Memories, you know. I have many fond memories. And some other memories of a more recent vintage which are not so agreeable."

The silence of the morning was suddenly shattered by the low, thrumming rumble of an approaching motorbike. Glancing out of the window, I was surprised to see a Harley-Davidson Electra Glide pulling into the car park. I knew it was an Electra Glide because I'd once been taken to see an old 1970s film called 'Electra Glide In Blue'. It was my friend, Justin, who'd dragged me along to that. He had an endless fascination for those old films: Easy Rider, The French Connection, Magnum Force – he'd dragged me along to see all of them. I hadn't liked the films all that much, to tell you the truth, but I'd ended up with a surprisingly wide-ranging knowledge of 1970s American police motorbikes and I knew that the Electra Glide was considered to be a classic.

So fascinated was I to see the Electra Glide that it took me a few seconds to give my attention to the man who was riding it. He was dressed in black leather in the classic style, by which I mean a Schott biker's jacket, the sort with little loops on the shoulders, zips all over the place and a buckled belt at the waist. He was wearing a decidedly retro crash helmet: one of those hemispherical pudding-bowl affairs with a black leather chinstrap; and goggles instead of the more conventional built-in visor. Clinging to the lip beneath the goggles was a thin, David Niven-style moustache.

"Shit," said Geoff. His economy of words was, on this occasion, entirely justified. At the sight of that tall, black-leather-clad, David Niven-moustached form slowly dismounting his classic bike, removing his pudding-bowl helmet, looping its chin-strap over the bike's mirrors then, with the index fingers of both hands, carefully smoothing out his moustache, Geoff's exclamation was about as appropriate as anything I could think of.

Smith stared at me with eyes wide open, "I can give him both barrels with my gun, if that's what's called for, son."

"He may be friendly," I said.

"Best to be sure," said Smith, holding the sapphire-blue imitation Glock in his mittened hands.

"I would be prepared to attempt to make a few friendly overtures," said Leila, "This biker has a sense of style that appeals to me."

"Leila fancies him," sniggered Geoff.

But Leila had already left our table and was moving through the foyer towards the main doors. The rest of us were hot on her tail. We met our leather-clad visitor in the wasteland of broken glass and discarded books mid-way between Martha's Coffee & Muffins and the destroyed newsagent's shop.

I was by no means as eager to make his acquaintance as Leila was. While the man might not be infected, there was no reason to believe that he had our best interests at heart either. He might be a looter, or a killer. He could be a rapist, or a sadist. As far as we knew he might be the outrider for a motorbike gang that would make the Hell's Angels look like a bunch of lily-livered softies.

"Good morning," said our visitor. He spoke in a pleasant baritone voice that sounded rather like the late Richard Burton, "I hope you don't mind the intrusion."

"No, not all," said Leila, smiling vivaciously.

"I thought you might like to know that there are some hostiles approaching and I would strongly recommend…"

"Hostiles?" I said. I wasn't sure what he meant. The term had a vaguely military sound about it.

"Possibly you call them 'Infected'?" he suggested.

Our various reactions showed that we knew that term well enough.

"Yes, well, it has not yet been confirmed that an infection is the primary cause of the problem. We prefer to use the term 'hostiles'. But it amounts to the same thing."

"We?"

"The CDC." – We gave him a blank stare – "The Civilian Defence Corps."

"Bloody Home Guard, you mean?" said Smith.

"I beg your pardon?"

"I knew a chap worked in the CDC back in the '60s," Smith said, "He'd been in the Home Guard during the war, so he claimed. Lieutenant or something. Jumped-up little twerp, he was. As far as I could see, the CDC is just full of jobsworths and busybodies."

"Ah, you are labouring under a misapprehension. You are thinking of the Civil Defence Corps which was disbanded many years ago. Quite a different organisation from the Civilian Defence Corps."

"They were a lot of pompous busybodies back then and from what I can see," Smith fixed the man with a gimlet stare, "nothing much has changed."

"Yes, well, er," the man smiled sheepishly which, if you've ever seen a sheep smile, you'll realise is not much of a smile at all, "We can but do our best. The thing is, we were a somewhat hush-hush organisation. Before the catastrophe. But now, of course, we aren't. I thought you might have heard of us."

"Not a thing," I said.

"Well, now you have. Captain Timms-Martin," he extended a leather-gloved hand to me; Leila shook it. She had homed in on the hand before it had had a chance to find its intended target. Leila was wearing her dark glasses, I noticed. To avoid awkward questions, no doubt.

"Are you the Army, like, then?" Geoff asked.

"In a manner of speaking, I suppose one might say so," Captain Timms-Martin's answer struck me as oddly imprecise.

"'Cos, I'd have thought if you was in the Army you'd have been riding a Triumph or an Armstrong or something. Not a bleedin' Harley-Davidson Electra Glide."

"Ah, the bike. You noticed? Yes well, it was requisitioned, don't you know."

"Requisitioned?" said Geoff.

"Stolen," Smith said in a loud stage-whisper.

"Acquired," Captain Timms-Martin said, "For the duration of hostilities. We are doing our best to work towards the restoration of order and the repair of infrastructure as speedily as possible, you see."

"And how much order and infrastructure has been restored and repaired so far?" asked Smith.

Captain Timms-Martin gave a wry smile, which was somewhat more successful than his sheepish one. "It's early days, but we have to start somewhere. Now, as I was saying, some hostiles have been observed heading this way. We would therefore strongly advise that you vacate the building, and the surrounding area, at your earliest opportunity."

"How many are there?" I asked.

"Oh, a couple of hundred, I should say."

"How far away?"

"About three miles. They are on foot and progressing at a rate of about two to three miles an hour, I would estimate. So I really would recommend most strongly that you leave immediately. Would there happen to be a convenience here, by any chance? It's been quite a long ride and…"

I pointed to the far end of the foyer. "Down there. But there's no water."

"Oh, that's quite all right. I'm used to that."

As he walked off, I said what all of us were thinking. "Do you think we can trust him?"

"The Civilian Defence Corps could be anything," said Smith, "Or nothing. How can we be sure he's even on our side?"

"I think he's making it all up," Geoff said, "If he was part of an official unit he'd be dressed like a soldier, wouldn't he?"

"Well, *I* trust him," said Leila.

Geoff and I groaned.

"No! No! Not there!" Smith suddenly shouted at the top of his voice.

We stared at him, uncomprehending.

"That bloke just went into the Ladies' toilets," he explained.

"Oh, for God's sake," I said, "I hardly think that matters."

"Oh, but it does."

From the direction of the Ladies' toilets came the sound of something heavy falling to the ground with a reverberating thump. This was followed immediately by an impressive list of obscenities shouted with great vigour in a rich, baritone voice.

We looked at Smith. He looked at us. "You remember I said I'd laid a few booby traps," he mumbled, "Well…"

21

We were stuck in the back of the Land Rover – me, Smith and Bobby – with Geoff driving and Leila in the passenger seat. We were following the route that Captain Timms-Martin had suggested, down the A421, south of Bedford, in the Cambridge direction.

"It was a sack of tinned fruit," Smith explained, "I'd filled the sack with tins to give it a good weight and then I got a step ladder and I climbed up and wedged it over the door to the Ladies' conveniences. It took me hours to get it right.."

"Where'd you get that daft idea?" Geoff shouted (he had to shout to be heard over the noise of the Land Rover).

"The Dandy, I think. Or maybe The Beano?"

"The what?"

"Comics," I explained for Geoff's benefit. It's what kids used to do for entertainment before computers."

"You could have killed the poor chap," Leila protested.

"Yes," Smith was smiling broadly.

I had been hoping that Smith would have declined Leila's offer of a lift. He had previously been emphatic that the one place among all others that he was most eager to avoid was Cambridge. However, when we gave him the choice of staying alone in the service station to face an advancing army of several hundred homicidal maniacs or roughing it in the back of a Land Rover on the way to the pleasant environs of England's most beautiful old university, he didn't hesitate for a second. Cambridge it was!

I kept the windows open to try to mitigate the heady odour of Smith but it wasn't having much effect. "It's a bit pongy in here," Smith complained once, "The dog, I suppose? You should put butter on his paws."

"That's to stop cats wandering," Leila said.

"My dear young lady," Smith replied haughtily, "there are no cats present so I fail to see the relevance."

If the roads had been clear we could have done the journey in under an hour. But the road was blocked by a mess of crashed cars at a place called Little Barsford and we had to backtrack and take some minor roads up to Eaton Socon and St. Neots. As with all the wrecks we saw on the roads, we were never sure what might have been the cause. I wondered at times if some of the crashes had been deliberate; if some joy rider, seeing the world dying, had decided to go out with one final, maniacal act of carnage.

And then, later on, we came up against a great ridge of concrete rubble blocking the road. It was the remains of a pedestrian bridge. Someone had blown it up. It must have taken a good deal of planning and a hefty explosive to cause so much damage. Why would anyone do that? The only reason I could think of would be to make a barrier to prevent people from driving further along the road. If that had been the aim, it was completely successful. We had to take a detour that must have added another thirty minutes to our journey. By the time we arrived on the edges of Cambridge, it was already twilight.

The approaches to the town were nondescript. We could have been in a suburb of almost any small town in England. There were little grey houses and bland little shops. The streets were littered with broken glass and rubbish. There were a few bodies too. The place had an air of bleak desolation.

We were about to turn left down a street when Geoff suddenly made a sharp U-turn to take us back the way we had come. I saw the reason before I'd even had time to ask him what he was doing. An armoured car pulled out of the street which we had almost turned down. It had a searchlight mounted on top and it appeared to be on patrol. We didn't know what it was looking for. But we were glad it hadn't found us.

Geoff drove more cautiously after that. He avoided the main roads into town, preferring to keep to small roads that ran through housing estates and industrial areas. It dawned on me then that we had no idea what we were heading towards. We'd come to Cambridge because the Colonel had told us that the Government had relocated there. I suppose I'd assumed that meant that there was some semblance of civilization there, that law and order reigned and basic services like electricity and water had been restored. So far there had been no sign of that. The streets were as dark and decrepit as they had been in London. More so, in fact. Though that was probably due to the fact that several weeks had elapsed since we'd left London. At least there was no sign of any gangs. Apart from the armoured car, in fact, there was no sign of anyone at all. I remembered the massacre we'd stumbled into at Chalk Farm in North London, when the tanks had rounded up a crowd into the entrance of the tube station and had then opened fire. Was that how law and order was being restored in Cambridge too? I wondered if that was why the streets around us were devoid of any sign of life. But when we got closer to town things changed.

We were going down a long, dismal road when suddenly a group of young people lurched out in front of us. Our headlights weren't on and we nearly drove right into them. Geoff slammed on the brakes.

"What the…!" Smith grabbed hold of me.

Bobby put his paws on the back of Geoff's seat and began barking.

"Accelerate, for God's sake!" Leila said.

"No," I yelled. I remembered the previous occasion when we'd ploughed into a band of red-eyes, that night after we'd been to the cocktail bar. The memory of that filled me with horror. I had no intention of repeating it. "Turn around, can't you? Drive away?"

But Geoff did nothing. He sat immobile. He was staring at the group of young people. They were staring back at him. Eventually, Geoff said, "They're OK. I don't think they're dangerous."

"You don't think…!"

"Look," he said, "They're moving away."

He was right. Very slowly and cautiously, the young people were walking back in the direction from which they'd come. As they did so, they kept a close eye on the Land Rover. They looked at us in the way you might look at a mad bull that you had unexpectedly encountered in a field, retreating while doing your best not to antagonise it.

"Are they afraid of us?" I said.

"I think so," Geoff answered.

I had assumed they were infected, mainly because of their age and the fact that they were wandering through the streets at night.

But now I wasn't so sure. It was almost fully dark so I couldn't see them clearly. There were four of them: three men and one woman. They were, at a guess, somewhere between eighteen and twenty years of age. All of them had that pale, dishevelled look that I associated with the red-eyes. But they gave every appearance of behaving rationally. They seemed to be talking quietly to one another. They showed no sign of the wild, animal ferocity which we'd seen in previous encounters with red-eyes. All in all, there was something very strange about them. And something very familiar. I realised, with shock, that they reminded me very strongly of Leila.

Leila had noticed the similarity too. "I'll go and talk to them," she said.

"No!" I grabbed for her shoulder but she shrugged off my grasp and was out through the Land Rover door before I could do anything to stop her. By that time, the gang of four had gone; a gated entrance stood to our left and they had run through the gate to get away. I opened the back door of the Land Rover, jumped out and went to take a closer look. The gates through which they'd gone must have been ten feet high or more and made of solid iron railings topped with rolls of barbed wire. To the left of the gate stood a squarish, two-storey brick building. Its windows, I noticed, were all boarded up. Beyond the gates spread out a great expanse of lawns dotted with trees forming what seemed to be a courtyard surrounded by long, low, elegant buildings in a neo-classical style. A rattle of keys close at hand distracted me from my observations and I noticed, at the other side of the gate, a small, plump man wearing a dark jacket and a bowler hat. Having locked the gate itself he was now engaged with the additional security of locking a heavy padlock to the ends of a chain that ran through the bars of the gate.

"You can't come in here, sir, madam," he said, "It's past gate hours and guests is not permitted in college."

"Where is this?" I said, "Who are you?"

"Not that it's any of your business, sir, who I am, but I don't mind telling you anyway. The name's Pipply. Augustus Pipply. And this is St. Dunstan's College, which is, as you no doubt know, the finest college in all of Cambridge."

"Who were those people who just came in?" asked Leila.

"I'm sorry, madam. I can't be giving out personal information about undergraduates."

"Undergraduates?" I said, flabbergasted, "You mean to say this is still a functioning college? People are still studying here?"

"Of course they are, sir. People have been studying at St Dunstan's for more than two centuries. And they've been studying at the university since the early thirteenth century. Wars, plagues, famines and catastrophes have come and gone. We try not to let these little things interfere with the life of the university."

The porter, having said his piece, decided there was no more to be said and was already walking away into the darkness of the college quadrangle.

"Hey, wait a minute!" I yelled, "Where can we go?"

"Go?" he called back, "There are plenty of places you can go."

"But we've come here to…" – what had we come to Cambridge for? We had never had any clear idea of what we would do when we arrived. We'd only come to Cambridge on the Colonel's recommendation. And why had I ever paid any attention to what the Colonel said, anyway? For the same reason that the people in the village had always done what he told them to do, in times of crisis and emergency. Because, quite simply, he had a natural air of authority.

"The Colonel told us to come here," I called out. I don't know why I said that. I had no reason to suppose that Mr Pipply, the porter of St. Dunstan's College, would have the remotest idea who the Colonel was. In fact, my words had a dramatic effect. Mr Pipply stopped dead in his tracks. He stopped. Then he turned. Then he looked at me and he looked at Leila and he said, "The Colonel?"

"You know him?" I replied.

"Now then, lad, which colonel would that be, exactly?"

"The…" – I had no idea what his name was. All I knew was that he was an antique dealer and that everyone in the village called him Colonel. Had he told me his name? I thought hard. In the Church Hall he had said his name was… what, Richard? Ronald? Reginald? Yes, that was it. Reginald. But what was his surname?

Geoff was standing beside me by this time. I whispered to him, asked if he knew the Colonel's full name. He shrugged – "Everyone just called him The Colonel."

"Reginald," I told the porter, "Colonel Reginald."

The porter looked unimpressed.

A voice called out from the darkness behind us – "Colonel McPherson. That's who they mean, Pipply, Colonel Reginald McPherson."

Pipply was back at the gates now and, miracle of miracles, he had the bunch of keys in his hand and was busy unlocking the padlock.

"Begging your pardon, Professor," he said, "I didn't see you there. I'd have had the gates open in a jiffy if I had."

"That's quite all right, Pipply. Be a good man, would you, and put the kettle on. We could all do with a good, hot cuppa tea, I think."

"Certainly, Professor Smith, I've got some biscuits in the lodge too, sir. Chocolate digestive."

"*Dark* chocolate digestives?" asked Smith, imperiously, as he strode up to the gates and entered with all the magnificence of Pompey returning to Rome.

"Oh, certainly dark chocolate, sir," Pipply assured him with cringing obsequiousness, "I wouldn't think of offering you anything less, sir."

"Lead on, then, Pipply. Lead on!"

As we sat in the porter's lodge, two things struck me at once: 1) The room was illuminated by an electric light; 2) the kettle was plugged into an electric socket.

The place had power! The porter's lodge was like a mysteriously preserved fragment of the world that had gone before. Soon we were drinking tea and we were eating chocolate biscuits and we were slowly beginning to relax. Smith, who it transpired really was a professor of the history of art, started to make arrangements with the porter to find guest rooms for us to stay in.

We'd been there about twenty minutes when there was the sound of a fairly large vehicle pulling up outside the gate. Pipply ran out with his keys jangling and, a few moments later, he was back again. There was no mistaking the tall, dignified-looking person standing beside him.

"Ah, I wondered if you'd make it," said the Colonel, "Still, I had every confidence that Smith would persuade you."

"Smith! What has Smith got to do with…"

"Oh, Smith has been pivotal to the entire operation, my dear chap. Without Smith, I really doubt if you'd be alive, let alone in Cambridge."

Smith said nothing but he raised an eyebrow meaningfully.

"I don't think I understand," I said.

"No," said the Colonel, "I don't suppose you do. It's going to take quite a bit of explanation, I fear. Still, plenty of time for that, don't you think?"

That night we slept in comfortable beds with crisp white sheets and duvets. Our rooms were in the guest wing at the far end of the quadrangle. Each room had electric lighting and an en suite bathroom with hot and cold running water. There was a telephone on a table next to my bed. I'd been told that if I needed anything I should use the phone to call the porter's lodge. A small bedside radio sat next to the telephone. I lay back on the bed and turned the radio on. It was playing music. Something with synthesizers that I couldn't quite place. As the song ended a familiar voice came on the air… "That was Blancmange with 'Blind Vision' and this is Peter Quinn with the All 80s Radio Show. You are listening to Radio True Britain. And now for another golden classic, The Human League with 'Dreams Of Leaving'…"

Just when I'd thought I'd begun to get used to the strangeness of this shattered world, things had started to get a whole lot stranger. I had no idea quite how strange until the next day when the Colonel told me about The Exodus Project. If I'd had any sense, I would have left while I still had the chance.

A MESSAGE FROM THE AUTHOR

Thank you for reading my book. I hope you enjoyed it. This is the first book in *The Exodus Plague* series and I am already busy writing another one!

Writing these books takes a great deal of time and effort. I love writing them and it is one of the best things in my life to hear from readers who enjoy reading them. But the biggest problem I face is trying to let potential readers know that I even exist. There are millions of books for sale on Amazon and elsewhere and it is really hard for my books to compete against titles produced by big publishing companies with huge marketing budgets.

You can help me!

Reviews are incredibly important to me. They let potential readers know if they might enjoy reading one of my novels. I would therefore be really grateful if you could take a few moments to leave a short review on Amazon. You can do that by clicking one of the two links on the next page or (on other Amazon sites) by clicking the 'Write a Customer Review' button on the book page.

Thanks again for reading my book!

Huw Collingbourne

To download **free stories** now and to be the first to hear about new books, join Huw's mailing list at:
http://www.darkneon.com/newsletter

Leave a Review

Amazon (USA)

https://tinyurl.com/y5mf38sn
or
https://www.amazon.com/review/create-review?asin=1913132102
or scan this QR code:

Amazon (UK)

https://tinyurl.com/yyqa8bvh
or
https://www.amazon.co.uk/review/create-review?asin=1913132102

Now Read On…

The story continues in **'Imprisoned'** – the second volume of *The Exodus Plague* trilogy. Here's the first chapter…

IMPRISONED

ARRIVAL

Cambridge: April

Perkins The Pardoner

"He's still there. By the gates."

"Are you sure it's the same chap?"

"There can't be two of them, surely." Sir Eric Martingdale poured another sherry. He'd had a tiring morning discussing college discipline with the Dean and, as a consequence, he now had a slight headache. He did not, as a rule, take sherry before lunch but he knew that his friend Dr. Ampleside was fond of sherry so he'd sent down for a bottle of amontillado from the Fellows' Cellars.

"You should get old Pipply to send him away."

Pipply was the college porter. He represented the third generation of Pipply porters at St. Dunstan's college.

"Pipply's no good," said Sir Eric, "I think he's afraid of the chap."

"Possibly you could get one of the bulldogs…"

Sir Eric laughed. "Ha! You are indulging in nostalgia, my dear chap. The days of University bulldogs are long gone. There's been no University Constabulary since the Great Snow."

"Ah, that had not occurred to me. What do you propose to do about the blasted fellow then?"

"Not much one can do. I suppose I could give old Pipply a call and tell him to round up a few undergrads to sort him out?"

"Give the man a good kicking, you mean? Good idea. He has no business lurking at the gates. A good thrashing would do him the world of good."

"I suppose it's worth a try, at any rate."

*

When the phone in the porter's lodge began ringing, Augustus Pipply had the distinct impression that it did not bode well. "This doesn't bode well," he said to the junior porter, Samuel Parker.

Pipply picked up the phone and answered in his most porterly voice, "Good morning, Master. Oh, yes, sir. I had noticed him. He's been there all morning. What's that? Get rid of him? How am I to…? With the help of some undergraduates, sir? Ah, well, now… I suppose… yes, yes, of course, Sir Eric. As you say, sir, nothing is impossible. When you put your mind to it."

Pipply slammed down the phone and scowled at Sam Parker who, at that moment, was leaning back in a chair with his feet resting on the porter's reception desk – a slovenly habit that Augustus Pipply particularly disliked. He swiped Sam's feet off his desk brusquely and said, "Sam, my lad, we got some business to attend to, me and you. The Master wants us to get rid of Perkins the Pardoner."

"'Ow we gonna do that, Mr Pipply?" said Sam.

"That's a good question, Sam. And one to which I ain't got an answer. He's mad as a hatter is that Pardoner. But he's just a skinny old fella', when all's said and done. I'm sure a young man of your strength and vigour won't have no problems seeing him off."

"Oh, I'm not gonna risk crossing the Pardoner, Mr Pipply. Not for all the tea in China, I won't."

"And why is that, Sam?"

"Don't you know, Mr Pipply? The Pardoner curses people. He's been touched by God, they say. And so his curses are good ones that always work."

*

Sam Parker was in his early thirties. He'd always kept fit. He cycled every day, played football on weekends, never drank more than three or four pints of beer when he was down the pub. It was thanks to his fitness that he had survived the Great Plague, so he reckoned, though some doctors from the University had their own ideas on that matter. Sam Parker was not, however, much inclined to acts of physical violence. On the contrary, he suffered from a marked aversion to it. Which is why he was not at all enthusiastic about getting into an argument with Perkins the Pardoner. Because Perkins the Pardoner believed that the spreading of the Word Of God was his sacred duty. And if anything came between him and his duty, God didn't in the least object to a bit of good, old fashioned, proselytising violence. Only a few days ago, Perkins the

Pardoner had knocked the Master of Christ's to the ground when the latter had informed Perkins that he was not entitled to be strolling barefoot over the grass of the college quad. The week before, Perkins had given the Praelector of Gonville & Caius a black eye following an altercation over an obscure element of doctrine.

No, all things being equal, Sam Parker did not at all relish the prospect of telling Perkins The Pardoner to go away from the college gates. Which is why Sam Parker strolled over to the college bar which, at ten o'clock in the morning, resounded to the sounds of snooker balls ricocheting off the walls.

"Morning, lads," said Sam Parker, "The Master's got a bit of business as needs doin' and I was thinking to myself you'd be just the lads for the job. Yow!"

The concluding "Yow!" was in response to a ricocheting snooker ball that made sudden and forceful contact with the tibia of Sam Parker's right leg. He knew it was the tibia and not, for example, the fibula because Terrence Farquhar (a student of medicine) informed him of the fact – "Got a nasty whack to the tibia just then, Sam," he said, "Want me to take a look at it?"

"No, no, that won't be necessary," replied Sam, who would no more trust his leg to a St Dunstan's medical student than he would trust his pet cat to a hungry Timber Wolf, "Why are you lot chucking billiard balls around the bar anyhow?"

"Snooker balls," corrected Angus Whitley-Stanton (a third year physics student), "And the reason we are doing it is to put to the test a theory of mine that Newton's third law of motion contains an error."

"Yes, well, be that as it may. I have important work for you, lads."

"Lads! Lads!" boomed a female voice (belonging, as it happens, to Fiona Chitterton-Ruddle, a second-year student of English), "I trust you intend that word in the mediaeval sense!"

Sam was starting to feel confused. When the undergrads got jabbering at him, it wasn't long before he started to feel as though his head was spinning. He decided the best thing to do would be to come straight to the point – "Perkins The Pardoner is at the gates again and the Master wants him got rid of."

"Oh, OK," said Angus, "I think we can do that. Can't we lads?"

"Oh, rath-errrr!" Fiona cried with enthusiasm.

When Sam had left the bar, Angus asked Fiona, "By the way, old girl, what is the mediaeval sense of the word 'lad'?"

"No idea, old man. The etymology is what is known in the business, as 'uncertain'. Come on, let's go and give this Pardoner fellow a jolly good thrashing."

ACCEPTANCE

Stony Cove: January

Sebastian

Sebastian had been planning to kill himself. He had considered throwing himself from the cliffs into the sea and he had considered jumping in front of a train but both of those methods seemed quite messy and might easily go wrong. In the end he'd settled on a couple of razor blades, a few bottles of cider and a hot bath. He'd heard somewhere that you could bleed out quite peacefully in a hot bath; a few bottles of cider would ease the process. But after the first bottle of cider, the razor blades started to seem less and less of an attraction. After the second bottle of cider, he couldn't even remember what he'd been planning to do. After the third bottle of cider, all he could think about was drinking a fourth bottle of cider. After that, he couldn't recall what exactly happened. All he could remember was waking up feeling very cold, very sick and with a head that felt as though it had been battered against a stone wall with a cricket bat.

In fact, it was another two days before he felt well enough to get up off the sofa and go and get a shower. He needed a shower to wash away the smell of stale sweat and vomit. He looked at himself with shame. He had never been so drunk that he'd vomited before. Why had he done it? He dried himself off and looked at his face in the bathroom mirror. His eyes were bloodshot and couldn't focus properly. Even after taking a shower, he looked a mess. He shaved and put on a clean tee-shirt and a fresh pair of jeans. It was only then that he remembered that he had planned to kill himself.

"Why would I do that?"

And then it all came flooding back. Freddie. He'd had the biggest ever argument with Freddie.

But wait, there's more…

More Books…
To be one of the first to hear about new books, join the mailing list at: http://www.darkneon.com/newsletter

Books by Huw Collingbourne

The Exodus Plague

Book 1: The Snow
Book 2: Imprisoned
Book 3: Escape

The 1980s Murder Mysteries

Book 1: Killers In Mascara
Book 2: The Glam Assassin
Book 3: Death Wears Sequins

Thank you for reading.

Best wishes
Huw Collingbourne

Printed in Great Britain
by Amazon

32036498R00138